Marci Giebels

The Francis Kelly Project

Published by Misty Morn Publishing

The Francis Kelly Project is a satire by Marci Giebels and is not intended maliciously. Marci Giebels has invented all names and situations in this story, except in cases when public figures are being satirized. Any other use of real names is accidental and coincidental, or used as a fictional depiction or personality parody (permitted under Hustler magazine v. Fallwell, 485 US 46, 108 S.Ct 876,99 L.Ed.2d 41 (1988))

Chapter One

1991

"The demo sucks." Benny Bernstein rendered his opinion through a mouthful of liverwurst sandwich.

"I'm sorry, what did you say?" Brain asked him.

Benny opened his mouth to clarify, displaying the condition of liverwurst and Wonder Bread once it's mixed together.

"I'm sorry, we can wait until you're finished. Just go ahead and enjoy your lunch, we're in no rush." Brian indicated that he was speaking for both of us. I saw him gesture because I had diverted my attention from Benny's mouth to Brian's handsome face, hoping my stomach would pull out of the spin cycle.

The entertainment attorney had evidently scheduled our meeting to coincide with his lunch. I tried to decide if having lunch at his desk was due to Benny's dedication or if it was an indication that he couldn't afford to go out.

Benny wiped his mouth with a thin paper napkin. "I said, 'The. Demo. Sucks.' We on the same page now?"

"Ah . . . no. I have to disagree. That CD was recorded and mastered by the top engineers at the finest studio in Manhattan; the musicians and the vocalist are examples of the most excellent talent available; and our songwriting is fresh, new, and cutting edge; so I can't understand how combining all of those elements could add up to a product that is anything less than the sum of its parts."

"I'm being straight with you, Brian...is it Brian?" Benny asked. "And Vi?" We nodded.

"Well, Brian and Vi, I could waste my time and yours. I could BS you and tell you that I know I can broker a deal between your band and a major record label. How about if I tell you you will surely debut on 'Rick Dees Weekly Top 40' within seventy-two hours, be on the cover of the next issue of *Rolling Stone*, and have your first single replace 'The Star Spangled Banner' as the national anthem'? Is that more along the lines of what you'd like to hear? Personally, I'd rather have someone be honest with me and tell me that my music sucks so that I could stop wasting my money and my life."

I began a counter rant. "There are newspaper reviews in our promo pack that call The Francis Kelly Project 'the best unsigned band in New York City.' *The Village Voice* called us 'revolutionary.' And I have the BDS play lists from several college radio stations around the country who have given us spins and wins on programs like 'Smash It Or Trash it.'"

"How old are you, toots?"

"Twenty-two." I replied, knowing exactly where his question was leading. The acts being signed to major-label record deals were teenagers or kids younger than that these days.

Benny almost choked on his fresh bite of sandwich as he started to laugh. "On your way out, make an appointment with my receptionist for ten years ago. And ask her for some singing lessons. She's better than you are, and look where it got her." Or at least I think that's what he said through the dump-truck sized payload he was trying to navigate around to form words.

"I'd be embarrassed to have a slob like you represent us," Brian said as we headed toward the door.

"I wouldn't take you on if you were the last band in America." Benny retrieved our demo CD from the machine, where it had been playing before the meeting took a nosedive. He slapped it into the case and I reached out my hand to take it back. My parents paid for the sessions to record the demo and to manufacture the CDs, and they were expensive. I wanted this one back.

Just before I grabbed the CD, Benny pulled it away from me and threw it towards the wastebasket at the corner of his desk. As the CD landed on the floor, he laughed an evil laugh, bits of liverwurst bursting from his mouth like spittle sparklers.

"I'll let the cleaning girl take that out with the rest of the garbage."

Brian reached for my hand and guided me towards the door. "You're a pig, Bernstein."

"Yeah, and The Francis Kelly Project is the next big thing!" He laughed some more as the door closed behind us.

Alone in the elevator, our hopes deflating more with every floor we descended, Brain winked at me.

"Good meeting," he said sarcastically.

"That was fun." I mimicked his tone.

"Hey, he's just one guy. One disgusting, vile, gluttonous guy." Brian grinned. "C'mon, are you going to be insulted that *he* doesn't like us? I don't know if you noticed but he isn't actually setting the standard for good taste."

The truth is, although the others had been far more professional about it, we'd been rejected by forty-eight other entertainment lawyers in New York. Brian and I moved here together from Stetson University in De Land, Florida, where we completed our junior year. We shared the dream of getting a record deal and had decided to go for it, having been given my parents' blessing and their platinum card. The blessing had strings attached, though. My parents gave me one year to pursue a recording contract. After that, if I wasn't successful, I agreed to go back to school and finish my degree. The year was up. The meeting with Benny Bernstein was the last appointment we had before my flight left in the morning. The *Rocky* theme song I had been singing in my head faded away as the elevator delivered us back to the lobby.

"I have to go home tomorrow, Brian."

"Vi, we're this close." Brian stretched his arms as far apart as they would go. "You can't give up now." He was smiling one of his gorgeous Brian smiles that made girls fall on their backs with their legs in the air.

"A deal's a deal."

We reached the lobby and the elevator doors opened.

We walked out onto Fifty-Fourth Street, heading for the train.

The reality of having to leave New York City never occurred to me -- even though I knew that the odds of getting a record deal were close to the odds of being struck by lightning. Like the music industry, lightning is unpredictable and it strikes without logic or discrimination. The percentage of people chosen by the natural phenomenon is a reassuringly small number. Unless you are playing the odds on the other side of the metaphor and are trying to summon a lightning strike. I honestly believed that I had control over my destiny, and that chance had little bearing on my success. It seemed impossible to me that I had to say good-bye to New York -- to my dreams -- and head back to school to pick up where I left off.

"Can we walk home?" I asked Brian. "I want to soak up the atmosphere."

Brain pulled me into his strong arms. "Vi, you love it here. You love me. I'm here." He wrapped me a little tighter for emphasis. "You belong here. You're too good to give up."

I tried to freeze the moment in time, but the world just kept on spinning. Even though it was late summer, there was a chill in the air. We held each other on the sidewalk under the colorless sky, amid masses of people moving like sections of a caterpillar contained by the sidewalk.

We both knew I'd go home. We both knew Brian would stay.

"Will you say good-bye to the band for me?" I whispered, feeling that speaking out loud would somehow make all of this more real.

"Nope. They love you too, Vi," he said softly into my hair. "You have to do that yourself."

"Will you get another girl singer and keep doing our stuff?" I asked.

"I haven't thought about it." Brian's reply tickled my ear as he held me close.

"Move it assholes." The accent was definitely Brooklyn. We started to laugh.

"See? You gotta stay. Where else are you gonna get that?"

Chapter Two

2009

Joe's Diner, La Cienega, Los Angeles

"Hey Joey!" Joe Cantone's favorite customer walked through the front door of his diner. Joe had been struggling to pay the rent until the day George had been photographed leaving here on his motorcycle. Now Joe didn't have to worry about the rent because he owned the whole plaza. Who says paparazzi are a nuisance? They're public servants as far as Joe was concerned.

"Mr. Cooper! Good to see you. How ya been? What can I do you for?" Joe embraced the movie star and continued the tradition of serving his most valuable patron himself.

"Stromboli please, sir." The actor took a seat at the counter and looked around at the nearly empty diner. "Has business been a little slow today?"

"We were in the weeds just an hour ago. You missed the lunch rush -- probably on purpose, hey?" Joe gave him a wink.

"I'm glad you're doing well, Joey. Just don't get so busy that I can't get my Stromboli**."**

"I'd clear the place out for you three times a day, Mr. Cooper. What can I get you to drink?" Joe placed a large, white charger plate in front of George and set his silverware on a linen napkin. Joe knew that in L.A., presentation was everything.

"Bourbon and water, hold the water." George waved a dismissive hand and grinned at his own joke. "Fine, just the water. But it's too damn quiet in here. Put on some music or something, okay?"

"I'll play anything you want to hear. What do you like?"

The cook brought Mr. Cooper's plate. "I don't care Joe, whatever you pick will be fine."

Joe's Diner had a new sound system that could really rock when the customers wanted a lively scene. But Joe didn't know how to use it. He fumbled around a little before hitting *power* on three different components and then *play*. He heard music. He didn't know where it was coming from, but there was music.

"That good?" he asked Mr. Cooper who was poised to take his first bite.

George became aware of the music and began to listen intently. He smiled, then laughed out loud. "Yes!" he shouted. Cooper was clapping now. "Joey, you did it! What band is this?"

"I dunno." He shouted toward the kitchen. "Hey, Cathy! What's this music?"

Cathy came out wiping her hands on a towel. Seeing George Cooper in person never got old. She willed her knees not to buckle.

"It's called The Francis Kelly Project," Cathy replied dreamily.

"So you like it," Joe confirmed with Cooper.

"Hell, you don't know, Joe. I need this song. This is the title track for my new film. I've been looking for the right song for six months and this," he slapped the counter, "is the song!"

"Give Mr. Cooper the CD," Joe said to Cathy.

Cathy ran to the CD player and hit *eject,* checking her reflection in the display window. Why hadn't she put on a little make-up this morning? George Cooper would never date a waitress who didn't look like she could walk the red carpet. *You're naturally pretty*, she told herself. *Just smile.* Had she mentioned to him that she was taking acting classes last time he was in? She couldn't remember.

"Cathy! Now, sweetheart!" bellowed Joe. "Don't keep Mr. Cooper waitin'!"

She ran back out front and handed George the CD. He looked at the handwritten title on the otherwise blank CD face.

"Is there a case?" he asked.

"Lemme check." Cathy ran back to look, but she didn't find anything. "There's no case," she announced as she returned to the counter.

"No big deal. My agent will know who to call. Joe, I could make out with you a little bit." Cooper held up the CD.

"You could do worse, Mr. Cooper."

6

Chapter Three

I had conquered my To Do list for the day and finished two major tasks that I had slated for tomorrow. Satisfied with my progress, I decided to call it a day.

"Henry, what do you say we go home for a little swim before the girls get out of school?" I pushed the chair back from my desk and took a few steps over to the pint-sized table and chairs arranged in the middle of my office.

"Yeah! Mom, can I pretend to be a shark and bite you?" My three-year-old little boy was beaming with excitement at the possibility of permission to bite.

"Can you pretend to be a shark who pretends to bite?"

"Nope. No way."

"We'll talk about it in the car." I hoped that he'd forget the conversation, but knew he wouldn't. "Let's pack up and head out." I helped him gather up his *Color Wonder* books and markers.

Except for my desk, every other piece of furniture in my office was for my kids. They had a TV/DVD, a miniature couch, shelves of books, stacks of games and puzzles, and a computer. Solid evidence that, even though I owned my own business, I didn't really work for myself; I worked for them. And it was my pleasure.

I placed my laptop in my briefcase and collected my purse before Henry and I went out onto the selling floor of my boutique. I felt as though we should have tiptoed so as not to be held up by patrons asking questions or . . .

"Sugar, honey, iced tea," I swore in code as my cell phone started to ring. "Vi Fancis-Gates," I answered.

"Mom, I thought we were going!" Henry protested. I winked at him.

"Can you put those details in an email for me? I am just stepping into a very important meeting." Henry returned the wink, but he's not entirely coordinated so it was more of a blink.

"I appreciate it. Thank you very much." I snapped my phone closed. If I wasn't a mother and a wife I would have turned it off.

The fashion shows were coming up and all the vendors wanted to invite me to spend my quarterly buying allowance on their labels.

"Ready, sir?"

"Let's say good-bye to everyone, Mommy. I wanna get some kisses for my kiss collection."

"Yes, your kiss collection is very important." I added one of my own to the top of his blond curly head.

"Ladies, we're going home." Henry announced. Doreen and Isabelle knew what that meant and they came over to hug and kiss him.

I am so lucky to have found such lovely people to work with me. I wouldn't know what to do without them. Having three kids and a husband who is an airline pilot isn't an easy gig to pull off by itself. Owning three boutiques in the Florida Keys would be an impossible dream if not for these women. They have been involved from the beginning and they are as proud of the business and as persoanlly invested in it as I am. And they love my kids.

"Will you be in tomorrow, Henry?" Isabelle made a coded inquiry about my plans.

"Wade is due in tonight, so Henry will stay home with his daddy tomorrow. I'll be here from open to close, so you can stack up my messages or have the vultures call back."

"We were good this morning so we get to play now," Henry explained. "We're going swimming and then Mommy gets to make us a nice dinner with dessert. Don't be sad without me tomorrow, okay? My dad misses me a lot for six days when he's gone, so I have to take him fishing."

"Have a nice evening, Vi," Doreen said in a commanding voice. She wanted me to have the freedom of not thinking about Francis and Company while she and Isa were on watch.

On the drive home I take in the beauty of my surroundings. The vegetation here is lush and tropical. The animals' native to this region range from graceful long-legged, long-necked birds to the prehistoric alligators who sun themselves in our low lands. It's a bit like a sun-drenched jungle where it's always Happy Hour. The further you go down the chain, the more immersed you become in the laid back, nature driven culture. We live in Key Largo, which is too close to the mainland for me; but Wade is based in Miami and, considering traffic, his commute is long enough from here. It's a bit of a compromise, but I'd be foolish to complain. It's February 20 and I am going home for a swim. The rest of the country is bundled up, looking at gray skies, and praying for an early spring.

I am prejudiced to be sure. I'm a Conch -- born and raised in the Conch Republic. I love sunshine, water, and palm trees. Nestled on this lush green island between the Atlantic and the Gulf of Mexico, I am surrounded by all three every day.

Our driveway is paved with shells and is covered by a canopy of overhanging palms. Every time I drive in I feel like I am entering the tunnel leading to paradise. The long narrow drive opens to reveal our two-story, Key West-style home, which seems to be an extension of the Florida landscape. I chose the light green paint to compliment the natural greenery surrounding it. I always dreamed of living in a home with wrap-around porches, and Wade wanted a crow's nest. The manifestation of our compromise is perched majestically on the bay, and we built a seawall and a dock out back to keep the boat in the "backyard."

I check the time and find that we have almost two hours until we have to pick up Megan from school. Lilly has cheer tonight so Wade can swing by and pick her up on his way home if the traffic isn't too bad. It's another fantastically average day.

Chapter Four

Captain Wade Gates eased into the seat of his Cadillac CTS-V. "Daddy's home," he told his car. The Cadillac was his reward for thirteen years of driving family vehicles with practical features like scotch guarded, stain resistant cloth seats. The Caddy was a museum piece and a performance dream. Wade thought it was unfair to limit the speed classification to 0-60 mph in 3.9 seconds. He thought it should be broken down into nano-seconds and that 60mph should be only the first milestone measured. Wade also appreciated the luxurious, comfortable cockpit and the cutting-edge gadgetry . It was like driving a work of art that had a soul.

There had been a tailwind on the way back from California today and Wade and his crew had made great time. He was going to get out of Miami before the rush and make it home before dinner. Wade looked forward to reuniting with his family after each flight rotation. The girls hadn't grown out of running to meet him at the door, and Henry acted like Santa just delivered a big bag of goodies every time he came home. Being away for six days at a time pulled on his heart, but Wade only flew twelve days a month. The rest of his time was devoted to family.

Vi made sure the kids were kept busy doing fun things while he was away and she instigated the celebration of every homecoming, holiday, and good report card. *It's not too often that you find a great homemaker who also looks as good as Vi does in a bikini*, Wade thought with a smile. Even after fifteen years of marriage and three kids, Wade got excited to see her after a trip.

They had met during Vi's senior year at Stetson. Wade was a senior at nearby Embry-Riddle Aeronautical University. The first time Wade saw Vi she was on stage singing with a band in a Daytona nightclub. He could still recall the black mini dress that displayed her beautifully sculpted legs. Her blonde hair was cut into a razor-sharp bob, much shorter than she wore it now. Wade had been awestruck by the fact that such a big voice was coming out of a petite five-foot-four-inch frame.

As a rule, Wade didn't go to nightclubs. He preferred to spend his free time playing basketball, running, or reading; but a buddy of his was having a birthday so Wade made an exception. He didn't own a pair of Z. Cavariccis, which seemed to be the "clubbing uniform" worn by every male in the place. He went out in Levis and a button-down, not thinking twice about wardrobe. Wade stood two inches above six feet and wore glasses, inviting girls to make the annoying and predictable Clark Kent connection. He had always been confident, though, comfortable that he could out think most people he encountered, including his college professors. He didn't need or want to feel that he fit in with the crowd. He felt like he was in his own world most of the time; but after he saw Vi, he was hoping to double his world's population.

He fell for Vi before he finished his first beer and hung around to meet her long after the buddies who had dragged him out that night had gone home. It took more than a year to get her to fall in love with him; but once she gave him her heart, he never had to question her devotion. They spent many years slugging it out with their careers, raising kids, and building a life together. It had all turned out okay because they didn't stop slugging until it really was okay.

Wade turned on the radio. He didn't listen to satellite radio or CDs much. He liked the feeling of being connected, and local radio gave him that feeling. Satellite felt so impersonal. His presets were a variety of formats to match his mood. He was tired. He'd had a hectic six-day sequence of several flights per day and lots of paperwork. The rotation finished with a long last leg and he needed a little pick-me-up. Classical music would put him to sleep today, so he settled on his oldest daughter Lilly's favorite station. He liked the music and he liked being able to talk about it with Lilly. He could tell she was surprised that he knew who The Jonas Brothers were. He liked keeping her on her toes.

He sipped a Starbucks Grande Black with nine sugars. That and the pulse of the music should get him home, he thought. He listened as the DJ talked about some young hot group with a cutting-edge sound.

"This is better than 'American Idol,' people, because these guys already have a deal waiting for them, they just don't know it. So here's the song again. We are going to play it every hour on the hour until we find the band. It's online, it's on every major radio station across the country, and no one is claiming the song! The name of the group is The Francis Kelly Project. That's all we know. Google 'em and you come up with a great big zipola. Nada. So we have a name that doesn't mean anything to anyone and this song. If you think you might know anything that could lead us to the band, call us, text us, or email us. We're dying to be the station that solves the mystery. It's streaming online and you can pull up the mp3 on our web site. Here it is…The Francis Kelly Project."

Wade almost spit up his Grande Black. Francis Kelly? Wasn't that the name Vi used when she was with the band in New York City? The song was playing and it did sound familiar. Then the vocal came in.

"Call home," Wade urgently ordered his car. What had the jock said? Why were they looking for this group?

"Daddy!" Henry answered the phone.

"Hi, dude. Is Mommy around?"

"Daddy, I am a shark and sharks bite people, right? So I can't get in trouble for biting because I didn't do it, the shark did, right?"

"Little man, can I decide later? I need to talk to Mommy." Wade was impatient. He didn't want the song to end before Vi could hear it.

"Daddy, just say I am not on restriction, the shark is on restriction, please?"

"You're not on restriction. Please, Henry, please get Mommy, okay?" Wade begged.

"Hey, babe." Vi was on the phone.

"Does this sound familiar?" Wade asked as she listened to the radio over the car speaker phone.

After a few seconds, Vi started to laugh. "My Lord. Where did you get that? I haven't heard that in years!"

"It's on Power 96 right now."

"Okay, Wade. That's funny. Really, where did you find it?"

"Vi, I swear on our marriage it's on Power 96 right now. I didn't really hear the whole thing, but the DJ said they are looking for this band!" Wade's excitement caused his voice to raise an octave.

"What? Why?"

"Listen, it's ending, maybe he'll come back on air." Wade found himself doing over 100 mph up the on ramp to I-95 South. *Ease off there*, he thought. Driving is so slow and tedious after flying.

"There it is again, The Francis Kelly Project. We're gonna play it every hour on the hour until we find out more about this song and the band. It's on our web site if you want to listen again before next hour or if you want to tell a friend about it. The first person who provides information that leads us to this new young band is gonna win a weekend for two to The Fountainbleu Miami Beach. Help us out. Power 96 wants to be the station that locates this band."

Vi laughed. "New and young . . . okay, well I guess they're in for a surprise!"

"Call this guy to see what this is all about, babe!"

Vi was quiet for a moment. "I don't know . . . I don't have any idea where this is coming from or what it's about. I mean, what if someone thinks we ripped off another artist and they want to dig us up to sue us?"

"What if a major recording artist wants to record the song? Maybe a corporation wants to use it for their advertising. You wrote that stuff, right? You own the publishing, don't you?"

"I do, along with this guy I was in the band with, Brian Kelly. Still, how would our local station have that? I shopped it in New York about twenty years ago. This is truly bizarre."

"Yeah, that guy, your old boyfriend. Fifteen years of marriage notwithstanding, I find him, I kill him. I'm going to call the station and ask some questions," said Wade

"I guess. Just be careful what you say."

"The DJ said it was on their web site, maybe you can find

out more there."

"I'll look it up.And, Wade, save the killing for someone who needs it, huh?"

"Daddy's gonna kill someone? Who? How?" Henry always picked up the tidbit of dialogue not meant for him.

"Good job, Vi. Explain that one to our tiny child," Wade laughed. "You go look online and I'll call the DJ."

* * *

On the way back to the pool, I paused at the computer desk in the kitchen and read the bulletin on the home page of the radio station.

"Nationwide Search for the Band That Recorded This Song . . . click here to play song. The Francis Kelly Project is an unknown, unsigned band with a fresh, new sound. Their use of combined of rhythms and time signatures is unique, ground breaking stuff. This talented young band deserves a chance at the Bigs and we want to find them and take them there. In this day and age, news travels fast, so forward this link to your friends and let's see how fast we can track down The Francis Kelly Project."

Hmmm. Still no real information. Why are they looking for us and where the hell did they get that song? I didn't think I could locate my own copies anymore.

* * *

"Power 96."

"I'm calling in regards to this band you're looking for. Can you tell me why they are being sought after?" Wade had finally gotten through.

"Here's what I know, sir." Great. The twenty-something addressed him as if he were ancient. "I got this mp3 this morning. All the stations in our broadcast group got it.

It came from California originally. All we know is that the owner of our stations wants us to find out who it is. Once we find the band, we give them a number to call in L.A."

15

"May I have the number?" Wade asked.

"Yeah, like I'm gonna give that out to just anyone."

"I know a member of that band. In fact, she's my wife," Wade told him.

"What's her name, sir?" the DJ asked skeptically.

"What difference does it make? You wouldn't know if it was really her or not."

The DJ thought about it. "All right. I'll give you the number if you swear you'll tell them you heard this on my show. Telly Taylor, okay? I want some credit for finding this band. The whole country is looking and I want to get some publicity outta this, okay? You sound like a very respectable man. Can I trust you to do that for me?"

"Okay, Telly. You have my word. Your name gets mentioned. I promise."

"Swear."

"Damnit, Telly, I swear. Give me the number!"

"Okay, okay, it's 818-979-6374."

"Thank you, Telly. I'll make sure you get your media attention."

"Have a nice day, sir."

It was shaping up to be an interesting day, thought Wade. "Call home." The answering machine picked up. Wade looked at the clock and realized it was time to pick Megan up from school. He'd try to call again later.

Chapter Five

"Daddy!" Megan and Henry bolted for the door as soon as Abrams started barking.

"Abrams, quiet, it's Daddy." Megan ran past the huge dog. My Great Pyrenees outweighed me and my two youngest children combined. Pound for pound, he was the most loving "person" in the house. He had conditioned us to feel that it was natural to share our home with an animal the size of a small horse who lumbered around like tank, hence his name.

"'Scuse me, Abrams!" yelled Henry as he slammed, full speed, into his furry big brother. Thank God Abrams is the gentlest dog who ever lived. I think the kids could skin him alive and he's just sit there.

"Good boy." I stroked his ear as I passed by.

Wade came bursting through the door. "Are there any kids in here who missed their dad?" Oh, the screaming. Lilly came through the door behind Wade. Sometimes I saw her in a certain posture or caught her graceful movement out of the corner of my eye, and I couldn't believe my little girl was thirteen already. She carried herself as if she was much older. She was very centered, unshakable, and unaffected by the awkwardness that afflicted most teens.

Megan was hanging from Wade's neck now. She was my heart on legs. Henry was the one I cherished, Lilly was the one I admired, and Megan was the one I worried about. She was much like me; dramatic, determined, and very emotional. Megan was gifted in art, music, and dance, which scared me because I knew where those talents lead. How did I teach her not to dream too big without breaking her gorgeous spirit? She was smart and charming and she idolized her big sister. Lilly was a good example and she took the responsibility of being a role model for her sister seriously. They both spoiled Henry. I already felt sorry for his wife.

Wade finally made his way over to me. "Hey, I've been calling and calling. I was starting to worry." He kissed my cheek.

"I'm sorry. I must still have the answering machine turned down. Megan and Henry fell asleep in the living room while I was making dinner, so I turned off the ringer and turned down the machine." I knew he hated it when I did that. Often he only got a few minutes to call us in between turns and he wanted to be able to get through. It was a constant issue between us.

"Sorry." I kissed him in a way that he knew I meant it without having to hear groans and gags from the kids.

"Dinner is ready. You're all gonna love it! Salmon burgers, cucumber salad, and homemade ice cream for dessert!" I lead the way to the lanai where the table was set. The sun was just beginning to fade into the bay, making the water appear deep purple. The orange, pink and lavender sky looked fake.

We had a huge pool deck, complete with an outdoor kitchen and a dinner table that seated ten. We had tiki torches and Christmas lights everywhere. The back walls of our home were sliding glass pocket doors, which we always had open to give the feeling that indoors and outdoors flowed seamlessly together. It was peaceful and festive at the same time.

Wade stripped down to his boxers and jumped in the pool; he started a trend. I went to get towels. I lived with a school of fish.

Once everyone was refreshed we sat down to dinner, caught up on the events of the day and heard all about Wade's trip.

"Every major media outlet in the country is looking for your mother right now, you know," he told the kids.

"Not really," I said, shooting him a look.

"Actually, they are. Turn on ET or Extra. I bet they have it too."

"What's up, Mom?" asked Lilly, her eyebrow raised.

"Oh, it's probably nothing. Your dad heard one of my old songs on the radio today. I can't imagine how anyone got a hold of it, but they were having some sort of 'name the band' contest on the air. The DJ was probably trying to find the most obscure song possible so that no one would win the prize."

"It's not a DJ, Mom, they're called on-air personalities now. Anyway, this sounds pretty interesting . . . what station?"

18

"I don't know . . ."

"Power 96, Lil." Wade stirred the pot.

"Holy Crap, you're kidding!" Lilly looked at me like I was someone she didn't recognize. "You're music was on Power 96?"

"Not really, it was just for a contest. It's not like it's on the play list."

Wade checked his watch. "Actually, they are playing it every hour on the hour. That's called 'heavy rotation,' I think. It's just a few minutes before seven; turn on the radio."

Lilly went running for the house's central music system.

"Which song is it, Mom?" she asked from the other room.

The sound of Power 96 filled the house and the pool area now. "I hope it's 'Close To You,'" said Henry, "Mommy sings that to me so pretty."

"That's not Mommy's song, it's someone else's," Megan corrected him.

"It's actually *my* song but you can sing it if you want to" said Henry.

"Okay, Mister. Want some ice cream? I'll get it for you." Megan always thought of her brother before herself.

"Power 96. Coming up on the top of the hour, The Francis Kelly Project. Again. C'mon, South Florida, we have been playing this song for six hours and still don't have any information on how to find this band. We're playing it till we track 'em down. I gotta say it's growing on me, but don't make me play it my whole shift tomorrow 'cuz I might OD . . . know what I mean?"

"I do know what you mean," I replied.

"Text me at . . . "

Lilly had her Blackberry going and she was tapping furiously.

"What are you doing?" I asked sharply.

"I want Ellen and Rachel to hear the song. I'm telling them to listen."

"No, no, no, no, no." I swiped the phone. "No one knows I have anything to do with this and it's like digging up bones from a million years ago. I think it might be better to just leave this buried."

Megan came back to the table with ice cream and some bowls. She was pretty efficient for a five-year-old. Yes, the bowls were plastic Princess breakfast bowls, but they would work. I stole away to the kitchen for the spoons and came back just as the first measure of the song started. It sounded a lot better on the house system than it had over the phone earlier. Still, I cringed a little. What a difference eighteen years makes. I screamed my head off with excitement when I heard this on the radio back then. I did get chills now, though.

"Your song is really nice, Mom." Megan was smiling from ear to ear.

"Thanks, Meg."

Lilly grabbed Megan and they started dancing. Henry laughed at them, but he had a bowl of ice cream and nothing was going to tear him away from that.

I felt Wade looking at me. "When I called earlier, they gave me a number to call. I left it on the machine about fifteen times, but I guess you didn't get the message. Call. Find out what this is about. C'mon!"

"Call, Mom. This is so cool!" Lilly showed her excitement.

Wade turned on the big screen TV on the lanai and flipped through the channels. Sure enough, ET was teasing the Band Search.

"This is crazy," I said. "Do you find this a little freaky? *Who* is looking for us? *Who* has enough money and pull to use radio and TV outlets? We would have found Bin Laden by now if we had used resources like this." I was getting unnerved.

"If it was an attorney or a criminal, they would have wanted the element of surprise not the attention of the whole country," Wade reasoned.

"Mom! There's a chat room online about you!" Lilly called from the kitchen.

"Oh my Lord," I said under my breath. The whole family circled behind Lilly. Wade and I were reading along over her shoulder as she read aloud from screen.

"It says that some guy from Colorado is claiming that he wrote the song and owns the publishing rights with a partner. Inside sources in Los Angeles say that he can prove his claim."

"Does it give a name?" I asked, speed-reading the text myself.

"Nope. I guess they're keeping it under wraps until they know the guy's legit," Lilly responded.

"Have you seen anything about why they are looking for the band, or how they got the song?" I was trying to focus on the page, but it was all a jumble as my mind raced.

"Mommy, I'm late for splashdown." Henry knew two times on the clock, lunch and bath time.

"You're right, little dude. Let's go. Lilly, clean up the table please, and, Megan, come on up so that you can go next." I was thankful to escape back into my familiar routine.

"You're serious?" Lilly asked. "Mom, people are trying to find you to make you famous. And you're gonna go bathe Stinky?"

"I'm sticky, Lilly, not stinky!"

"We have no idea who is tracking down the band or why. I am not hastily going to get involved -- I have a family to protect. This is the last word about this for now. And, kids, all of you, it was cool hearing Mommy on the radio tonight, huh?" Three faces beamed. "But we're not going to tell anyone at all. It's a family secret, okay? Keep it Inside the Gates," I said, using our family code for something discussed only at home.

Like the fact that the neighbor drinks too much.

Wade looked more disappointed than anyone. "I'll give the kids their baths, you take a nice glass of wine down to the dock and relax. You have a lot to think about and I hope you'll come to your senses. It's *my* job to protect this family, by the way."

"I don't think I'll change my mind."

"That's what the wine is for. It worked before." Wade winked, holding up Henry. Yup, there was wine the night Henry was conceived, I remembered.

I did just what Wade suggested and tried to get in touch with the feelings this event has created. What good could possibly come from subjecting myself to national exposure? I could only see the disruption, however temporary, of a life I really loved. I didn't want to do anything that might tip the balance. It *was* kind of cool hearing my young, strong voice on the radio, but I didn't even remember the lyrics to sing along. It was like I was listening to someone else. I was. And that was my decision. I was someone else then and I didn't want to risk a moment of who I am now to resurrect the past. I finished my wine. The Decision was made: I would remain in hiding.

Unless someone "outed" me. I took a deep breath and tried to think who could track me here. I'd lived in Key West my whole life and I still owned a business there, so I wasn't not exactly in deep cover. I still used my maiden name -- another stealthy move. I never needed to hide from anything so I didn't exactly cover my tracks. The wine was hitting my head now. I'd worry about this tomorrow, and go upstairs now to make Wade glad to be home.

Chapter Six

Englewood, Colorado

Brian Kelly woke up early as usual. He gently kissed his long-time girlfriend, who lay sleeping beside him, before he quietly left the room. He slept in his sweat pants and tank top so that he woke up dressed for his morning workout. He crept downstairs and could smell that the coffee had automatically started brewing right on schedule. It would take more than a strong cup of java to clear his head this morning. Yesterday's developments were starting to re-enter his consciousness. One of his high school band students had told him that there was a search going on for the band who had recorded "some song that goes, like, dah da duh, *so beautiful so beautiful* and then it gets slow and fast."

Brian's heart had stopped. Certainly the words "so beautiful" weren't unique, but he and Vi had written a song using those words in the hook. Their song also changed time signatures between a ska-style and a slow reggae beat. Brian had always loved the way that song made him feel. There was a little magic in the melody. It was a little too off-beat for most people, though. He had gotten a lot of negative feedback on the cut because it was hard to dance to.

After the student had told Brian where he heard about the search for the band, Brian went online to hear the song for himself. He was transported back in time almost twenty years as he listened to the intro. It was his song. His and Vi's. And he was listening to her clear, strong, sometimes wild voice. He couldn't believe it. When the song had ended there was a tag asking anyone who knew anything about this band or the song to call this phone number.

Brian dialed from his cell phone as his intermediate band class filed into the room. After a brief conversation that left him with more questions than answers, he was given another number with an 818 area code. He had waited until after class to call. The person on the other end answered, "Warner Brothers Studios,

Brooke Taylor's office."

Brain explained who he was and why he was calling, and was immediately put through to Brooke who, in addition to being his new best friend, was in the middle of a power breakfast with her boss, an executive in charge of licensing music for use in Warner Brothers' films.

Brian convinced her, by reciting the titles of other tracks on the demo she apparently had, that he was the leader of the band they were looking for and the songwriter.

"Don't worry about anything. I'll take care of everything. You're about to make it big, Kelly. I'm going to send over some paperwork for you to sign. Congratulations!" she had said.

As soon as someone told Brain not to worry, he knew he should be worried.

"Actually, it's Brian. Brian Kelly. When you offer to 'take care of everything,' could you hone in a little bit more on what exactly you mean?" Brian felt as if he had been excused from a conversation that he thought really should involve him. "What type of paperwork and how does this relate to my music?"

"Your song is going to be used in a major motion picture with an A-List cast, Kelly. Brian…can I call you Kelly? It rolls off the tongue better."

"No, I respond mostly to Brian because it's my name. What's the film, who's in the cast and can I see it or read the script to make sure it's a project with which I want to be affiliated?"

"Brian. Okay, this morning when you woke up, how many songs did you have placed as the title track in a film being released by Warner Brothers Studios?"

"None." Brian understood her argument. He should go with the flow and let it happen. It couldn't be a bad move as far as his long-defunct music career was concerned. Maybe someone would actually listen to the volumes of music he had recorded and something else would sell or get licensed. He wasn't exactly in a position to bargain so what the hell. "You can send the paperwork to my home in Colorado . . ."

As Brian ate his oatmeal and mulled over the conversation

he had yesterday with Brooke, he knew he had to have one more conversation before things could develop further. He had to call Vi. She co-wrote the song and owned half the publishing rights.

He rinsed out his bowl, grabbed an apple, and headed down to his home gym in the basement. He started warming up with a light jog.

Vi. How to call Vi? He had promised, so many years ago, that he was going to stay in the city just six more months and then go back to Florida to live with her. The daily phone calls became weekly, then bi-weekly. They were both busy…

The promise to come back got pushed back by a tour he got hired to do with an up-and-coming vocalist who was opening for a national act. He missed Vi's graduation because he was on the wrong coast. That seemed to be the offense he couldn't forgive himself for, and he grew more distant after that, in spite of Vi's best efforts to understand. She said she wasn't serious about anyone, and he believed her. But days and nights on the road ran together and he started spending every waking and sleeping moment with the up-and-coming and he could no longer bear to hear Vi's voice on the line telling him she loved him. He just stopped calling. The up-and-coming got dropped from the label so the tour -- and the fling -- were over.

Brian had called Vi's best friend after the tour and she told him about Wade. How he was crazy for Vi and treated her beautifully, and how he had waited almost a year for Vi to give him a chance. Brian knew she had spent all that time waiting for him. Now she finally took her life off of pause and moved on. He had wanted to move back to Florida and try to get Vi back, do it right this time, but he didn't. He let her be happy with Wade and he hoped she was. He heard about the wedding and then, years later, that they were expecting.

Calling Vi. "So, what's new?" just wouldn't work. It had been a lifetime.

He got off the treadmill and started lifting. With every rep he thought of a new, witty greeting. He wondered if Vi had heard the song and knew about the band search. Probably. Certainly.

Hearing from him might not be a big surprise under the circumstances. He'd Google her to get her number after his workout and call on the way to school. The East Coast was two hours ahead, so that should be good timing. If she still lived there. He had resisted the urge to Google her so many times before, although he knew her new last name.

He didn't need any more complications in his relationship with Sarah, though. She had been waiting for an engagement ring for seven years. He still introduced her as his girlfriend. He wanted to want to marry her. He didn't look back because thinking about the past might affect the present, so it was best to leave it where it belonged, in the past. Not that he really could, but he tried so hard. Until today.

Brian moved onto leg extensions. *This will probably be good for me*, he thought. To see that all this about Vi was just romantic fantasy. A longing for simpler times, dreams that still seemed to be within reach -- and youth. It wasn't that Vi was the only one for him, it was that he wasn't ever free to move past that period of time. Maybe somehow this connection would give him whatever the hell he needed to let go. After eighteen years. He could end up on "Oprah" if he didn't man up.

He did love Sarah -- very much -- and couldn't imagine life without her. He was happy, very content actually. That was one reason he hesitated to get married. Things were good the way they were. You heard about it all the time, marriage ruining good relationships. That was why. Nothing to do with Vi.

Chapter Seven

I was always first to arrive at Francis and Co. because I loved stealing a few moments alone with my boutique. It was a great feeling to be the solitary occupant in the 2000-square-foot world I created, especially in the morning. I loved to flip the sign from Closed to Open, welcoming the new day and all the untold potential that waited. I liked the sound the overhead lights made as they woke up and combined with the glow of the sunshine outside.

I enjoyed brewing iced tea and coffee and arranging lemon cookies on a silver platter to welcome the ladies of Key Largo who made "Vi's" their gathering spot. Over time, my place had become their destination after dropping the kids at school, tennis lessons, or in between scouring the bathroom and grocery runs. I was flattered that people felt comfortable here, and I loved sending women home with an outfit that made them feel like walking with a little sass in their step.

My concept was to model the store after my dream closet. Our merchandise was displayed to make you feel like you might be peeking through the private collection of your favorite celebrity. I had a few hanging racks, but most of the clothes were in armoires and bureau drawers. I had an eight-foot round ottoman in the middle of the store where we casually arranged the newest arrivals. The shoe room brought tears to every woman's eyes. Rows and rows of shelves, from the floor to eye level, were filled with wedges, heels, peep-toes, sandals, and casual footwear. In Florida that meant stylish flip-flops.

Wade and I painted the walls a toasted almond color that was set off by the heavy, dark wood furnishings we chose. Cream colored, billowy drapes separated the shoe closet from the main floor. The decor chosen by most retailers in the Keys is Gulf-blue walls adorned with pelicans aplenty. My clothing was a little different as well. Better than the inevitable run-of-the-mill resort wear outlet you found in every strip mall. I carried lines from European designers and offered both cutting-edge big city fashion and upscale, yet comfortable island attire.

My alone time came to an end as my dedicated assistant manager arrived earlier than expected.

"Hi, Vi! Good Morning!" Doreen called out from the back room, letting me know that it wasn't an intruder I heard back there.

"Good Morning!" I called back to her, already smelling the gardenia fragrance that always accompanied Doreen.

"We're getting an order today, right?" she asked, coming onto the selling floor where I was just finishing setting up the coffee service.

"J Brand jeans and some pieces from Tria Reno, that new designer I'm trying out," I said as I gave her a quick hug.

"Not loading up on too much inventory before the shows, are you?" Doreen asked, as she sneaked a cookie.

"I hope not. It wouldn't hurt to make a pact that no one leaves here today empty handed, though," I laughed.

The phone rang and Doreen got it before the machine picked up. It was still a few minutes before we were open.

"No, I'm sorry, Mrs. Francis-Gates is not in. May I take a message?" Experience had taught her to conclude that any person using my full name must be a vendor.

"Oh. *Oh.* Oh!" Doreen's eyes were huge. "You know what? She just walked in. One moment please." She put the line on hold. "I think you better take this."

"Who . . . ?"

"Just take it." She went into the back and I took the line off of hold.

"This is Vi," I said.

"Good morning, Vi. It's Brian Kelly . . . uh, Brian. Did I catch you at a bad time? I understand you're just walking in."

Brian's voice. After all these years. I almost froze, but one look around at my reality reminded me that I'm not twenty-three anymore and this isn't the phone call I waited for every day for months on end. "No, Brian. It's a fine time . . . how are you?"

"Well, I am the proud co-writer of the biggest hit in the land right now. I'd say I'm doing pretty well. Have you heard it, Vi?"

"I have. Over and over again. It's creepy and fun at the same time."

Brian laughed. "I know what you mean. Listen, Warner Brothers would like to use the track for a film they have set for release." Brian explained. "They're sending me an agreement . . . I don't know the details yet, but I'm hoping that you'll let them use it."

The picture had come into focus. "So, Warner Brothers is behind the search to find the band." It made me feel a little better that the band search had been conducted by a well-known and reputable source. "Do you know how they got a hold of the song?"

"No. I called a local radio station yesterday after one of my students told me about it, and that lead to a phone number in California which turned out to be a rep from Warner. All she told me is that they want to use the song in a movie with an A-list cast." Brian paused for a moment. "Vi, you're as excited about this as I am, right?"

"I'm not sure what to be excited about," I answered. "You mentioned your student, you're a teacher?"

"Yup. I teach beginning, intermediate, and advanced band at a high school in Denver."

Lilly had found out last night that someone in Colorado was claiming the song. It was obviously Brian. "That sounds like a good fit for you. You must really enjoy passing on your love for music," I said.

"I like it, but I think I'd like to try life as a hit songwriter just to see what it's like on the other side," Brian laughed.

"Sounds like this could be a long overdue and well deserved break for you, Brian. If success in the music business was based solely on talent, you'd have been recognized decades ago."

"Well, you too, Vi. You're selling something too. Not just as a writer, you're the lead vocal. This could just as easily be the start of a new career in music for you."

"Oh, Brian, I'm not sure how to explain this, but if you were to visualize that I have a cart and it's full of bright, shiny, ripe apples . . . " I laughed at myself and heard Brian chuckle on the other end of the phone. "My life isn't only about me anymore. It's about my husband and the kids, the business, and balancing it all. I don't have dreams of being a rock star anymore. I'm happy to let someone else, someone much younger, chase that rainbow."

"But you don't have an objection to letting Warner use the song, do you?" Brian asked. "We're already 'out there.'"

"I know." I've felt the burden of being "out there" for less than twenty-four hours now and it's almost crushed me. "What if I assigned my rights to you and you take sole credit for writing it? You can put whatever name you want to in the lead vocal credit --"

"Really, Vi? All the ambition you had -- all those hopes and dreams? You're willing to just give that up?"

"Sure. And I don't feel like I'm giving anything up. I'm giving it to you." I head Brian make that sound that I've heard so many times before when he hears something that touches him. It was a familiar exhale with a faint "mmm" inside of it. "I have new dreams that took the place of my music dreams."

"I understand, and that's really gracious, Vi. But I know I don't deserve it, and I don't think I can take you up on it. This woman from Warner made it sound like she needs to have this deal done yesterday. She already has the contract on the way to me. I gave her both our names as writers. She wants me to sign it, overnight it to you, and get it back to her ASAP. She made it sound like any sort of delay in the process would be a major snag for the studio."

"I see. Well, could you give me her number, maybe I could talk to her and explain things? Another day couldn't be that big a deal, could it?" I asked.

"When I talked to her, I didn't get the impression that she's in the mood for bargaining. She got a little feisty when I started asking questions about the project, and her response was something like, 'Do you want your song in the film or not?' I'd like to make this as simple as possible to be sure that it gets done." Brian took a deep breath. "I guess I still do want to be a rock star, in a way. I still think about what it would be like to have an artist take one of my songs to number one. I still think about performing.

I look forward to playing in high school band concerts with my kids. I don't want to do anything at this point that could mess it up before I get the chance to see where this might go --"

"Okay. How about this? I'll sign the contract for Warner to get the ball rolling. All they want is rights to the song, correct?"

"That's my understanding. The mastering was genius, remember? They can use it as is. She made it sound like we sign the papers and the song is on the soundtrack. End of story."

"Fine. I'll have my lawyer draft an agreement assigning you my rights to all of the other work we wrote together so that you can have the freedom to do whatever you'd like with it. I'll sign that and have him email it to you today. If you want to send me a copy after you sign it, you can. In the meantime, I'll sign the Warner contract when I get it and return it to them."

I was still leaving myself in a position I didn't really want to be in because I was still affiliated with this song, but I felt an obligation to do this for Brian. I'd just have to hope the fallout was minor. The important thing was that after they use this one piece of music, I'd be out of the picture.

"That sounds great, Vi. Thank you very much. I really appreciate it. I'll send an email to the store so you have my address. I found your site through Google, by the way." Brian sounded very relieved.

"Go get 'em, Brian. I hope I hear more of your stuff on the radio," I said.

"You don't have to make this as easy for me as you are, Vi. I realize what this sounds like -- I drop in after eighteen years to ask for a favor . . . " His voice trailed off.

"Bygones," I said, putting an end to that conversation before it began.

"All right. Take care of yourself. . . . It was great to hear to hear your voice."

"You too, Brian," I said and hung up the phone.

Doreen must have been close by because she came back onto the floor right on cue as my conversation with Brian wrapped up. "Vi, is everything, okay?" she asked with a face full of concern.

"Yes, why?" I asked. "What did he say that made you so sure I should take the call?"

"Well, when an agent from the IRS calls and mentions the word audit, I figured it was best to address the matter right away because I know that our accountant couldn't have possibly done anything wrong and the sooner the IRS knows that, the sooner this whole thing will be over," Doreen blurted.

I guess she didn't expect me to react with peals of laughter because her concern took a turn towards confusion. Musicians were scared to death of the IRS, and Brian and I would leave phone messages for each other that said, "Hello, Mr. Kelly, this is Agent Francis from the IRS . . ." or vice versa.

I explained to Doreen that an old friend was referring back to an inside joke as I dialed the house to let Wade know that the mystery was over.

Chapter Eight

Brian lived close enough to the high school to go home every day for lunch. He was thankful that he had a good excuse to avoid eating in the teacher's lounge and having to struggle to identify with the other educators. He found his interests were more akin to those of his music students, and he was secretly proud to be so in tune with those who determined pop culture.

The home he shared with Sarah was a traditional two-story farmhouse in the midst of newly constructed tract housing. He felt his property had more character than the newer cookie-cutter designs that repeated themselves up and down the cul-de-sacs in the community. A few years ago, a builder had bought up the vacant lots around the few existing homes in the area. The development of the newly formed gated community meant that Brian's house had nearly tripled in value since he bought it, a reward that made it easier to ignore the fact the he had unwittingly become a resident in the very type of community he had intentionally avoided.

He took the stairs leading to his front porch two at a time and saw an overnight letter propped between the screen and the front doors. It was from one Brooke Taylor of Warner Brothers. He tore it open, anxious to see what the terms of the agreement were.

He quickly scanned past the declarations and carefully read the pressing items. Brian and Vi would spilt compensation as "work for hire," the absolute worst deal in the music industry. . .. Warner Brothers acquired the rights for the picture, 'So Beautiful' being part of said picture, and could license the rights from the picture to other companies.... Warner Brothers would pay a one-time payout of five-thousand dollars to own the song.... Brian and Vi would get credit in the film crawl and on any product to which the song was licensed, a CD soundtrack for example....

Brian began to make his lunch and mentally sifted through the points of the agreement. He knew that the rule for making money on a song was to never give up publishing rights – exactly what

Warner was requiring.

Before going to school that morning, Brian consulted his well-worn copy of Donald S. Passman's *All You Need To Know About The Music Business*. He had read that unknown artists generally get between five and ten thousand dollars for a title song deal. He had hoped they would be closer to the top end of that scale, considering the nationwide search the movie studio had undertaken to find the writer. He had also allowed himself to dream about receiving royalties. Warner obviously really wanted this song. Maybe he should get a lawyer. This was a lousy offer.

But, like so many naive artists before him, Brain wanted to sign any deal they offered so that he could get his foot in the door. Brooke's words came back to haunt him again: How many songs had he placed in the title track of a film? Did he want to gamble away a sure thing by negotiating?

Brain finished off his PB&J with banana slices and chugged an energy drink. It was one of those containing fifty times the caffeine a person can safely consume, with high fructose corn syrup added. Good stuff. Pot was illegal, but these were fine. Have a few and get behind the wheel. Brian wondered if road rage or just good old-fashioned rage of every variety had increased since the introduction of this type of beverage.

His mind snapped back to the contract. He decided to forget about the seemingly unfair terms and focus on the fact that he was about to sign his first deal and sell his first song. His first deal wasn't the one he expected to secure his retirement anyway. After twenty years, the moment had arrived and he didn't want to rob himself of the satisfaction he deserved to feel. He dismissed his momentary disappointment and was overcome by genuine excitement.

He wished Sarah was with him. He'd take her out to dinner tonight to celebrate. Maybe $2,500 could buy them a California getaway. They hadn't taken a vacation in a long time and they both loved the coast.

He wanted to make a copy of the contract before he sent it to Vi, so he carried the package to the den. He noticed for the first time that there was another page to the contract. A Performance Agreement. As Brian read it, his eyes grew wide and his stomach seized up. Here's where it all fell apart. The studio wanted "The Artist" to do promotional appearances including, but not limited to, performing for talk show appearances made by the cast and a performance at the studio premiere party.

Oh no. No, no, no, Vi will never agree to this. And The Francis Kelly Project they were expecting was "young, fresh and cutting-edge." Brain knew the recording could still be considered all of those things, but the live version was a little more problematic.

Brain's mind raced. He could pick some of his best students and teach them the song -- but Vi would still have to sing . . . that was not going to work. He paced back and forth across the den. The energy drink was kicking in and he was thinking as fast as his feet were moving.

Brooke never mentioned performing. *Oh, by the way, there's a performance contract.* Nope. She left out that little tidbit. Maybe they'd concede the secondary agreement and just buy the song.

Brian fished his cell out of his cargo pants pocket and scrolled through the numbers he had called yesterday. He saw Brooke's, selected it, and hit send.

"Warner Brothers Studios, Brooke Taylor's office."

Seconds later, Brain had been forwarded to Brooke's cell phone once again.

"Hi, Brian." She answered on the first ring, emphasizing the use of Brain's first name. "Did you receive the contract?"

"I did…"

"Good, good. Sign it and get it to the other party, okay? I have to get this sewn up."

"There's just one issue."

"No issues, Brian. We have to get this done." Brooke sounded less friendly now.

"There's a performance contract here. You didn't mention that yesterday."

"Came up after our conversation. I figured you'd be thrilled to get the media attention. You can thank me when we meet in L.A. next month."

Brain was holding the performance agreement and quickly scanned it for . . . *dates* . . . there were dates. One month from yesterday. He hadn't noticed that part in his caffeinated panic. "Shit," he muttered under his breath.

"What's up Brian? This is great for you! You have *no idea* what the studio is doing to move up the release date on this film. I mean, it's been slated, but Mr. Cooper couldn't find the title song till he heard yours and now it's got the green light and we want to capitalize on all the publicity generated by the search so we are releasing the film in a month. I mean, it's almost impossible on our end." Brooke hadn't taken a breath.

"Mr. Cooper? George Cooper?" Brain asked.

"When you meet him, you had better bow down and kiss his feet, Brian. You owe all of this to him. He loves your song and he pulled every string in L.A. to get it -- and you -- and finally get this film out of the can."

"I don't understand . . ."

"My God, Brian, catch up. Pay attention, okay? Mr. George Cooper," she was speaking slowly and over-enunciating, "heard your song. He loved it. He has a film that he produced and directed called *Lovetime* that has been ready for release for six months, but he hated the title track and didn't want to release it until he found the perfect song. You know how 'Friends' had that Rembrandts song? It was part of the identity of the show. He wanted a song like that."

"Like 'Cheers' . . . where everybody knows your name, right?"

"Cheers to *you* Brian." Brooke obviously had no idea that Brian was referring to one of the most successful sitcoms of all time. *How young is this magpie?* he wondered. She babbled on, unfazed. "He loves this film; it's his child, right? Somewhere, he heard this 'So Beautiful' song from The Francis Kelly Project and he freaked. This is the song he has been looking for -- if the studio gets him this song, the film is ready for release. Everyone who has seen it says it's the next *Titanic*, you know? Big money maker. Great big love story. Cooper thinks this is *the* film of his career. He feels so strongly that the song sets the tone for the movie that he wants it performed when he goes to promote it. You know, Leno, Letterman. You still there, Brian?"

"I'm . . . yeah."

"Are you getting the picture? Instead of being just some filler while the important stuff plays out on the screen, your song is central to the identity of the film. Soooooooooooo, you get tons of national exposure that every other band in the world would die to have. You'll be the new, hot, fresh commodity and you'll be assaulted by labels, management, lawyers . . . you have won the lottery, my friend. Mr. Cooper gets what he wants. Period. It's your lucky lifetime because he has decided he wants your band. So, Brain, don't tell me there's a problem. If you have finals next month, tell your parents you won't need your diploma or degree or whatever, and then buy them a nice house to show them gratitude for their support."

"I don't know if I can pull this together . . ."

"I already told you not to worry, that I was taking care of everything. You'll have a handler for the members of the band. Read the contract, Brain. That's decent money for ten or fourteen days. There are provisions in there for you to use our resources to help you handle offers . . . I have never seen a deal like this Brain. If you start having trouble 'pulling it together' on your end someone might look a little closer at this thing."

"If the song is so important, why are you only offering five grand to get it?" Brian asked.

"Don't do that. You get national exposure, which is priceless, performance money, and per diem. You'll be able to steal tons of gear, I'm sure. Don't get petty with me, Brian. Like I said, if someone starts thinking about this rather than just saying, 'whatever Mr. Cooper wants,' you're out in the cold. Sign the damn contracts, send them to Vi, and get your little asses out here. I'll send you travel information and your itinerary in a few weeks.

And Brian, don't call my cell anymore, I could be meeting with someone important." Brooke was instantly perky, as if a switch had been flipped.

"Have a great day, see you soon!" She hung up.

Brian stood with the phone to his ear for another ten seconds. He felt as if he was still under the spell of Brooke's high-pitched tirade. She reminded him of his teenage students. He checked his watch. Shit! He'd be late for class. He grabbed the contracts and raced out of the house, his mind filled with obstacles, possible solutions, excitement, and dread. "This just gets better and worse at the same time," he muttered.

His seven-year-old Ford Explorer responded to Brian's urgent turn of the ignition by making three failed attempts before coming to life. He had just shifted into reverse when his cell phone rang.

"Damn, damn dammit," he said as he reached to answer the call. It wasn't his principal as he expected. He didn't recognize the number, but the area code was New Jersey.

"This is Brian."

"Hey man, had any rhythmic chocolate lately?" Then Brian heard a very familiar, jovial laugh.

"Jackson! Man, it's good to hear your voice without having to look at your ugly face. How ya doin'?"

Brian was glad to hear from the heartbeat of The Francis Kelly project, Jackson James. Vi and Brian had met Jackson at The Bitter End in The Village. Jackson was breaking down his drum kit after playing with a four-piece band as Vi and Brian were setting up to play the next set. The Francis Kelly Project was a duo at that time, but meeting Jackson had been the first step to forming a full band. Brian loved Jackson's funky playing style and, after Jackson heard Brian and Vi's set of originals, they made plans to get together the next day to rehearse. The other band members were added soon after and, as Jackson had predicted, the duo became a stronger, more dynamic product as a full band.

Jackson's rich baritone boomed through Brian's cell. "I'm great, dude. Really good. Sharon and I have two little girls who rule my world and I'm happy to be in service to all three of 'em eight days a week." Jackson was laughing his good-natured laugh. "I can't believe you still have this number, dude. I figured I'd give it a try though just in case. I'm glad one of my friends shows some stability."

"I don't like change Jackson. I take it you heard the song, right?"

"Ain't that the shit man? I told Sharon I thought someone was punkin' me. We're still livin' in Newark. I sell Buicks during the week and play in a band on the weekends. Anyway, I first heard the song on a test drive. I thought one of the assholes I work with put it in the CD player just to get me, you know?"

"Jax, you're not going to believe what's happening, but I'm two minutes away from having to start class. I teach music at a high school. I have quite a story for you and maybe an opportunity if you're interested."

"I don't wanna ease in on your thing, brother. I just love hearing us on the radio. You paid us fair and square for those sessions. Having it come back is cool and it reminded me of good times. Don't think I'm trying to get any action, 'cuz we're square, dude."

"Well, I need something that only Rhythmic Chocolate can deliver. You said you're playing?"

"Every weekend, man. It's a cool bunch of cats who have 'real jobs,' but have pretty good chops. We do bar gigs mostly, but we get some wedding and convention work now and then. Why?"

"I'll have to get back to you tonight, but do you think Sharon and the kids could do without you for a couple weeks?" Brian was committed to using the original band over any other option. Hearing Jackson's voice again made him certain.

"Sharon's still cool, man. She knows her husband. We got a gig?"

"The gig of a lifetime, Jackson. Can I call you at this number around six your time?" Brian had parked the car and was running into the music department. The bell had rung about three minutes ago.

"I'll be waiting, Brain. You have that serious tone like you have somethin' good cookin'. I'm game."

"Talk to you later, Jackson." Brain snapped his phone closed and joined his students in his classroom who were sitting in a group talking among themselves.

"Sorry I'm late guys. You ready to get started?" Brian settled into his real life gig and spent the rest of the day thinking about the overture for 'The King and I,' this spring's production put on by the drama and band departments.

Chapter Nine

Brian and Sarah dressed in their finest and dined at Chez le Bear in the lower downtown section of Denver. The local young professional set had dubbed the area "Lo Do." They moved into the formerly depressed part of the city, bringing their development dollars and "just add water" clientele. The formula had been very successful.

Brian and Sarah enjoyed every moment of the decadent evening. Over Pino Gris, chilled lobster salads, and caramelized pears, Brian laid out the whole opportunity/dilemma to Sarah and they had thought it through together. They agreed the best course of action would be to get the rest of the band on board first thing in the morning, leaving Vi as the last contact. If the other band members were willing, maybe she could be influenced by peer pressure. Hopefully Vi was an easily swayed and still attractive forty-year-old woman. Demi Moore was never hotter than when she hit the big 4-0 milestone. Maybe Vi had fared as well as the movie star. Brian felt physically ill knowing that Warner Brothers had assumed the band was "young, fresh, and new." At least they were new.

"To The Francis Kelly Project." Sarah raised her wineglass one more time for the final sip. She beamed with pride and excitement for the man she loved. Sarah knew that Brian enjoyed teaching music, but the evidence of his real passion was all over their home. Band posters hung in the gym; newspaper clippings and articles featuring Brian were laminated and carefully catalogued, and the *Musician's Friend* catalogue arrived monthly so that Brian could ostensibly "look for gear for the school band program." Sarah was worried, though. A band of forty-somethings? How would the movie company feel about that?

Sarah had seen the old band pictures so many times. She had studied Vi, and was even a little obsessed with her after she found out that Brian had dated her for such a long time. Sarah's insecurity and need to measure up had faded with time. She and Brian had been together for nearly seven years. Maybe a break like this would give him a new outlook on his life and their life together. They didn't talk about marriage very often because it always started an argument. Sarah was thirty-four and the alarm on her biological clock had been going off for about four years. She knew she was facing a difficult decision. If Brian was so slow to make the ultimate commitment to her, how likely would he be to jump into having kids right away? This professional break might be the difference, though. Brian had told her that he wasn't sure he could ever provide a comfortable life for them on his teaching salary and that he wanted to be more financially secure before marriage.

Sarah studied Brian with objective, critical eyes as he finished his dessert. He looked forty -- not older than that, though. He worked out six mornings every week and he was in great shape. His hair, however, was a problem. How could she convince him to let go of the ponytail? It screamed *clinging to my youth!* It didn't make him look young at all, like he thought it did. And it had some gray running through it. In his old band picture Brain had wavy hair, short but shaggy. She made him over in her mind. How would a present-day shaggy cut work for him? He definitely needed color to cover the gray. How about a forty-year-old Zac Efron type cut? That would be pretty good she decided, if she could convince him.

And the glasses just had to go. Sarah knew he hated contacts, though. Maybe she should suggest an update to the glasses. His frames were so big he looked more like Harry Potter than the High School Musical star she was picturing earlier.

Thankfully, Brian's job had kept him in practice musically. He wouldn't have to be nervous about his performance. As if reading her mind, Brian broke the comfortable silence.

"Wanna be my audience for a private concert at home? I want to rehearse the song and you can pretend to be my groupie."

"You got it, rock star." Sarah reached out to grab his hand. She would have the makeover done this weekend. They could go to the Cherry Creek Mall and take care of everything all at once. After the new glasses, the new hair, and some funky clothes, Brian would be looking the part. Sarah wondered about everyone else, though.

Too bad for Warner Brothers, she decided. They made the mistake of assuming, and you know what they say about that. They offered a performance contract to a band they had never seen or heard. Since when was that good business?

Chapter Ten

Mayor Sam Wintner placed the old-fashioned telephone receiver back in the cradle. He sat straight and tall in his leather wing-back chair, looking over the town square through the window of his law office. From the hand-laid brick streets to the familiar faces he saw going about their business, it seemed that the day was progressing in the same manner as it had each day of the past twelve years. But son of a bitch if that last phone call hadn't changed a little bit of the world as he knew it.

Sam was surprised and pleased to hear from his old friend Brian Kelly. They'd quickly caught each other up on the most noteworthy events of the past eighteen years.

Neither had any children, which was a sore subject with Sam. After he had won the mayoral election in the town of Commerce, Texas, two years ago, his wealthy and influential supporters began to groom him for a run at the Senate. The same group had brought a university campus extension to the small town. They made plays and won political games when they had personal interests at stake. They could hand-pick their representative; but they mentioned, on more than one occasion, that Sam would be easier to sell to voters as a family man. Sam had always wanted children and thought it was important to carry on his family name. But his young wife had no intention of destroying her body "to give birth to a little leach" who would require her every waking moment. Worse yet, a baby would cost her some beauty sleep and she liked to sleep in after her evening escapades. Cassandra Wintner wanted to be free to jet into Dallas for shopping and cocktails at her leisure.

After a few minutes, Brian revealed the motivation for the out-of-the-blue call and told Sam about Warner Brothers' interest in their song. Sam hadn't heard about the search for the band, and it had taken a few minutes for Sam to grasp what Brian was getting around to.

Sam didn't share Brian's excitement. The mayor of Commerce, Texas, and hopefully the next junior senator from

Texas couldn't play keyboards in a band and maintain his credibility with the voters. Hell, if it was a country band it might not be so embarrassing, but playing top forty dance music just wasn't going to fly with the good folk of Commerce. The men were successful in various professions ranging from medicine and law to ranching and oil. Manly men. Texans. They could drink you under the table till four a.m. and be in the office making million-dollar deals by seven. Their women were well taken care of, and they took good care of their men in return. For that reason, there were already questions about Sam Wintner among his backers. Sam couldn't even knock up his own wife. If he couldn't call the shots in his own home, could they really count on him to carry out their agendas in the Senate?

Sam knew touring the talk show circuit playing keys in some fruity dance band would not do much for his already questionable image. It was true that Clinton had played sax, but he was a Democrat. It was expected for those guys to be softer. Huckabee played bass on "The Tonight Show," but he didn't get the nod from the GOP. Sam Wintner wasn't going to consider taking a potentially career-ending risk for something as far removed as loyalty to a band he left eighteen years ago. Although, playing in the band had given Sam a freedom that he had never felt before and had not been able to duplicate since. It was the only time in his history that he felt like himself. At that time he lived an authentic truth: he was being Sam, for Sam, and by Sam.

Linneava Harper-Wintner, his mother, had been well bred, as they say. According to her, exposure to the arts made for a well-rounded child, and she had insisted that Sam learn to play piano. She forced him to take lessons until he graduated from high school. During his time at NYU he had found that playing in bands was an easy way to make money, get girls, and score free beer. His choice to go north for school made it easy to keep the secret that he was playing in bars. His mother never would have approved and his friends would have laughed him out of Texas for good. Guitar or drums might have been easier for them to take, but there's something kind of feminine about tickling the ivories. Sam never wanted to risk what the reaction to his playing would be, so he kept it to himself. It was just part of his college life before he came back to Texas to attend Baylor Law School.

For one free-wheeling moment Sam daydreamed about accepting Brian's offer, but he knew his life had to go on according to plan. A flashback to his college days could ruin his chance at the Senate. He had never used the name Sam Wintner on stage. He called himself Sammy White and took payment only in cash or beer. There was no trail leading from New York City to Commerce, Texas.

Once the connection was made, Sam could imagine his political opponent's campaign commercial showing him spending college breaks healing the sick in Nigeria while -- flash old picture of Sam playing keys with one hand and swigging a beer with the other -- "Sam Wintner was squandering his family's wealth and neglecting his studies." Sam shuddered at the thought of giving the opposition that type of ammunition.

He wondered what Cassandra would think if she knew he had played in bars around lower Manhattan. She might find it sexy. Sam worried that the only thing about him she found truly sexy was the substantial inheritance he had acquired when his mother passed away. She had started discussing marriage soon after the will had been read.

Brian had been disappointed that Sam wasn't going to accompany the band on the tour. Even though he couldn't participate, Sam felt good knowing that he had been in demand and the whole country had been looking for him. There was something kind of surreal about the whole thing. Considering his future ambitions, Sam knew he had made the right decision. But he wrote down the number still showing on his caller ID, just in case he ever wanted to call Brain to say hello. He always was a hell of a nice guy.

Chapter Eleven

Brian understood Sammy's reluctance to be a part of the tour. Brian was pretty sure he was the only person Sam had ever given his real name to in the music scene in the City. Brian always felt there was something Sam was hiding from. At any rate, they had parted on good terms after Sam graduated from NYU. In a drunken "I love you man, you're my brother" moment, he had written down his name and parents' home address in Commerce and told Brian if he ever needed anything, not to hesitate to contact him. Sammy sounded like he was wound pretty tightly these days. *What the hell happens to some people*? Brian wondered.

Now Brian had a keyboard player to find. There was also a makeover on his agenda for later today if Sarah had her way. He wasn't crazy about cutting his hair, but he knew she was right. Maybe they would go into Boulder tonight to try out his new look and hit some of the bars. He was bound to find players there. Boulder was a cool, eclectic college town.

For a brief moment he had considered giving the opportunity to one of his best students, but then he would be babysitting a minor and he wanted to enjoy this ride. Besides, he really needed someone with stage experience. Maybe Jackson's keyboard player would work out; he'd have to ask about that. It would be good to have two people in the band that had been working together recently.

He had yet to locate Adam Richards, their bass guitarist. Brian hadn't heard from him since he left Manhattan. During Brian's last weeks in the city, Adam had become withdrawn. He was depressed over breaking up with his girl and when Brian got picked up for the national tour and disbanded The Francis Kelly Project, Adam's dream of making it big with the band was crushed. Adam wasn't the kind of guy to go out and find a new situation or make things happen for himself. He was unbelievably talented and could cover any hole in any band like he was playing his primary instrument. Need a drummer? If you have a kit, Adam could play for you. Bass? No problem. Keys? Give him three boards so he doesn't fall asleep from boredom. Brian had heard about him before they actually met. He had a rep for being a monster musician and he was described as "the best, fill-in any instrument here, player in the City."

Google searches on Adam Richards had returned approximately sixty kabillion hits. Brian had added "band," "music," "New York City," and anything else he could think of that might shake the right Adam loose. He decided his next step would be to call some of the talent agencies based in Manhattan. A player as well-known as Adam had been should still be in someone's address book. He hoped he made the connection quickly.

Brain had planned to wait until everyone else was on board to call Vi, but he had to get her to sign the contracts and he had already lost a day trying to assemble the band. He should have forwarded the package to her yesterday after he signed. All his effort to fulfill the performance agreement could be a waste of time if Vi said no to the tour. He could use any competent musicians as band members if he had to, but it would be impossible to find a singer who could mimic her vocals. He should know -- he had tried.

When Vi left the City, she had let him keep the demos. She just took a few as souvenirs. He had tried to find another singer who sounded like Vi, but no one had the bite she had to her voice. She was very versatile and a very emotional singer. From one song to the next you would swear you were listening to different people. That should have made her easy to replace, but Brian was used to writing material for Vi's voice. He could be as whimsical as he wanted to be. He wasn't restricted by style or sound. It was hard to find a singer open to being a chameleon; most wanted to establish themselves and develop a signature sound. Pigeon holed -- that's what it felt like to Brian. He wanted to record different styles and draw from different genres. In fact, that's how "So Beautiful" came to life. Two different styles and a few different time signatures came together to create one great song. Finally, someone else agreed!

Brian finished his morning workout with a light jog on the treadmill and decided to make some calls to try to find Adam. He would call Vi once he had a commitment from Adam. He knew he'd need a little luck to get this wrapped up today, but he was determined.

Wiping his face with a towel and taking the stairs two at a time, Brian made his way to the den and his laptop. Before he began his search for talent agencies in the City, he noticed he had new mail. He clicked his inbox and saw an unfamiliar address. The subject read, "From Adam Richards' sister." Damn, the Law of Attraction did work. He opened the mail and noticed it had been forwarded to his personal email from his school email address. He had set that up so he didn't have to keep up with two accounts.
"Dear Brian,

I don't know if you remember me, but we met once in New York when you were playing in The Francis Kelly Project with my brother, Adam Richards. I was very excited to hear one of your songs on the radio recently. I still have a copy of that CD you guys made. It was really good. I still listen to it every so often.

I Googled you and found this email link on your school's web site. I hope you don't mind me contacting you and hope I don't sound too presumptuous when I ask if the recent interest in your song and the band might lead to an opportunity for Adam to work with you again. He was really happy when he was working with you and Vi. You made him feel like he was a part of something special.

Adam has been down a very hard road. He has been arrested for DUI three times. He served his time for that and he has been through rehab twice. This last time was a 28 day program and he did very well. He just got out two weeks ago and is living with me, my husband, and my two children in Long Island. He's working at Wal-Mart, the 10pm-6am shift to try to avoid the temptation to drink. Adam was taking pills as well, I don't know what, but he's been clean since making it through the program. He's trying really hard. As long as he stays sober, he has a place with us. Still, I know it's best for him to have his own life, not just adopt ours.

Brian, I know Adam needs some good luck to stay on the right track. He was playing with a band before he got well, but he's afraid to do that again because of the environment. I know you are good people. It would be so great for him to be around good people. Playing music is as natural to Adam as breathing and he isn't himself without it. You wouldn't even have to pay him. My husband does well and we could work something out so Adam wouldn't know. I understand this is a bit of a burden, but I have faith that Adam is determined to stay straight and I want him to have every possible opportunity to do that. Again, I'm sorry if I overstepped by contacting you. I love my big brother. That's my excuse. Thanks Brian. If you want to contact me, here's my number . . ."

Brian looked at the clock on the wall. Six a.m. local time, eight a.m. in Long Island. It was Saturday, but even if the rest of household slept in on weekends they should have been awake by now. He knew that Adam himself wouldn't mind being awakened to hear news like this. Brain picked up the phone and dialed. Three rings later he was talking to the greatest musician he had ever heard play. The country was finally going to get to hear Adam Richards play bass . . . or keys, whatever he chose.

Chapter Twelve

The Gates home was always a flurry of activity on Saturdays. There were games to play in/cheer for/practice for and lessons to take. The kids' schedules kept us all running and I longed for summer. Saturdays during the summer usually meant packing the fridge on the boat, fueling up, and heading out onto the water. Even Abrams liked to hear the big engines roar to life. He ran down the dock as fast as the kids to get on board. It was just a few more months until school was out. I looked forward to summers more now than I did when I was the student.

As I poured my breakfast from the blender, I looked at the calendar hanging on the freezer door. Megan had soccer at nine, Henry played at ten, Lilly was cheering that night for boys' varsity basketball -- oops, almost missed something -- Henry had a birthday party at one. There were a few hours in the afternoon when I planned to run to the boutique to make sure all was well. I expected to have an overnight letter from Brian waiting for me there. I wanted to be sure to get that taken care of so I could send it on its way for Monday before ten a.m. delivery.

All of us usually went to the soccer field together. Lilly had a crush on a boy from school who reffed the Under Six games, so she was thrilled to come along. Even before she had extra incentive, she tried to make it to all of the games. She knew how much it meant to the little ones to have their cool big sister there.

"Hey baby." Wade swooped in for a sweaty kiss as I leaned back out of the way. "What?" I'm not that wet."

"Your nose is dripping." I blew him a kiss. "I'll take a rain check on that pucker. Good run?" I winked at him.

He grabbed his Gatorade from the fridge and headed for the stairs. "Yup. Felt great. It's already hot, though. How much time do I have before the first game?"

"We should leave in half an hour." I told him. "Wake Lilly up if she isn't moving around, okay?"

"Lill? Get up Lilly, hit the shower!" I heard him knock on her door as he ran down the hall.

Megan and Henry had been up since 6:00 watching Disney Channel and devouring the Breakfast Bread I made last night. The difference between boys and girls was truly amazing. Megan and Lilly were good eaters, but Henry wouldn't quit. He'd eat all the livelong day if I'd let him. They sat at the breakfast bar watching the flat screen in the kitchen. Yes, there was a TV in every corner of the house. During football season Wade liked to be able to make a sandwich without missing a snap. And take a lap in the pool, visit the bathroom, tinker in the garage . . .

I took a minute to stare at the little faces sitting behind empty plates and full glasses of milk. Megan was wearing her princess nightgown with a tiara, necklace, bracelets, rings, and high-heeled shoes. Henry had on his Mickey Mouse jammies. His blond curls were going every which way and he had a few crumbs on his little chin.

I leaned over my side of the breakfast bar and gave them both kisses. "Drink your milk, soccer players."

"Oh toodles" they yelled at the TV and grabbed their glasses. Megan wasn't really interested in the Mickey Mouse Clubhouse anymore, but Henry loved it, so they traded off on TV time.

I glanced at the clock.

"Have you guys seen this one before?" I asked.

"Mom, he's seen this, like, fifty times. Is it time to get ready?" Megan wasn't one to get distracted; she had an adult awareness of things like schedules and timing.

"Yup. Let's get upstairs and get your teeth brushed, faces washed, ears cleaned . . ."

"Mommy, I don't want my hair done, okay? I'm gonna wear my sweatband anyway." As he lobbied for his way Megan helped Henry get down from the tall bar chair.

"Sounds reasonable, dude. Meg, can you get him started while I clean up a little down here? I laid out both your uniforms on your bed."

"Aces Mom. I'm all over it." They raced up the stairs giggling and pushing the whole way.

I quickly rinsed the dishes and dropped them in the dishwasher. I wondered what would happen if I didn't wash the dishes before I put them in the washer? Seriously, why? The phone rang just as I headed for the stairs. The caller ID said it was Megan's friend Anna's house.

"Gates residence" I answered.

"Vi, it's Mary. How are you?" Anna's mother was a funny, "real" person. I got along with her very well which was great because our kids were best friends.

"So far, so good!" I laughed.

"Oh, well I'm happy for you. I have a wildlife situation and I wonder if you can take Anna with you guys to soccer to buy me some time?"

"Yeah, sure. What happened?"

Mary started to whisper, "Fuzzy the ferret. He went to ferret heaven last night. Anna hasn't noticed because she's busy getting ready for soccer, thank God, but I need to sneak away to go get another Fuzzy. I know I should use this to explain death and that everything dies," Mary had that dah, da, dah, da, dah, rhythm to her speech. "But geezus H., it's a damn rat. I'll just replace it. It's not like Grandma kicked the bucket right?"

"This is going to sound really weird and morbid, but take Fuzzy with you. Then you'll be able to match him better. You know size, weight. They can probably dispose of him for you too." I whispered myself to keep the secret from curious ears.

"Oh yeah. Good Vi, I'm gonna drive an hour with a dead rat on the seat next to me."

I started to laugh. "Henry plays at 10:00, so we'll keep Anna with us and bring her home after his game. You'll have more time, okay?"

"Thanks Vi. You're a lifesaver. I'll send Anna over."

"That's fine, just have her come in the lanai, it's open. I'm waiting for her."

"She's on the way right now."

"I'll have my cell if you want to call. If I don't hear anything I'll just drop her off after the game."

"She just went through the hedge do, you see her?"

A dark ponytail and a "Francis and Co." soccer jersey bounded up to the screen enclosure door. Of course I sponsored the team.

"Good Morning Anna," I said. "Megan's upstairs, so surprise her and tell her to hurry." Then into the phone, "The eagle has landed."

"Good. Fuzzy and I are going for a ride." Mary hung up and I went upstairs.

Lilly's door was still closed, so I knocked. "Lilly? Are you up honey?"

"Oh Crap! C'mon in Mom!" Lilly moaned from the other side.

"Hey sleepy. Are you comin' this morning?" Lilly sat up and threw off the covers. Her bedroom was the perfect fantasy bedroom for a thirteen year-old girl. Pottery Barn Teen met their monthly quota when I decorated in here. Lilly and I had done it together last summer and we had a blast painting, choosing furniture and accessories, and hooking up her wall mounted flat screen which she could also use as her computer monitor. Our kids had better do well in college because they were used to the good life.

"How much time do I have?"

"Only about fifteen minutes, I think." I gave her a kiss on the top of her head. "Stay up late watching movies?" I asked.

"No. I was reading and the next thing I knew it was two a.m. I knew I had to get up, but I thought I would hear everyone."

"Tell you what. You jump in the shower. I'll tell Dad to grab some "to go's" from the kitchen and you guys can meet us there. Anna's here, so I'll take the kids now. Still hurry though, okay? Megan will be upset if you see Henry's game and miss hers." I kissed Lilly's head one more time.

"Dad will let me have a coffee." She smiled and raised her eyebrows at me. I didn't like her having coffee, but Wade pointed out that soda is just as bad and I can't ban everything.

"Just one Java Jane. I don't know what it is about you kids having to have coffee. I made Breakfast Bread, it's down there."

"Great Mom, I'll be quick." Lilly headed for her bathroom and I made my way toward the giggles. Megan and Anna had Henry dressed and they had soapsuds all over Henry's face. They were "shaving" him with Megan's Barbie comb.

"Mommy, I'm shaving my beard!" Henry's eyes gleamed above the foam.

"That's . . . great. The car leaves in five minutes. Let's go!" I wetted a cloth and removed the froth. "Awwwwwwww," the collective groan was magnified as it bounced off the tile in the bathroom.

"Wade?" I entered our bedroom where Wade was fully dressed and sitting at the computer. Our bedroom was Wade's retreat . It was really the only room in the house that he got to decorate without input from me or the kids. I liked it in there because it made me feel more a part of his world. The antique furniture was typically oversized and made from solid dark walnut. The wood floors were whitewashed oak and the bedding was rich in texture and color. Wade chose layers of blues from midnight sky to the turquoise blue you can only find in the waters surrounding the Abacos. I thought of it as "The King's Quarters." He thought of it as a man's room with manly colors. I went to his desk and cashed in the kissing rain check from earlier. "Did you hear Anna?" I asked him, still nose to nose.

"I guess we are taking her along? Are you ready to go?" he asked.

"Lilly got up late, but she'll be ready soon. Do you mind bringing her just a few minutes behind us?" I kissed him again.

"Nope, I like the way you asked."

"I'm gonna get going; make sure Lilly grabs something to eat."

Wade started typing again. "I'll grab a couple "to go's" from the kitchen," he said as he read my mind and used my name for the on-the-run meals I put together and kept in the fridge so the kids didn't resort to junk food when they needed something quick.

Wade and I made a good team. We covered all the bases and rolled with the swells. When you practiced that technique with the easy things, it was easier to do during tough times. I grabbed the bag I had packed with snacks, water, sun block, extra socks, and the camera and joined the kids who were already strapped into the car.

Just before I started the Jeep, I heard the phone ring. I hoped it didn't hold them up.

Chapter Thirteen

Wade reached for the phone, "Gates residence."

"Is this Wade?" asked a male voice that he didn't recognize.

"Yes it is," Wade responded in his usual easy-going manner.

"Wade, my name is Brian Kelly. I was in a band with Vi years and years ago."

"Brian, yes. The Francis Kelly Project. You guys have had some excitement lately." Wade leaned back in his chair. "I'm glad you called L.A. I couldn't get Vi to do it."

"Well, it seems that the situation has gotten a little more exciting. I was calling to tell Vi that our licensing deal has, well, evolved a bit."

"She just left with the kids to take them to soccer, but I can give you her cell number." Wade felt a little strange talking to the man Vi had been in love with before she had ever met him. They had never spoken until now -- not that he had much interest in becoming friends with her former lover, even if the relationship ended decades ago.

"Well, Wade. Maybe you can help me here. You said you tried to get Vi to call L.A.? So you're okay with all of this?"

"I was the one who called the radio station and tried to get Vi in touch with whoever was looking for you guys. I think it's great that your song is going to be in a movie. You know I never wanted Vi to quit singing in the first place. She loved it and she was so good…of course I don't need to tell you that."

"Well, here's the thing. The movie was produced and directed by George Cooper and it's a pet project for him, so he's doing a rare promotional tour. The studio wants us to go out with him and perform the song on some TV talk shows and at the premiere party."

"That's awesome!" Wade imagined Vi, looking gorgeous on TV, singing her heart out.

"Yeah? That's great. I'm, you know, really glad that you

think so…but you think Vi will think it's awesome? I mean, she made it pretty clear that she doesn't want anything to do with music anymore. She told me she's really happy with her life just as it is and doesn't want to risk changing any part of it." Wade was glad to hear that. "I have the rest of the original guys on board -- well, all except one -- and we really need Vi to do this. Hell, I'm scared to even ask her."

"Listen. You give me the details, I'll talk to Vi. It's a lot easier to say no over the phone to someone you…" Wade thought quickly, "don't see very often. It's a lot harder to say no when your husband and kids are tugging on you, and I know we'd all love to see Vi get to do this. This is rare, Brian. You guys are getting something really rare. Second chances don't show up too often."

"Wade, I can't thank you enough. For, well, you wouldn't have to be this cool, you know?"

Wade laughed. "I'm sure your wife is being cool about it too. When you love someone you want them to reach for the stars, right?"

"Well, I'm not married, but you're right about that."

Not married? Shit. Wade hadn't seen that coming. At their age, who wasn't married? Someone who's waiting for that rare second chance? Wade's stomach flopped. The moment of panic passed and Wade started typing the details Brain was dictating into his laptop. It wouldn't be easy to sell Vi on this, but Wade thought that she would be very happy that she had done it once it was all over. And wasn't life about taking those wild rides and making the memories that can give you pleasure every time you call them up? His wife shared that philosophy. He just had to get her to put it to action.

"Lilly!" Wade called when he hung up the phone. "You aren't going to believe this!"

Chapter Fourteen

Wade and Lilly arrived at the soccer field soon after the game got underway. I caught sight of them as they were walking towards us from the parking area. Luckily, Megan was playing on the field closest to the parking lot.

I took off my straw hat, tied to look tired, drooping cowboy-style, and waved it so that Wade and Lilly could pick out where Henry and I were standing. It was amazing that at 9:15 a.m. in February the Florida sun could be that strong.

"Do you have enough sunscreen on, dude?" I asked Henry.

"Mom, my shorts are so long they go past my socks and this jersey covers all my arms." He stood with his arms out to his sides to prove his point.

"You look super-cool, Henry. The sweatband is the thing that really sets off the whole uniform. And I know something about that, it's my business," I remind him.

"Then, Mom, can I tell you something?" He looked very serious.

"Go." I gave him my undivided attention.

"Mom, you're really petty. You look like that lady, Helen, in the movie where the kids have to teach her everything. Prettier, Mom. But that hat is something awful. You have to get a new hat. It's your bizzzzz-ness, Mom."

I got down on my knees to be eye to eye with him. "I know it was hard for you to say that, buddy. I'll think about it, okay?" I gave him a big squeeze. "Thanks for saying I look like that lady in the movie. Her name is Kate Hudson and she's very pretty."

"You're way prettier, Mom."

Wade and Lilly had been standing behind us for some time now and heard most of our conversation. "That hat is God-awful and I've been telling you that for years. It smells too. Stale Summer if I had to call it something." Wade gave me a one-armed hug and lifted up Henry with the other.

I crinkled my nose at him. This isn't the first time

my hat drew friendly fire.

Lilly started yelling and gave me a break from the assault. "Go Megan!!! Go Megan!!"

Megan had the ball and was taking it down the field with Anna beside her. They got to the other end and Megan took her shot. She missed, but she was really proud of herself for taking the ball away from the other team. One of our players trapped the ball and kicked it hard in the direction of the goal. Megan's head was in the wrong place at the right time, it ricocheted and she got to finish what she started, she scored! "Ow! Dang-it!" Megan was rubbing her head. "You kicked me with the ball!" she yelled at her teammate. We all laughed hysterically. "You scored Meggie!!" Shouted Lilly. "Nice shot!"

"Yeah, Megan!" Henry was jumping around like a true fan. We all were. Megan realized that everyone was cheering for her and she came over to the sidelines to give hugs all around. I noticed she was still wearing her princess jewelry form earlier. I had to laugh. Both Mother and daughter failed Accessorizing 101 today and she was a walking billboard, wearing a Francis and Co. jersey. Hey, we had our own style.

Megan's goal was the only one of the game. Henry decided to spend most of his game on the bench drinking juice and eating the snack the Team Mom had brought. His game was even less eventful.

We grabbed our stuff and we headed toward the parking lot.

"I have to run to the store for a while this afternoon," I told Wade.

"Okay. We're all headed home right now though, right?" he asked.

I had driven the Jeep and we had reached where it was parked. "Yup. Who wants to go with me and who wants to go with Dad?" I asked.

"I want them all to come with me if that's all right with you. I missed everybody." Wade had a weird look on his face. Maybe they were planning to pick up lunch to surprise me.

"You missed me too, Mr. Gates?" Anna asked wide-eyed.

Wade lifted her in first, "Of course, Anna." He looked at me. "Race you home," he said.

We only lived about ten minutes from the field, but it was nice to get some alone time. I didn't get much of that at all. Once I made it home, it was confirmed that Wade had won the race. He had passed me on A1A, so I wasn't shocked.

I expected there to be whitecaps in the pool from all the post-game activity, but it was quiet everywhere around the house. Totally quiet. I set my bag down and hung up my keys before the panic hit -- did someone get hurt?

My clan all jumped out at me at the same time. "Surprise!" they shouted. Anna had gone home.

"Umm . . . what's the occasion?" Everyone looked as though they had a secret they were dying to spill.

"Lilly has news," said Megan.

Lilly came over and grabbed my hand, leading me to the kitchen table. She pulled out a chair for me, and Megan and Henry perched themselves on the breakfast bar. Wade and Lilly joined me at the table.

"Mom," Lilly began, "you always taught us to follow our dreams and to take on all of life's challenges head-on, right?"

"Dad and I will help you any way we can," I said.

"You know how you have always sung that song to us about how *when you have the choice to sit it out or dance, I hope you dance?*" Lilly had tears in her eyes now.

I leaned forward and reached for her hand. "What is it, Lill?" I looked from face to face and they all were tearing up, except Henry who looked like he might have to go potty.

"Mom, it's your turn to dance." Lilly was smiling as tears streamed down her face.

Wade took over from there. "We always said that our biggest job as parents was to set an example for our kids, right?" I nodded. "And we have raised some fearless, beautiful children."

"You guys are incredible," I told my kids. "But you're all going to be on restriction if someone doesn't tell me what's going on very quickly."

"I spoke with Brian Kelly this morning. George Cooper wants The Francis Kelly Project to accompany him to promote the film. It will mean appearances on the talk show circuit and at the premiere party. George Cooper wants you, babe. How can I say that to my wife with a smile on my face?" Wade asked no one in particular.

"How does George Cooper know about The Francis Kelly Project? There is no Francis Kelly Project. There hasn't been for eighteen years!"

"There is, though. Brian talked to the other band members. They're all really excited. You're going to get the celebrity treatment!" Wade was hugging me now.

"Mom, you're going to be on TV, and maybe you'll meet everybody from *High School Musical*!" Megan shrieked.

"How did you find out about all of this?" I asked Wade.

"Brian called here just as you were leaving this morning. He told me that Warner Brothers was offering a better deal than the original offer to buy your song. They added a performance agreement and he wanted to talk to you about it."

"You didn't answer for me, did you?" I was horrified.

"Of course not, but this is great news, isn't it?" Wade asked.

All the kids yelled at the same time. "Guys, guys, guys. . . ," I said. "Mommy isn't going to go to Hollywood or wherever to sing. I don't sing anymore. I couldn't if I wanted to."

"It's one song, Vi. Over and over, but it's just one song. You can do that, for heaven's sake." Wade sounded like he was giving a pep talk to one of the kids.

"Mom, I hope you dance." Lilly and I were still holding hands. One by one each of my corny but loving family members came over and added their hands to ours.

"Mom, I hope you dance," said Megan.

"I hope you dance, Vi," Wade said softly.

"Will you dance with me, Mommy?" said Henry, his sincerity blowing my heart up.

I looked at Wade and gave him the evil eye. "I love you guys so much."

Chapter Fifteen

Lilly had gone out for pizza with her friends after the boys' varsity basketball game. Henry and Megan had fallen asleep in the car on the way home. Wade and I tucked them into their beds and looked forward to some time alone. Wade grabbed a bottle of our favorite cab-syrah blend and two glasses while I lit the candles and started to undress. I caught my reflection in the huge leaning mirror in "The King's Quarters," and I stopped to assess myself the way they might in Hollywood. I had been considering the television appearances all day, although we hadn't discussed it again since this morning.

I pulled my eyebrows apart the way a Botox shot might. Yup, that was first on the list. I had avoided the temptation to get started on that slippery slope, knowing it would lead to an eye-lift in a few years, collagen injections, Restalyn, lipodissolve, etc. I had watched too many of my girlfriends become obsessed with their appearance once they began "fixing." My boobs looked like they had been through three pregnancies. Without a good bra they were pretty much sagging nipples. The skin above my knees drooped slightly. Lilly and I shared jeans, but we didn't look the same in shorts.

Being in the fashion industry had forced me to stay up to date with my hair and I loved to keep up with make-up trends. But my face was a canvas flawed by freckles and wrinkles left behind after so many wonderful days in the Florida sun. "Ugh!" I threw myself on the bed beside Wade.

"Thinking about it?" he asked, handing me my glass.

I stared at the ceiling. "They said I was too old at twenty-two for God's sake! I don't know if I can get my voice in shape in a month. I don't want to embarrass myself, or you guys, in front of such a huge audience."

"You could find a voice coach," Wade suggested.

"Maybe, but when am I going to find the time? I have to buy for next season; the shows are coming up. Isabelle and Doreen could handle the stores for a while, but what about the kids? Who will stay with them while you're working?" I had a million more objections in my head fighting to become words, but the magnitude of all of them overcame me and I settled for taking a deep breath.

"I can stay with the kids. I have plenty of time coming to me. I'll call my chief pilot. I'm sure he'd help someone with my seniority work out a few extra days off. Actually, if I put my days off back to back, I might not even need to dip into vacation. I'll figure that out." Wade gently turned me onto my side to face him and brushed the hair from my face. He gave me a soft kiss. "The question is, do you want to do this? You decide that and we'll follow through. If this was a democracy, I know the kids and I would have the majority rule. It's all up to you though, Vi." Wade's kisses gradually moved from my face to my neck to my chest.

"I want you guys to come with me." I said. "I could do it with you there." I closed my eyes to concentrate on the delightful tingling on my skin.

"Not an option," Wade said softly. "You need to be free to move without worrying about getting kids ready and making all of us comfortable. You don't need the distraction." Wade kissed my eyelids. I opened them to look at his face. My strength was there. "When was the last time you got away for a few days, anyway? You need that," he told me.

"I haven't gone away without my family since . . . ," I stopped to think. "God, I think it was before Lilly was born!" I laughed.

"It was." Wade confirmed. "My work forces me to be away. I love coming home and I think about home the whole time I'm gone. But I can't lie to you, it's nice walking fast through an airport without having to stop a hundred times or carry Henry, Lilly's laptop, and Megan's Big Bear. You would get to sleep through the night." Wade dangled the most appealing carrot. Both of the kids got me up a few times per night. I mentioned it a lot. In a complaining, frustrated sort of way.

"Think about how much fun this would be, Vi. Aren't you

even a little tempted to see the entertainment world from the other side? You wanted that so badly at one time, I can't believe that desire completely vanished."

"Eighteen years erases and replaces a lot of stuff, Wade. You know that. Do you still want to take a Harley across the country by yourself?" I challenged.

"Absolutely."

"You do?"

"Yes, and I am going to do that. I owe it to myself. It's on my list."

Wade had started rubbing my feet. I was very ticklish, so I squirmed and giggled a lot. He thought it was romantic, so he still did it after all these years.

"What . . . list?" I asked, willing myself not to kick him.

"My list of things I promised myself I wouldn't give up. Things I will do because I promised myself. Everyone has a list."

"I don't."

"Yeah, you do. Vacations you want to take, things you want to experience. You've forgotten how to think that way for yourself because you have a habit of thinking that way for the kids right now, but you'll remember."

"I love my life. Right now, right this minute," I tried to explain. "I want to live in the moment and appreciate every minute with the kids and every moment we're together in this house. I don't dream about anything else."

"This. We . . ." Wade made a wide, sweeping motion with his arms, "will always be here. You do need to do something for yourself and I think this is the right thing and the right time. You do have to call Brain in the morning and let him know, though. Everyone else is on board, except Sam, he said."

"Why wouldn't Sam want to do this?" I asked. Then I heard the irony of my own words.

"Dunno. Sam's obviously an idiot not to jump on The Francis Kelly Project's tour bus." Wade roughly rolled me over on my back and moved on top of me. "What happens on those tour buses, anyway?" he asked.

"I wouldn't know!" I cried knowing the attack was coming. I laughed with anticipation.

"You had better learn how to knit," Wade told me just before he showed me exactly what he thought happened on those rock-n-roll tour buses. It was nice not to have to go any farther than my own bed to have rock-star sex.

Chapter Sixteen

On Sundays, Brian gave himself a day off from working out, but he still got up early. His internal clock didn't allow him to sleep late. *Damn clock*. He threw on his robe and went to the front door to get the paper. He caught his reflection in the hall mirror on the way and didn't recognize himself at first. He had honestly thought there was someone in the house.

Yesterday, Sarah had taken him to some fancy salon where all the stylists wore black and the guys pretended to be gay even if they weren't. He looked really good at the end of it. His hair was still a little shaggy, like he liked it. He looked like a lot of the kids in his class, actually. A finely crafted, organized mess. They had returned him to his once-natural sandy brown color as well. He felt younger and hipper. The new look put a little swagger in his step; and it was a good thing, because when he opened the front door to get the paper, camera flashes started going off and there were guys shooting video.

Brian stood on his front steps looking surprised and feeling like he stepped out of his door into another reality.

"Brain Kelly?" someone shouted.

"Yes," Brain answered, which caused another flurry of flashes.

"How does it feel to have instant fame, man?" some guy asked.

"I didn't know I had fame of any variety. Who are you guys? What's up?"

"All right, this isn't what I want." The photographer closest to him turned off his video camera. "Dude," he addressed Brian, "just be natural and do whatever you came out to do. Act annoyed to have paparazzi on your street like everyone else does."

"Paparazzi? What do you care about me?" asked Brain, still stunned.

"Our source told us where to find the leader of The Francis Kelly Project, the writer of the hottest song in the land. You know, the whole search to find you and everything." He turned to the guy next to him. "Shit, man, we have the wrong guy."

His colleague pulled out a picture. Brain thought it looked like they had gotten it from the school yearbook. "That's him man; he looks better, that's all."

"Thank you." Brain's reflexes responded.

"Okay, dude, can you go in again and come out like you don't know we're here? Try not to look like a deer in headlights this time, 'cuz I don't want to take that to my boss. Okay? Gimme something. You can't give me squat Sunday morning -- I missed mass for you."

"Um. Yeah, I don't . . ." Brain gave them all a look of disgust, the cameras worked overtime, and he went back into the house.

Sarah met him in the foyer. "What's going on out there?" She tried to see past him out the window.

"It's paparazzi, they're trying to get the first shot of Brian Kelly from The Francis Kelly Project."

Sarah looked for telltale signs of lying. "Are you serious?" she asked.

"Just one of the drawbacks to fame," Brian said, as he feigned arrogance.

"You're bad." Sarah punched him in the shoulder then kissed him, jumping into his arms. "This is gonna be so cool!" she screamed.

Chapter Seventeen

Lilly checked her favorite web site, TMZ, while the rest of the house was getting ready for church. She had to know what her favorite stars did last night. Saturdays in New York and L.A. were good times to capture celebs being themselves. Lilly loved to see who they were with and what they were wearing.

Florida Soccer Mom, Lead Singer of The Francis Kelly Project Watches Her Kids' Game in the Keys Saturday. Click here for the first pictures of Vi Francis-Gates . . . Lilly sat frozen in disbelief as she clicked and scrolled through the pictures. No way! She was in some of them too!

"Mmmooooommmm!"

"Megan, you wore that dress to school Friday, pick out something else . . . ." I was pleading with Megan because we were running late for church when I heard Lilly's scream. I covered fifty feet in a half-second to get to her.

"Mom, look at this!" she showed me the web site and allowed it to sink in before she started dancing around. "How cool is this? Look, here's a good picture of me right beside you. I'm on TMZ! Thank you, mom!" Lilly was acting every inch a teenager.

"What is this?" I asked her.

"TMZ, Mom, it's paparazzi shots -- they follow celebrities!"

I was appalled. Making the same wail as Lilly had earlier I screamed, 'Waaaaaaaaaaaaaaaaaaaaaade!" who came bounding in seconds later.

"My God, Vi, I heard Lilly yell, but I thought it was a fashion disaster . . . what's wrong?"

Lilly and I pointed to the screen.

"How did TMZ get these?" asked Wade. *He knows TMZ?* I shouldn't have been surprised. He got out of the Keys more than I did. I isolated intentionally.

"You look good, babe." He winked at me. By now Megan and Henry were pushing to see what we were all looking at.

Lilly searched for "Vi Francis-Gates" while we stood watching. She clicked on a chat board.

So awesome to see this happen to someone like myself . . . a soccer mom! Makes me think I might still have a shot to make a dream come true . . . right after I finish the laundry . . . ." Mya from TN.

A nice family lady makes a positive role model for our kids, not the drunk, crazy, naked young girls getting so much attention right now." Jan from WI.

How old is she? She looks great! I'm gonna put the Twinkies down! Kathy from MA.

I'm so glad this turned out to be a grown-up woman. I'm sick of watching fifteen year olds sing, dance, and act. How am I supposed to identify with that? Take note Hollyweird. Sandy from VA.

"People on the Internet are chatting about *me*?" I asked no one in particular. "That's *nuts!*"

"Kind of makes up your mind for you huh, Vi? You don't want to let down the other soccer moms living vicariously, do you?

"Mom, you're not still thinking about this, are you? I thought we talked you into it yesterday." Lilly sounded so disappointed…then a tad bit feisty. "Well, if you want to wimp out it isn't like anyone knows. Oh yeah, they do! The whole world will know by noon. You can't chicken out, Mom --"

Wade interrupted. "Now Lilly, we shouldn't be talking to Mom that way. She has no one to answer to but herself. She'll do what is right for her -- make her own decision with no pressure from out in the world or Inside the Gates, got it?"

"I'm doing it," I said softly. Then, for the sake of hearing myself say those tiny but powerful words again, I repeated, "I'm doing it." I started to laugh and jump around like Lilly.

"All right, Mom!" Lilly, Henry, and Megan were jumping and dancing with me. Wade leaned against the doorframe to Lilly's room. "Good for you, baby." He was beaming with pride.

"I'm gonna dance! I'm gonna dance my ass off!" I told him.

74

"Mommy!" Henry looked like he had just seen a ghost. "How could you say 'ass?' We don't say that!"

"I'm sorry, dude. Mommy forgot her manners. I apologize." I picked him up and squeezed him. Before I knew it Meg climbed into my arms as well.

"You had better say ten Hail Marys in church, Mom," she said solemnly.

"I promise." I kissed her forehead. "Everyone finish getting ready quickly. I'm going to call the band leader on the way to church to tell him he has a singer."

Suddenly I was desperate to get to church. Not just because I hated walking in late. I had a lot of praying to do. I was going to need a lot of divine intervention to get me through what I had just decided to get myself into. I was scared to death, but I felt energized. I'd never have to wonder what might have happened if I had taken this gift and run with it. I was going to dance.

Chapter Eighteen

Across the country in Studio City, California, Brooke Taylor was also logged onto TMZ.com. It was five a.m. and she had just gotten in from a particularly great night. She had started at Koi where she and her friends had run into a young actor whose first film was being released this summer. Brooke had met him a while ago on the set and had an instant crush on him. He was going to be the desire of every woman and gay man on the planet in a few months, and Brooke had spent most of the night making out with him. It was a big no-no to socialize with the actors from the studio. There was an unwritten rule about the office getting involved with the talent. Hell, it was Hollywood -- you could always find some other shallow, beautiful actor to hook up with and leave the Warner Brothers talent pool alone. But Brooke couldn't resist unwrapping this tasty bit of eye-candy. When he greeted her using her full name, Brooke was so flattered that professional sensibility was replaced with girlish fantasy. "Hello Brooke Taylor" had bought the young actor her undivided attention to some of his favorite body parts.

As Brooke, Dirk (not the name his mother gave him), and their friends were climbing into Dirk's Escalade last night, paparazzi were taking pictures like crazy. If her boss saw a picture of Brooke with Dirk...

She kicked off her Christian Loub Feet Killers and waited for the page to load. "C'mon, c'mon . . ." Then she saw it. "Florida Soccer Mom . . ." Brooke took a sharp breath and exhaled a low "Noooooooooooo!" How could it be that Vi Francis was an old woman with kids? The Francis Kelly Project was supposed to be the fresh, new young group on the music scene. Who first said that they were young? Was it her? Did they just assume? Brooke searched her alcoholsoaked memory bank. When the movie studio had first launched the search, they did think they were looking for a young band with a fresh new sound. The radio stations and television shows ran with that. Brooke traced the events in her mind trying to recall if it was she or someone else at the studio who represented the band to the public as "young."

Brooke looked at all the photos from the soccer game. "Nice hat, Vi," she said out loud as she reached for her box of BC Powder. As she analyzed the pictures, Brooke wondered how much older she was than the girl who appeared to be Vi's oldest daughter. Were heads going to roll over this? Vi was actually quite pretty for an older woman. *Is this really going to be a big deal?* Of course this was a big deal. This was Hollywood where youth was preferred over talent, money, health, love, or security.

The studio was more than committed to this project and the song was what it is. Mr. Cooper loved it, but he thought he was giving a big break to an undiscovered young band. *Would it matter that Vi appears to be like, God, thirty-five or something?* Lots of the pictures were taken from far away, but the lens was good.

Vi appeared to be average height judging by the man standing next to her. Brooke guessed she stood about 5' 6". She had an athletic build and longish blonde hair. The close-ups revealed crinkling around the eyes and parenthesis on each side of her mouth. Brooke had always worn her sunglasses to reduce squinting. "Where are your shades, Vi?" she asked the photo. Brooke promised herself never to smile again as she looked at at Vi's laugh lines.

Then she groaned out loud as she thought about Brian; how old must he be? She had talked to him like he was a dumb teenager and if he was Vi's age he could be her uncle. *Great. This is just great.* She'd dug up a band from the crypt. It was the band Mr. Cooper wanted, though. Brooke only did what she had been asked to do -- which was an impossibility that she had managed to make a reality. She hoped it wasn't a nightmarish reality.

Having taken the BC Powder, Brooke shuffled from her living room/bedroom to her tiny bathroom. She washed her face and slathered on some La Mer. She'd live on the street before she'd give up using this stuff. Someday she would be Vi's age, in like a hundred years, but she wouldn't accept looking any different than she looked today. The cream promised a miracle and the price implied that nothing less than a full-blown, bible-worthy, raise-the-dead miracle was crammed into each small jar.

Brooke changed into a tank top and boxers and went back to the computer. She refreshed the TMZ home page where newly added pictures of Brian Kelly popped up. Another old person! He was good looking. But old. He looked like one of the Kennedys. Thick, tousseled hair and good teeth. Still, twenty years had to be taken off him. She'd have to find the best stylists available and that doctor from 90210. Her head hurt so badly, and it wasn't entirely due to the champagne she drank with wild abandon until just a half-hour ago. She had to get this band here and make them camera ready before they were seen on television. Brooke just hoped the paparazzi left them alone in the meantime.

She refreshed the page again then decided to get some sleep. Dirk… The paparazzi probably just shot her group of friends because they looked like they might be someone. Further research probably left them empty-handed. She hoped they didn't keep the photos until Dirk's movie came out this summer. All she needed was for someone to realize they had some old shots of him in the archives. She'd worry about that later. For now, makeovers and hangovers were taking priority.

Chapter Nineteen

"Good Morning from the flight deck, ladies and gentlemen, Captain Brett Katrell speaking. First Officer Dan Julian and I would like to welcome you aboard flight 1050 non-stop to LAX. We are currently climbing through twenty-eight thousand feet on our way to our cruising altitude of thirty-six thousand. I anticipate a smooth flight and will give you local weather as we get closer. Our expected flight time is five hours and fifteen minutes. We'll be arriving at approximately nine-fifteen a.m. local time. Breakfast service will begin in a few minutes. Enjoy the flight."

I listened to Brett's greeting from first class comfort. Warner Brothers had sent my airline tickets and when Wade saw that I wasn't flying on company or in first class, he made me a D-2 reservation so that I wouldn't have to sit elbow to elbow on the long flight. It was nice flying with the company because the crew treated D-2 passengers very well. D-2 was a designation for the tickets usually used by family of crewmembers. They took care of their own. I was happy to see Brett this morning as I was boarding. He and Wade were just a few seniority numbers apart and got hired at the same time. They went through training together and their movement through the company had been very similar.

Relaxed comfortably in my seat, I realized that this was the first time I had remained seated for more than ten minutes in the last three and a half weeks. I had been in perpetual motion, preparing to be away from my family and the business. I got the boutiques ready for my departure and sent Doreen and Isabelle to the fashion shows. They were excited to be trusted with purchasing.

Things at home were far more difficult to organize. Wade was able to take two weeks off to be with the kids, which he was looking forward to. Lilly and Henry were excited to have the time with Daddy, but Megan was far more skeptical. "How is he going to know what to do?" she had asked me over and over again. Wade was right -- I should have taken a few trips alone, just to increase their independence. I had always organized family vacations around my buying trips, so whether Wade could come along or not, I took the kids with me and I worked in something fun for them.

I had worked with a voice coach and together we did a three-week crash course, helping me to regain control and smooth out vocal transitions from my head voice to my chest voice. I had to remember how to breathe to support the notes, especially at the top of my register. It wasn't at all like riding a bike. I felt comfortable with my range, but I still lacked the power I once had. Mrs. Tremont, my voice coach, assured me that the engineers would make sure I was comfortable and they would ride my level to make sure I sounded as strong when singing falsetto as I did when singing full-voice. She felt I was ready. I supposed I was as ready as I was going to get.

I brought half my wardrobe along so that I would be sure to have something that made me feel confident. The contract didn't address the issue of wardrobe, so I had guessed that we were on our own. I did get Botox shots in my forehead and around my eyes. It felt like my forehead was a foreign object resting on my face. I'd never have this done again. And whoever classified the pain as "mild discomfort" was a masochist. I had three natural childbirths, I was no dainty flower. Still, that was no "mild discomfort" I'd pay to endure again. I looked good though. My brow line levitated a bit and my formerly wrinkled areas looked smoother.

I thanked the First Class Flight Attendant for my toast and eggs and wondered about the rest of The Francis Kelly Project. When we talked on the phone two weeks ago, Brian had said that he, Jackson, and Adam were rehearsing on their own, as I had done, and that they were really excited to play together again. I would miss seeing Sam. It wouldn't be the same without him. He had a unique flavor to his playing and his personality complimented the others' in the band. He had kept to himself mostly, but he was very kind and easy-going. Sam's gentle spirit and southern charm had made me feel more at home during my time in New York.

I was looking forward to seeing Jackson and Adam. Brain

had filled me in on their lives. Jackson was now a family man. I imagined he was a fun, but strict father. Brian hadn't found out too much about his personal life, so I was looking forward to asking the important questions men don't think to ask each other. Adam was always a fragile soul, but a great guy. He could be lead down a good road or the road to hell just as easily. Dear, talented Adam. I should have stayed in touch with him, but my past and my present didn't overlap anywhere in my story. There was a definitive ending to my old life. Some people had a seamless blending from one stage to the next, and it was easier to carry over relationships when that happened. I had made a clean break and a fresh start. Self preservation, I supposed.

Brian was a separate matter entirely. I had no worries about old feelings or anything remotely related to our romantic past. But I worried that it might not be as easy to fall into a comfortable working relationship with him when you factored in all the baggage from the past. I knew that I'd forgiven him completely and released all the negative feelings that held me back for a while. The decision not to continue our relationship was Brian's, so I guessed he resolved his own issues before I even knew we were over.

I finished my breakfast and settled back into my seat to watch the in-flight movie. Disney's *Enchanted* gave me the first terrible pang of my trip. I had taken Megan, Henry, and Lilly to see the movie when it first came out in theaters. We went out to dinner and then pigged out on chocolate at the show. Megan loved the music and Henry loved the chipmunk. Lilly liked "Mc Dreamy" or was he "McSteamy?" *What am I doing on a plane headed away from my children for two solid weeks?* Too late now. Deep breath.

On the ground at LAX, I checked my cell phone messages. There were four from home, so I listened to the most recent one first. It was Wade. "Hi honey, we're fine. No worries. Ignore Megan's 911 calls from earlier. We found the Paul Mitchell Sculpting Lotion for her curls. I was looking for something that looked like lotion, but we're fine. Her hair's all curled up and ready for school. Love ya, knock 'em dead, and call when you can."

I deleted the rest of the calls from home, worried that hearing Megan's upset voice might just send me for a departing flight straight back home. *It's just hair. She's fine. They're all fine.* I saw a sign reading "Gates" and headed that direction. I introduced myself to the man holding the sign. He was about twenty-five and was definitely out here to become an actor, model, or anything other than a driver.

"Hello, Mrs. Gates. Welcome to L.A." He revealed a Midwestern accent as he shook my hand. He seemed to be a well-mannered, sincere kid. His mother was probably worried to death every day he was out here. "Did you check any baggage?"

"I did. Three bags -- is that too many?" I knew I over packed. I was worried that the L.A. Green might drive only Prius', and the Prius' I've seen would have needed a trailer to accommodate my luggage.

"Of course not. I'll be happy to pull them for you. Your baggage is arriving at this carousel." He pointed the way.

Once settled in the car, Todd (he had introduced himself while we were waiting for the bags) told me that we were headed straight for a meeting at the rehearsal studio with the execs. As I primped in the backseat, I asked, "So what brought you out west, Todd? Are you an actor?"

"No, ma'am. My grandfather had a stroke and I came out to help take care of him. My whole family is from a small town in Wisconsin. Grandpa came out here a few years ago on vacation and fell in love with the weather. After all his years working the farm and getting up at four a.m. to start the milking, he felt like he'd found heaven, so he stayed. Grandma was gone by then, so he felt free to move out here."

Not at all what I expected to hear -- but I had been in town five minutes and already found a husband for Lilly. "That's incredibly admirable, Todd."

He let out a genuine laugh, "Have you ever been to Wisconsin in the winter time, Mrs. Gates?"

"Well, no, I can't say I have." I didn't think I had ever even driven through Wisconsin on my way to another destination.

"It wasn't a tough choice. I called it first, but I have cousins aching for the chance. It's pretty brutal weather there. The girls sure are nice, but they aren't as pretty as they are here."

I laughed with him. Todd pulled into the studio gate and spoke with the guard. My stomach flipped over a little as I looked around. This was the entrance to the back lot at Warner Brothers Studios. Incredible. *I am actually here.*

"Do you know if anyone else from my group is here yet?" I asked.

"I picked up Mr. Kelly last night and I know another driver brought in Mr. Richards this morning, ma'am."

"Todd, I'm forty and trying to look twenty-seven, please don't call me ma'am. You're killing my self-confidence."

"Sorry, ma' . . . sorry. My Mom is a stickler for manners. We're here." Todd had parked in front of the last building on the right side of the street. It was the tallest of the studios lining both sides of the little road. There was a large 16 on the side; other than that it looked rather nondescript.

"You can go ahead on in. I'll take your luggage to the hotel if you have everything from it that you need."

"Yeah, I'm fine. Thank you, Todd," I said, handing him a twenty.

"You're all covered, ma'...Vi. The studio has you in their tender loving care now," he said, waving off my tip. "Have a great time."

Chapter Twenty

My eyes adjusted from the bright sunlight to the dimly lit interior as I walked through the gray metal door into a large empty area that looked like a warehouse. A table and chairs had been set up in the middle of the baron expanse. I could see that a few people were helping themselves to a coffee service off to the right. A very perky, pretty, petite blonde was chatting at an unbelievable pace, just riding the edge of being impossible to understand. The person she was talking to sensed the presence of a new arrival and turned towards me. It was Brian. For a flash of a second he was my Brian. The way his face exploded into an electric smile, the way his eyes conveyed intimate tenderness, and the way he gestured towards me as if expecting me to take my rightful place at his side. He was an older version, but he was still more attractive than ninety-nine percent of the human male population. My palms began to sweat and my mouth dried out completely. I was glad he spoke first. As he called out, his voice reverberated throughout the empty space: "Ladies and gentleman, on lead vocals, the voice, the brains, and the beauty of The Francis Kelly Project, Vi Francis!" The small crowd went as wild as possible as three people could go and I laughed out loud.

Brian grabbed me into a tight squeeze. "I can't believe I'm here, let alone the fact that you seem to be here too." I laughed. Then I realized that Adam had been standing quietly behind Brian. "Adam!" I gave him a hug, but he stiffened a little inside my embrace. I respected his discomfort and stepped back. "How are you? It's so good to see you again," I said with genuine warmth.

"You look great, Vi. I'm really happy to be here." Adam looked down at his shoes. I wondered if his complexion was truly as gastly as it looked or if the lighting was just that bad. He was skinny and drawn. Under different circumstances, I might not have recognized him. "We couldn't do it without you, Adam. Wouldn't want to either," I assured him.

Adam took a sip of his orange juice and nodded a little. Just as I started to question my decision to be here for the umpteenth time, I heard Jackson's deep throaty greeting. "If the house is a swayin' Francis Kelly must be playing!" He sounded very much like James Earl Jones. Our drummer sauntered across the floor. Jackson had gained about a hundred pounds since I last saw him, but he still kind of floated with his internal rhythm. His white smile glowed against his black skin. I ran to him and got snatched into a huge bear hug.

"Hey, girl." He held me out for inspection, "You look like heaven had a leak and an angel fell right down to earth." Jackson had the worst lines in history but his delivery was golden, so he scored big points with phrases that would seal another man's doom.

"Sharon is a lucky woman."

"She must be a damn good cook too, judging by the size of you, man." Brian eased in to put a hug on his friend.

"Not that great, but she gets pissed if we have leftovers -- and if Momma ain't happy, nobody happy. If you ever get married, you'll find out Brian. Ain't that right, Adam?" Jackson caught sight of Adam hanging back.

"I'm single, bro. Can't find a woman messed up enough to want me." He gave a half-hearted chuckle.

"Bull. Shit," said Jackson. "Welcome to the land of broken toys, baby. We'll have you laid and paid or married and miserable before two weeks are out. Your choice." Jackson made himself laugh. Thankfully Adam laughed along.

It surprised me to hear that Brian was single. Divorced maybe? I shook my head. It didn't matter.

"So," I asked, "who's playing keys?"

The pretty, perky, petite blonde answered. "We hired a studio musician. He's toured with everyone from Billy Joel to Justin Timberlake. He's great, you'll love him. Hi, I'm Brooke, by the way." She held out her hand. "I'm from Warner and I am your contact. I'm sorry we could only get one handler for the whole band, but your schedule is fairly easy and you'll all be sticking together so you'll be well taken care of. Whatever you need, just ask the handler and she will make it happen." Brooke looked at a file she was carrying and flipped a few pages. "Her name is Jane and you'll meet her later today after you meet with your stylists."

"Let's have a seat over here once everyone has what they want from the coffee bar," Brooke said. Adam poured himself another glass of juice and I grabbed a bottle of Arizona green tea. Jackson opted for coffee, Brian grabbed a can of one of those high-octane energy drinks, and we settled down around the table.

"As you know," Brooke started, "we have an eight-event publicity tour. Here are your schedules. You'll start in L.A. and end up in New York. The premiere party is in New York. That will be your last engagement. You'll tape a video for use at our discretion before you leave L.A. in case we need something later." Brooke didn't seem to require air like the rest of us mere mortals. "Today will be spent with individual stylists. The studio is giving you each a budget for wardrobe. It's modest, so listen to the stylist. They know how to make several looks from a few pieces." *So much for my three bags of luggage*, I thought. Still, I was glad to have the option to wear my own clothes as a safety net.

"Tomorrow will be your first of six rehearsal days until your first taping which is . . ." Brooke consulted her file again.

"Looks like we get to do 'The Tonight Show' first," said Brain, following along on the schedules Brooke had handed out to us. "At least we'll have the chance to work out the nerves on a small show that no one watches." We all laughed.

"No nerves, Brian," said Brooke. "You're in the big-time now, so you'd better rise to the occasion." Brooke was dead serious. "Mr. Cooper doesn't usually do this many talk show to promote a film. He simply doesn't have to. But this is an important project to him and you are a very big part of it. He has taken a huge chance on you guys, don't fuck it up."

Brian smiled an overly sweet sarcastic smile at the twenty-one- or twenty-two-year-old.

"Don't worry about us, Brooke. We've been doin' our show since before you were born, girl. If we don't have it polished by now, six more days ain't gonna matter," Said Jackson.

"Uh-huh. Part of my job is to make you look like…well, a new, fresh band. Not a resurrected eighties flashback."

I laughed. "You're not alone, Brooke. I think that's my oldest daughter's greatest unspoken fear as well."

"Okay, well that's what today is all about. I'm taking you via studio transportation right now if we are all ready." Brooke looked from person to person.

"I'm all for it," said Jackson. "When they see me on TV, I gotta look fly."

"No one says 'fly' anymore, Jackson." Brooke rolled her eyes.

"What about the keyboard player?" asked Brian. "When do we meet him? Doesn't he need to see a stylist?"

"Tomorrow at rehearsal, and no."

Adam was the first on his feet.

"You excited about this, man? They're gonna make us look like women," Brian said.

"It's been a while since I bought new clothes. I am kind of relieved. I packed a lot of jeans," Adam confided.

"White boys," said Jackson.

I was nervous, excited, and on my way to meet with a Hollywood stylist.

Chapter Twenty-One

We climbed into the studio van and Brooke gave an address to the driver. I had read every fashion magazine published since 1995, but I still couldn't imagine what a professional stylist would suggest to help me make the most of my looks. I tried very hard to be objective about my appearance. It was one of my pet peeves to see a middle-aged woman trying too hard to hold onto the "good years." My goal was to age gracefully. I wanted to look good for my age. I didn't want to get sucked into following trends like I did when I was too young to know better.

Giving voice to my thoughts, Brian blurted out, "Sarah's going to kill me if I cut my hair. She insisted on this style and I really like it too." He sounded like a little boy. "It's a brand new style. I just had a makeover. The guy was even gay!" he announced.

"Relax. You'll be in the best hands in L.A.," Brooke assured him. "Do you think Mr. Cooper decides what to wear to events? Every A-List celebrity has help deciding what looks best on them and what's appropriate for the occasion. You're getting the star treatment, just enjoy," she said from the passenger seat, poised to take a call on her Bluetooth.

"Your woman tells you how to cut your hair, dude?" Jackson laughed.

"Bite me, Jackson. You're too scared to tell your wife that you're full and don't need three more helpings. You're not exactly wearing the pants at your house either,"

"You're a good man, Brain Kelly. Just like the rest of us good men, you fell in love with a good woman and gave up your balls to make her happy." Jackson's laugh filled the van.

"All right, that's about all the wife bashing I can take," I chimed in. "Listen, Wade is a brilliant man. He's a great pilot and a great dad. But if I didn't take care of running the household, he'd be homeless. If you called him right now and asked him who has our mortgage, he'd have no idea. I don't even think he knows where we bank."

Jackson laughed again.

Adam spoke up from the back, back seat. "You're breakin' my heart back here." His thick New Jersey accent loaded his words with sarcasm. "Poor guys, havin' women cook for you and pick out your hairdo. How do you stand it?"

"I have a sister, dude -- she'll boss you around 'til death parts you," Jackson offered.

Adam was more sincere now. "You know what? I never thought I'd find somebody, but I gotta be honest. This thing that's happenin' to us right now, it makes me think anythin' is possible, you know?" He was suddenly animated. "This is like a dream come true for me, man. Like I've been rescued. I let go and let God and look what he did."

"It's pretty cool," Brain agreed.

The driver rolled up to a very posh looking salon on Melrose. "Here is your first stop rock stars. You'll be here for three hours. I'm going back to my office. Call if you need me. Ciao." Brooke's send-off made me feel like I had to jump out of the van before it came to a full stop.

We spilled out onto the sidewalk and Brian held open the door so we could all go inside. It was a very trendy, upscale salon. I did a double take when I saw Michelle Pfiefer being escorted to a private area in the back.

"Welcome Francis Kelly Project!" we were greeted by a paper-white smile, perched on impossibly high stilettos. "We have all been so excited to meet you!" Can I get you anything? Coffee, water?" I didn't want anything, but I had to wonder if anyone out here ate. Our coffee service this morning was just that. No pastry, fruit, yogurt, or anything resembling food. Maybe coffee was the meal in L.A.

We all shook our heads as two more sharply dressed and coiffed girls joined us. "Hello Vi. I'm S'iva, I'll be your stylist." the one with jet-black, pixie short hair reached out for my hand. "Nice to meet you." I replied. I said a silent prayer that she had an appreciation for blondes and didn't try to make me a version of her.

"I'm with Jackson," said the first girl from her ear popping elevation.

"That's me, baby. Make me over." Jackson stepped forward with a bright smile and gentlemanly handshake.

"Then you must be Brian," said the girl who appeared to be the youngest. Skipping school young, if I had to guess. She was soft spoken and looked rather understated in spite of her hot-off-the-runway jumpsuit. Perhaps her natural beauty gave the impression that she was younger than she really was. I instantly wanted her for my stylist. She seemed safe and she had good taste.

"Adam, your stylists sent a text saying that she will be joining us momentarily, so let's sit for a little chat before we start." said the ringleader. She lead the way through a doorway I hadn't noticed before, just off the waiting area. We entered what must have been a VIP waiting area complete with couches, beverages, and a big screen TV. Ringleader perched in the middle of one of the couches and patted the cushions on either side of her. She relocated her long, blonde hair from one shoulder to rest on the other and I could see that she had a name tag . . . Summer. Of course. When she sat, she kicked off her shoes. So that's how she got through the day in those giraffe feeders. We made ourselves comfortable on the heavenly soft couch and the chairs that were arranged to face it.

"You are all individuals and I don't want to imply that you have to look alike just because you are a band, but it would be good for you all to have the same general style." Summer was smiling so widely that I couldn't believe words were being formed through her mouth, the movement was so slight it was almost imperceptible. I wondered if she had additional teeth implanted; I couldn't help but notice that she wasn't opposed to artificial enhancements to her person. "We've heard your song and we get a real organic California feel from it. Like surfer-ish. Does that ring true with you guys?"

Jackson burst out laughing. "Yes, Summer, I take my huge black ass out to the beach every day to hang ten."

Summer looked offended for a minute, but then responded

to Jackson's hearty laugh.

"Well, I mean care-free and easy-going." Summer explained.

"Summer, we are going to have a great time together, but I'll tell you this, I am from the city. I like to wear black because it's slimming and smooth. I like my hats, baby. I like nice black pants, a black button down that I can move in; I'm the drummer, you know. And a nice, stylin' hat that I can bring down over this eye so I can look at girls without my wife noticin." Jackson's speech made each of us chuckle.

"I'm from the city too." Adam chimed in quickly. "These legs haven't seen the sun or a beach in fifteen years, okay? When I do go to the beach, I wear cutoffs. Hear what I'm sayin'? I'm that guy. The one who swims in jeans."

S'iva took over the conversation. "What mood do you think the song sets?" she asked us.

"We didn't set out to write a reggae song. I think it gives that type of relaxed vibe, but when the time signature changes it gets a little crazy." Brian tried to pin it down. "It has both a soft side and a hard edge, really. I guess people will identify the best with the part they feel more comfortable with, you know?"

"Okay, so it's back to an individual mind-set. You are four talented individuals, so let's just bring out the individual personalities so that each of you feels confident." S'iva hit the nail on the head and I was glad to have her as my stylist after all.

"When you see each other again, you'll all be surprised." said Summer, invoking the great talk-show reveal that has become so common over the past few years.

Just then a fourth girl joined our little meeting. She wore all black and had long brown hair. She wore a lot of make-up for L.A. "Oh gawd I am so sorry I'm late. I know, I know, the gawd damn freeway is a mess again," she addressed Summer and her New Jersey accent stuck out like a sore thumb.

"We'll talk later." Summer said curtly. Then she turned to sweetly address Adam. "Adam," face barely moving, smiling broadly, "This is Tracey. She'll be your stylist." That was it. It was done. I could tell by the look on Adam's face that he was at the mercy of this woman. I had just witnessed love at first sight. *Be gentle with our Adam, Tracey, or the wrath of the Project will be unleashed* I told her with my eyes.

"Good," said Tracey. "My room is this way." She grabbed his hand and they were off.

S'iva asked again if I wanted anything to drink and then we were headed to her room as well.

"I have some really great ideas for you," S'iva said as I got settled in her chair. "Do you have any ideas?" she asked.

"You're looking at it," I laughed. "I did all of this on purpose."

"You look great, Vi. Really. You make my job easy." She started lifting my hair with her fingers. "You don't color you hair." It was a statement rather than a question. "It looks like you spend a lot of time in the sun. You're slightly parched. I think we could come up a few inches on the length to rectify that and to give you more fullness right around your face. What do you think about bringing it up to just below the shoulders?" S'iva turned the ends of my hair under to demonstrate her idea.

"As long as it's still long enough not to fall into the category of 'Mom Hair'. Every mother at my kids' school has the same bob cut which tends to get shorter and shorter with each passing year." I desperately did not want to be a member of the Bob Cut Club.

"Definitely not 'Mom Hair'. I hear you." S'iva was misting my hair with Evian spray. "I see a little wave coming to life here."

"I straighten my hair," I explained. "It's really wavy naturally."

"Awesome. Let's work with your natural wave to make it look soft and sexy. I'd like to see you add some dimension and depth with color as well. How do you feel darkening the base a little and making a rich blend of caramel and buttery highlights on top of that?" S'iva's eyes met mine in the mirror. I looked at my long, blonde hair. It hung to the top of my shoulder blades, but I could stand to get rid of a few inches. S'iva was right, the ends had seen a lot of sun, wind, and chlorine. I did what I could to treat my

95

hair well. Heaven knew I spent money on my products and services. Still, S'iva was an expert at working on Hollywood A-listers. Styling hair was an art and a science.

I felt the excitement of trusting her and making the change. I wondered what a professional stylist would suggest and now I know.

"S'iva, work your magic," I said with a big smile.

"I think you're gonna love it Vi. I see you in flushed, natural make-up so I think a shade of color in your hair will frame your face beautifully so that you don't wash out under the lights on stage. I see you radiant and glowing. Naturally full hair with lots of dimension like Jennifer Aniston.

"I'll be uncomfortable if the base color is too dark. I wouldn't feel like myself if I get too far away from the blonde spectrum and my husband loves blondes." I had to get that off my chest so I knew we understood each other and so that I could relax.

S'iva nodded. "I'll go mix your color. I'll be right back. Can I bring you anything? Coffee, water?"

"No thanks, I'm fine." I reached for my cell as S'iva left the room. I had slipped it in my pocket before one of the girls commandeered my purse. I dialed Lilly's cell and waited for her to pick-up.

"Hi Angel, it's Mom. Do you know who Jennifer Aniston is and do I want her hair?"

Chapter Twenty-Two

If you thought you were doing everything possible to make the most of your looks and cultivate your own signature style, you're wrong. Professional stylists exist for good reason: they're better at it than we are.

S'iva spent three hours formulating, snipping, styling, bronzing, and dressing me to transform me into a "natural" beauty.

I had a great time selecting stage clothes from the wardrobe sent over by the studio. I chose various designs, cuts, and colors of mini dresses which we paired with various styles of Monolo Blahnik footwear. I was particularly excited about the butterscotch calf-leather knee-high boots with fur trim and five-inch heels. Zipping them up gave me an instantaneous attitude of absolute confidence. When fashion had a tangible effect on your senses, it couldn't be perceived as frivolous.

"S'iva, I can't thank you enough for making me feel so self-assured." I gave S'iva a hug.

"Knock 'em dead, okay? There are a lot of people in this town pulling for you guys. And not just out of loyalty to Cooper. This is a great story for all of us who came out here to make it big. What happened to you guys is inspiring. It makes you believe that your wildest dreams may not have a shelf-life." S'iva grabbed my phone. "Shall I take a picture of your new look to send home to your family?"

I smiled for the photo and S'iva handed my phone back to me to approve the shot. Looking at the picture made me realize that a makeover isn't merely external. My eyes reflected conviction and readiness.

"Let's go see what the guys look like," S'iva suggested.

Jackson and Brian were waiting for me in the foyer. Their conversation came to a standstill when I entered the room.

"Baby, baby, baby girl!" Jackson stood up and gave a low whistle.

"Oh stop it," I said, feeling the heat rise in my cheeks.

"You look like you belong out here," said Brian. Poor

Brian. His stylist had practically shaved his head. He had been so proud of his "shag" or whatever it was called.

"You look great too," I said to them.

"They said this is the Maroon 5 look. I feel naked. I'm practically bald. I'm gonna need to look through Jackson's hat collection," Brian said.

I tried to make him feel better. "With a face like yours, bald would be beautiful," I said. "I know you aren't used to it, but it does look good." He looked like a longhaired dog after you shave him -- totally humiliated.

Jackson looked pretty much the same as he had when he walked in this morning. "What did they do to you?" I asked.

"No work was needed, baby, just a little maintenance. I had a facial, a manicure, and a pedicure. That pretty girl started to wax my damn eyebrows, can you believe that shit? I put a stop to that right now."

I looked around. "Where's Adam?"

Brian said, "Oh, you're not going to believe Adam. First, he looks like Orlando freakin' Bloom. That girl made that pale, skinny thing really work for him. They're in her room 'talking.'" Brain made the quote marks with his fingers.

"We're supposed to get him when we're ready to go."

"I saw a little spark there when he first saw her," I said, but I didn't want to gossip. "What kind of wardrobe did you guys pick?"

"Suits," said Brian. "Versace suits. I hope I don't have to give them back."

"I'm gonna look so good, nobody's going to notice you guys," Jackson said matter-of-factly. "I picked out some silky black pants and shirts, and some nice vests...oooo-oooo!" he howled.

"What about you, Franny?" Brian used his old nickname for me. He was the only one in my life who ever called me that and it felt more intimate than if he had touched me. It was such a personal familiarity that the conversation skipped a few beats of its previously easy-flowing meter.

I regrouped. "Well, I wouldn't have predicted it, but really short dresses." I laughed. "I hope Wade and the kids don't suffer post-traumatic stress disorder."

Brooke breezed through the door. "Ready?" she asked. She didn't react to our changed appearances at all.

"We have to get Adam," Brain told her. "And lunch. I'm starving."

"Hmmm." Brooke looked irritated. "We're due back at the studio to meet your handler, and then I have a surprise for you. I'm not sure we have time for lunch. Get Adam." She was looking at Jackson.

"Did I marry you and forget about it?" Jackson asked her. He was on the move though.

"Let's stop at Subway or some place like that, Brooke. We all have to eat. It doesn't have to be a fancy sit-down," said Brain.

"Kraft services will be set. We can swing through to pick up something once we get to the studio." Brooke referred to the cafeteria-style set up in the commissary on the Warner lot.

Jackson had retrieved Adam and they rejoined our group.

"Hurry up and get into the van. I have to make up ten minutes in our schedule so you kids can eat." Brooke rolled her eyes.

Chapter Twenty-Three

Brooke ran us through Kraft services at the speed of sound, and we were seated once again at the table where we began our day in the middle of the huge, empty sound stage. I was happy to be feasting on roasted turkey breast, cheese, and fruit. The guys had piled their plates high, and we were too busy eating to attempt conversation.

Brooke had dropped us off and had gone to search for Jane, our handler. Brooke was such a high-strung girl, I thought. *She's gonna look sixty by the time she turns thirty.*

A familiar voice boomed through the room. "Hello Francis Kelly, welcome to L.A.!" With a mouth full of turkey breast, I looked in the direction of the voice. I almost choked. George Cooper was making his way to our table. What to do? Spit it out? Chew in front of George Cooper? *Oh my Lord, he's close enough to see me now. Swallow it whole.* I gulp. *I'm going to die in front of George Cooper. How humiliating.*

Thankfully Jackson stood up to greet him first. "Mr. Cooper. Thank you for bringing us out here, sir. I am prepared to have the time of my life." Jackson shook the actor's hand firmly.

"Jackson, it's great of you to come." George Cooper was an awesome presence. Whatever "it" was, he had it. It was impossible to believe that he could have been better looking in person than on film, but he was.

"You must be Vi. My powers of deduction are awe-inspiring, I know." He held out his hand to me.

Thankfully I had washed down my turkey with a gulp of Evian only a moment before he turned his attention my way. "Mr. Cooper it's truly a pleasure to meet you." I took his hand and swore that I felt a zap. There was a tangible feeling. To me, he was honestly *that* electric.

"I understand that you left behind three children, a husband, and a very big dog."

I was shocked that he knew anything about me.

"Yes, I did, but my family is in good hands. The dog is

very well trained. He cooks, he cleans, he failed his driving test so he can't chauffeur anymore, but . . ." When I got nervous my mouth operated on its own.

Thankfully, Mr. Cooper laughed politely. "She sings and she's funny," he said. "Adam, thanks for coming all this way to play for me." He shook Adam's hand.

"I'm really impressed that you took the time to come meet us," said Adam. "I'm sure you are a very busy man. It really says something to me about who you are. This whole deal does, Mr. Cooper. You gave us the greatest break without knowing anything about us. We are going to make you proud, sir. I promise."

I mentally kicked myself. Adam was suddenly perfectly eloquent when appropriate. *Why couldn't I have said something so sincere and wonderful? No, no, no, I have to paint a picture of my dog behind the wheel of a car like in a bad children's movie.*

"I echo Adam's sentiment, sir. I am Brian Kelly." Brian stood and held out his hand.

"Ah-ha. The songwriter…well, along with Vi. Brian -- and please call me George, everybody -- you're a music teacher, aren't you?"

"Englewood High School, just outside of Denver."

"Important to keep the arts in the public schools," said George.

"I agree. Kept me off the streets and popular with the girls. Without my guitar I would be a lonely man."

We all laughed along and George asked us to sit down to finish our lunch. He pulled up a chair. "I don't want to interrupt, I just wanted the opportunity to meet you and to express my personal thanks for taking the time to come all the way out here to do this promotional tour with me," he said. "Geez, where'd they take you for lunch? Kraft services?"

"Yeah, but it's cool. We're eating, we're good," Jackson assured him.

"No, no. I am picking up the tab for you to be here. I don't want that to sound like it's big deal because it isn't. If you have to eat lunch meat and grapes, I'll increase the budget; but I'll let

102

Brooke know I want you guys to have whatever you need."

George switched gears and placed his forearms on the table, clasping his hands. He leaned forward and we instinctively followed his lead as if under his spell. "You know what this is about? This whole thing?" he looked from face to face around the table. "It's about originality. Integrity. Your music is unique. It seems like there are a lot of bands out there these days trying to chase what's selling rather than being themselves. I want you guys to be yourselves, play your music and have a great time with this. This is a great song and it's the perfect match for my film. So, be proud of your work and show it off, okay?"

George got up from the table and pushed his chair back underneath. "And get some real food for God's sake, huh?" He winked at me. Zap.

As we watched him leave, it sunk in that George himself -- we were on a first name basis now -- was footing the bill for our trip. He must have really believed in this song if he was putting his own money behind it. Relatively speaking, it probably wasn't much for him, but I felt a deeper responsibility to do a great job so that this whole thing came off fabulously well for him.

"Great fuckin' guy," Adam said, devouring his sandwich and reverting to his regular vernacular.

"I love me some George Cooper," said Jackson.

"For such a smart, beautiful woman you aren't any better at meeting men than you were twenty years ago," Brain said teasingly. Evidently he hadn't forgotten our first meeting at Stetson University. I roller bladed past him while "commuting" from one class to the next on campus only to trip and fall headlong into a row of bicycles parked at a bike rack. Brain came to help me get back on my wheeled feet and he lifted the weight of my backpack to give me a fighting chance at stability. To show my gratitude for his kindness, I said, "Thank you for your handsomeness." I never forgot those words because Brian had reminded me of them whenever he needed a good laugh.

"I'm charming in my own way," I said defensively.

"I'm not saying that's a bad thing, Vi." He laughed and

took another bite of his sandwich.

Brooke came bounding in with a pretty brunette behind her as we were finishing our lunches. "Francis Kelly, this is Jane, your handler," she announced, and we all stood to meet Jane. "And in a few minutes, I have a surprise for you," She teased us.

"Wouldn't be George Cooper stopping by to assess our lunch situation would it?" Jackson spoke up.

"Awww. . .are you kidding me?" Brooke was visibly disappointed. She tried to compose herself and took a deep breath. "What did he have to say?" asked Brooke.

"One thing he mentioned is that he's footing the bill for us and he had hoped that what he spent could buy us a better lunch," said Adam with a surprising grin. Tracey had flipped a switch in him, I think.

We all laughed. "Brooke, we're good. No worries, okay?" Brain tried to make her feel better. "Let's just continue on with our day and forget that Mr. Cooper was completely pissed off that we had this crappy lunch and no breakfast."

Brooke's eyes grew wide and her mouth dropped open. I was glad to see that Brooke had human weaknesses just like the rest of us. She had been void of emotion until now. Still, I hated to watch anyone squirm.

"The boys are having a little bit of fun at your expense, Brooke. Mr. Cooper wasn't upset with you at all. We had a very pleasant conversation with him." I felt motherly towards the young girl when I looked into her eyes.

"Take this any way you want. Stay on my good side." Brooke broke the sympathetic spell I had been under and stomped out of the room.

We burst out laughing after Brooke slammed out the sound stage door. Jane began to apologize for Brooke. "She's been really stressed out getting ready for the junket . . ." , but she couldn't maintain composure and started laughing again.

"All right, all right, if she has an aneurysm it's on our heads, so let's not be too proud of ourselves." Brain quieted us down, displaying his classroom skills. "What's next Jane?"

"I can take you guys to the hotel. You must be jetlagged and we want you fresh for tomorrow morning's rehearsal. We have to be back here at ten sharp."

We all agreed and loaded into the van for transport to the hotel. Upon our arrival, it made a fine first impression.

The Renaissance Hollywood Hotel and Spa was to be our home away from home for the next week. The ultra-sophisticated entrance gave way to a contemporary lobby, heavily influenced by 1950s' decor. The highly polished floors were a stark platform for couches and chairs upholstered with primary colors, and floor lamps with cylindrical shades. It looked like a cover photo for the 1951 Sears catalog.

I couldn't wait to call home and tell my family about meeting my new friend George. *Lilly is going to die!* I mentally kicked myself for not asking to have a picture taken with him. I also couldn't wait to see what tomorrow would bring.

Chapter Twenty-Four

I showed up for rehearsal fully made up and dressed to impress. After George's surprise visit yesterday I wanted to be ready for anything.

The studio had provided the equipment we requested along with a knowledgeable sound engineer named Manny, who gave us a tutorial on the history of our rehearsal space as we set up.

Stage 16 was completed in 1935 and was the tallest sound stage on the Warner Brothers lot. Manny told us that *My Fair Lady*, *Ghost Busters*, and *Jurassic Park* were filmed there.

I had a not-so-secret adoration for Humphrey Bogart. I especially loved seeing him on-screen with his fourth wife and greatest love, Lauren Bacall. I owned every one of his films that made it to DVD.

"Warner contracted Bogie in 1935, so is it possible that he ever filmed here?" I suddenly felt reverent.

"Oh yeah," said Manny, "Bogie and Bacall did *The Big Sleep* right here. Mr. Bogart's been all over this lot. *The Maltese Falcon* was shot on Stage 17, *Casablanca* was shot on Stages 17 and 18, *Key Largo* was on 18, *Dark Victory* was on 27A . . ." Manny laughed at himself. "I'm obviously a film geek. I love the old ones especially. You gotta take the studio tour while you're here."

"Wow. Humphrey Bogart might have stood right here..." The idea thrilled me, which was a fabulous distraction because I had been nervous about rehearsal all morning. The guys started to tune up and my stomach began to flip. I never used to get nervous when performing was a daily ritual. I tried to imagine Bogie standing next to me, his confident grin lending me some of his trademark courage.

Brian seemed to be completely at ease and in his element as he assisted Manny. "Kick drum," he prompted Jackson so he could get a level on the kick mic. Brian and Manny dialed in levels on the soundboard.

"Good. Snare." Brian nodded. "High hat." After another

quick adjustment, Brian was ready to move on. "Okay, Jax, gimme the whole kit." Jackson gave us the roll from "Brick House" and grooved along with his sound check. It was obvious that he had been playing regularly.

Brain had already tested his own mic and guitar so he moved onto the bass.

"Adam, you ready, man?" Adam, wearing one of the new outfits his stylist had chosen for him, popped and slapped around on the bass a bit. Brian prompted Jackson to join Adam. After a few tweaks, it was my turn.

"Okay, Franny. Let's get some levels." Brain winked at me. I think he could tell that I was nervous. I swallowed my last sip of green tea and stood behind my mic stand. I had requested an industry standard Shure Beta 87A, wireless. It was a great road mic.

I felt like a newbie and hoped the voice work I'd been doing would carry me through. I started singing the first line of "So Beautiful." My voice filled the rehearsal studio and sounded a little shaky. The sound was nice and round, though, and I summoned Bogie. I closed my eyes and kept going, trying to calm down and sing, but I was still shaky. I heard Brian's guitar accompanying me and I opened my eyes to give him a grateful glance.

By the beginning of the first chorus, I sounded pretty good; but then I tried to push it, singing full voice through the point where my voice naturally breaks instead of relying on my breathing to make an even transition into my head voice. Rather than trusting what I had perfected in rehearsal with Mrs. Tremont, I hit the gas and tried to force it. The failed attempt sounded like an old train locking up its brakes on the tracks. Brian kept playing. I closed my eyes and tried to pick up the song again.

"I'm sorry, I'm sorry…" I said into the mic. Brain stopped playing. "I know how to sing through that, I'm just really nervous."

Jackson came to the rescue. "Don't worry, baby. We've got nuthin' but time. We won't leave here until you feel good. Hell, we all need to work this up. I haven't played this in a while either, you

108

know."

"You sounded good, Vi. Right up until you laid that fast pitch on us." Adam tried to hide a grin.

"Okay, all right. I'll be fine. I didn't think we were running the song anyway, I thought I was just giving a level on my mic." I made a lame excuse.

Brooke popped into the studio with Jane in tow. "Good Morning. Do you have everything you need?" she asked Brain.

"I think we're all set," said Brian. "We'll be ready to run rehearsal in a few minutes. Where's your guy?" Brian referred to the studio musician.

"He's on the way. He might not be here until this afternoon, though, so start without him."

"That's not as easy as it sounds." Brain told her. "We kind of need his part; it's the core of the song. I can cover it, but then I don't get to practice the guitar parts."

"Do what you have to do to get by until he gets here, okay?" Brooke turned to leave and then spun back around to face us, "Oh, your catered lunch will arrive at high noon. Don't make any distress pleas if you start getting hungry at eleven-thirty. If you need me, call my cell."

Jane looked a little uncertain as to whether she was expected to stay or go with Brooke. "I'm gonna hang here in case they need anything," she stated to Brooke's back.

"Good," Brooke said and mumbled something inaudible under her breath.

"That girl needs a good rodgering, you know?" Jackson gave himself a ba-du-bump on his kit.

Jane smiled. "Do you guys mind if I stay? I know some groups like closed rehearsal sessions."

"What happens here stays here," I said. "If you can promise that, have a seat."

"I'm here," said Jane, taking a seat at the table where we hung out with George Cooper yesterday.

"You guys wanna try to take it from the top then?" asked Brian.

"Let's go." Jackson counted the tempo off on his sticks and then started playing. Adam missed the first lick, but jumped in and Brain gave him an eyebrow. "I missed the count, whatever," shouted Adam over the band.

The band played my intro. I took a deep breath, closed my eyes, and sang the first line. I sounded good -- less shaky and more confident. Then we got to the chorus and my voice cracked just as the drums crashed as if Jackson had fallen off his throne.

"What the . . . ?" Jackson asked himself. "Sorry, dude, I know that's where we change meter, I just couldn't get there." He regrouped. "Again."

Jackson counted off the intro and we started over. I asked him with my eyes if he did that to save me and he shrugged. We were playing as we would be on stage, all facing the same direction; but I felt better turned around looking at Jackson, so I grabbed the mic and sang backwards with my monitor behind me. I had to be careful not to feed back, but I had more connection looking at the guys than at the empty sound stage.

We got through the first verse and the chorus; I smoothed out a little bit, relying on what I had been taught and letting the mic do the work. Still, I could tell we had a long way to go. As we changed time signature again and headed into the bridge, a train wreck ensued, assaulting all of our senses.

"Woah." Brian held up his hand for everyone to stop.

"We change keys there; it modulates to A-flat minor," Adam told Brian.

"No, man. There's no key change. Just time signature," Brain corrected him.

"I've been listening to this for a month," Adam told Brian, "It modulates there."

"The second time around, Adam. Not both times. Let's run it again."

Jackson counted off the intro. Every time the song took a turn, we derailed. I stole a few glances at Jane to see what her reaction was. She was expressionless. I looked at my watch. It was 11:45; we had been at it for an hour and forty-five minutes and hadn't made it through the song once yet.

"I wish the keyboard player was here," said Brian. "Can you find out what's up with that?" he asked Jane. She grabbed her phone and headed towards the door. "Let me make some calls."

I looked around the room and everyone seemed a little shell-shocked.

"This morning is for working out the rough spots. We've all been practicing on our own, but it's different when we put it together. You guys know that," Brian reminded us.

"This is a mother of a song too," said Jackson. "It works so perfectly that one false move throws off the whole damn thing. Must have taken some OCD SOB to write some shit like this." He looked at Brain out of the corner of his eye.

Brian had been re-tuning. "Vi wrote it," he said.

We all laughed.

A light above the metal door started to flash, indicating that someone was outside. I opened the door to find our catering in the hallway. Perfect timing, I thought. We could use a few minutes away from the music.

"I have really bad news, guys," Jane announced. She had answered a phone call while I was answering the door. "The player we had lined up had emergency surgery early this morning and he won't be able to work for another two weeks."

"There have to be hundreds of studio musicians here. We can get someone else, right?" Brain asked.

"It's not that simple with such short notice," Jane said. "Brooke has been on the phone all day calling in favors, but the few available players who heard the song said they wanted sheet music. Brooke asked me to get it from you," she told Brian.

"I don't have that scored," said Brian. "Sam just played what he played." Brian slipped inside his mind where, undoubtedly, he was going over the song. Brian played many instruments, including piano. He sat down at the keyboard and started tinkering and writing. "You guys eat, I'll try to figure this out."

A half hour later, Jackson, Adam, and I were full of crab

cakes with raspberry sauce, spring mix salad, and chocolate crème brûlée. Brian was cursing intermittently at the piano.

"How goes it, man?" asked Adam, placing his napkin over his plate and heading toward Brian. Adam, by rights, was the better all-around musician. I think he let Brian take the lead out of respect. If anyone could hear the quality of the chords, it was Adam.

"I'm having a real bitch of a time finding the voicing of some of these chords. I can't figure out..." Brain played a few for Adam, "if the B-flat is at the root of the chord or the third." He experimented a little and Adam nodded.

"Then, here..." Brain played something else. "This sounds minor, but only because of the chord before it." He played that chord.

"That's like The Beatles' 'I Feel Fine,' man," said Adam. "Same thing."

"Yeah." Brain nodded back.

"I am so glad I am not a musician," I laughed.

"Me too," Jackson said.

Brain scrolled through his phone and hit send. "Hey Sam, it's Brain Kelly. I need your help."

I listened as Brian asked Sam if he could chart out the song and send it out.

"The musician who was supposed to start rehearsing with us," I said to Jane, "he must have charted the music, right? Why can't we get that from him?"

"He's in ICU," said Jane. "I don't know if he's conscious."

"Do we wanna know what happened?" asked Jackson.

"Sadly, I don't think anyone cares to find out. He's just not available, so you solve that problem. Ugly, huh?" Jane shivered a little.

"You're kidding me, man. Don't tease me now." Brain laughed out loud. "Okay. That's fantastic. I'll see you in the morning!" Brian ended the call. "Sam's coming!" he shouted.

"No shit?" Adam looked surprised.

"Well, all right! It'll be nice to see that cat again." Jackson sat back down on his throne behind his kit.

"With the time we don't have, it's the best possible solution," said Brain.

"How in the world did you convince him, Brain?" I asked. "I thought Sam was worried about his political career."

"Maybe he decided the publicity could only be a good thing. Hey, love him or hate him, at least people will know who he is and see him as a whole person not just a stiff politician."

"Well, he's gonna be stiff. That boy never let his guard down, even after a few beers," Adam reminded us.

Jackson counted us in and we played straight through the song. It wasn't perfect, but something felt better about it. Maybe it was simply the knowledge that the Francis Kelly Project would be complete tomorrow.

Jane applauded as the last notes faded away. "Sounded great!"

"Here we gooooooo . . ." Jackson was already counting us in again, smacking his sticks together in tempo.

As I waited for my part, I felt my phone vibrate. I looked at the display and saw a picture of my family. All faces were tanned and smiling. Abrams was holding a sign in his mouth that said, "Vi Francis Rocks!" I laughed out loud.

Chapter Twenty-Five

By the end of rehearsal my throat was aching but the quality of my voice had increased tenfold. The band had gotten much tighter as the day progressed and we all felt a sense of relief and accomplishment.

After the studio van had dropped us at the hotel the guys decided to go to the lobby restaurant for dinner, but I passed. I couldn't wait to get back to my room, call home, order from room service, and take a long hot bath.

I experienced a terrible pang when Megan answered the phone and I heard the familiar sounds of my household in the background.

"Gates residence, Megan speaking." She sounded like a thirty-year-old receptionist.

"Hi, Meggy!" I wished I could crawl through the phone. "Thank-you for the picture you sent me earlier today. It was fantastic!"

"No problem, Mom." She took the phone away from her ear. "Henry, don't try to jump down by yourself. Wait for Lilly or Daddy."

"He's on the stool by the breakfast bar?" I guessed.

"Yep. I think he wants to talk on the phone." Megan took the phone from her ear again. "You'll get your chance -- don't worry, okay?"

"You're such a great big sister. What did you do today?" I asked.

"Well, we went out in the boat. At first Abrams didn't want to go, but when we pulled away from the dock he jumped in the water and tried to follow us, so Daddy had to go back and let him climb up the swim platform."

"Daddy made us sandwiches and he brought lots of fruit and juice on the boat. We had a great time Mom. We caught grouper, but we had to put them back because of the band." I chuckled to myself. Megan was referring to the "ban" on grouper fishing. "We pulled in some yellowtail so Daddy is going to make it for dinner."

"Okay, Mom. Lilly's getting Henry down, so he'll want to say hi."

"I love you Megs. I'll call you tomorrow. If you need me, my phone is always on." I wanted to make sure that she knew I was always available to her.

"I might call you sometime, Mom, if I'm not too busy." I held in another laugh and answered very seriously, "That would be great, if you have a spare minute."

"Bye, Mom. Love you." Megan handed the phone to Henry.

"MOMMY! I LOVE YOU!" Henry shouted into the phone.

"I love you too, little man. How was the boat today?" I wanted to be there so badly. I pictured his chubby cheeks and wanted to give him little kisses, to smell Megan's hair, and hold Lilly's hand. Not to mention what I wanted to do with Wade. . . .

"Mom, Daddy went really fast and Abrams stood on the aft-back-deck and barked at the wake. Megan helped me catch a fish and Lilly helped me with my sandwich. She cut the crust off because Daddy didn't know."

"Sounds like you're taking good care of each other." I said.

"Mostly they are taking care of me, but I caught the fishy we are eating for dinner!" Henry sounded very proud.

"Wow, dude. That's awesome! Good thing they have you there!"

"I know Mom. We have to drop Lilly at cheering practice and then Megan and Daddy and I are going to go to Publix to get cupcakes for dessert."

"Mmmmm. Chocolate or vanilla?" I asked.

"I don't know Mom. Megan and I will have to ah-gree."

"You let me know tomorrow. I'll be interested to hear." I told him.

"Okay Mommy. I love you! Daddy made a calculator so I know how many more days until you come home. Also, Daddy said we can stay up late and watch you on TV."

I laughed. "He did? Wow. You better not grow up too much in these next few days. I better ask Daddy to put a book on your head. Can I talk to him?"

Henry put the phone down and I heard him ask Lilly if Dad was still outside giving Abrams a bath.

"Hi, Mom. How are you?" Lilly picked up.

"We had a good rehearsal today. I miss you guys though." I loved hearing her voice.

"We missed you today too, Mom. Dad and I are going to keep everyone busy so that before we know it, you'll be home."

I try to do the same thing when Wade is flying. "Thanks for filling the time, Lil."

"Dad is outside bathing Abrams, did Megan tell you he dove in?"

"Yes. I hope he didn't go in the main salon on the boat." I pictured him shaking salt water everywhere in the main cabin before he sat down to make a puddle on the interior teak deck.

"Oh, no. You know Dad. Abrams stayed on the aft deck and didn't set one wet paw in the house. I asked Dad if he wanted me to help bathe him, but he said he'd rather have me stay inside and watch the midgets."

I laughed at my oldest daughter's politically incorrect description of her siblings. "Thanks for being such a big help, Lilly. You're a very reliable person. I'm proud of you."

I'm proud of you too, Mom. I can't wait to see you on TV." Lilly perked up. "You have to tell me all about George Cooper."

"I didn't see him today, but he is even more handsome in person and he's exceptionally charming."

"I meant to ask if you took a picture with him yesterday or were you were too freaked out to think of it?" Lilly asked.

"The second thing." I laughed.

"I'd probably forget how to breathe with that hottie in the room," Lilly laughed. "Do you want Dad to call you back, Mom?"

"Sure honey. Tell him I love him. I love you too."

"Love ya, Mom. Have fun, all right? We're okay so don't worry."

"I feel good knowing you're there, babe." I said my good-bye and hung up. I thought about calling the store, but I was too exhausted. I drew a bath, ordered my dinner, and embarked on some "me" time.

Chapter Twenty-Six

I was submerged in hot water with a fluffy towel folded behind my head, Borghese eye compresses covered my eyes and Fango mud frosted my face. This was my definition of heaven on earth. I breathed in deeply and inhaled the fragrant Banjo di Vita Body Soak also from the luxuriously pampering line of beauty products. The Italians knew an awful lot about how to enjoy life. The gentleman from room service had told me that it would be at least half an hour before I should expect my broiled Dover sole salmon and Pinot Grigio. Just as I entered a state of total bliss and relaxation, my phone rang. Just like at home, I thought. I lifted one eye compress and looked at the display, it was Wade.

"Hi Honey." I answered before the voice mail took over.

"Hey Hollywood, meet any heart-throb actors today that I should know about?" Wade teased.

"Shhhh, George, it's my husband," I whispered, playing along.

"Funny. How was your day? First rehearsals go okay?"

"It started out pretty rough and we're going to need more time before we're ready to be heard, but it was a lot better at the end of the day than the beginning," I reported.

"How were you?" Wade wanted to know.

"I started out badly, ended pretty good."

"By the time I talk to you tomorrow you'll be chomping at the bit to get the show on the road." Wade always expected the best outcome and that is usually what he got as a result.

"Hope so. Sounds like you guys had a great day. I'm sorry I wasn't there," I said.

"It was perfect. We had smooth water, sunny skies, and severe clear." Wade used aviation slang for the type of weather they had experienced.

"I really had a homesick attack when I talked to the kids earlier. It helps to hear your voices, but it makes me want to come home at the same time."

"Don't let yourself think like that. This is going to be over before you know it and you have to enjoy every minute of it so that you can hold on to the memory until we're old and eating soft foods." Wade's low, soothing voice did the trick.

"I know you're right."

"I know where you're coming from though. The down time is probably hard because you start thinking. It's probably better for you to stay busy out there."

"I don't think that will be a problem. My days are full, but I do have some free time the next few evenings. I'll probably go to the hotel gym after rehearsal from now on. Then, by the time I get to the room, I'll be too tired to mentally torture myself."

"Actually, being tired is probably part of the trouble. You might still have a touch of jet lag and you weren't sleeping well for weeks before you left. Everything feels more intense when you're tired. Get a good night's sleep tonight and call us in the morning, okay?" Wade suggested.

"I will." Just then there was a knock on my door. "Oh, that must be room service. I need to get out of the tub and grab the door, honey."

"Look through the peep-hole." Wade was protecting form a distance.

I sighed a little as I got out of the water. "Yes, sir," I said.

"I love you Vi."

"Miss you and love you too. I'll talk to you in the morning." I hung up and threw on a robe. Aware that my face was still covered in green mud, I chuckled that Wade was worried for me when it was the unlucky delivery person who was at risk.

"Just a second, please!" I called out, securing the robe. I swung the door open wide enough for the cart to come through, and found Brian standing in the doorway.

"Whoa!" He did a lousy job containing his surprise.

"I was expecting...you're supposed to be room service..."

"I, uh, well, I just wanted to talk to you for a minute." It looked like Brian had had a few beers.

"Can it wait until tomorrow?" I asked "I'm kind of in for the night."

"Can I come in for a few minutes?"

"I'm . . ." I held out my arms to indicate the obvious. Not dressed, dripping wet, wearing a mask, alone in a hotel room . . ..

"I want to make sure you're okay, Vi, that we're okay, and I think there are some things that were left unsaid that I need to say." Brain looked pitiful.

"You mean things from eighteen years ago, Brian? Because, honestly, I don't think what happened between us back then matters much today." I leaned against the open hotel room door, keeping Brian in the hallway. I intended to be firm yet not mean, but I really didn't want to revisit the past. The possibility of rehashing that was one of the reasons I didn't want to do this tour in the first place.

"Vi, I . . . I am just very sorry about what happened between us, and seeing you again brings back all that regret."

"There's no need for regrets. When you look at me today, see a happy wife, a mother, and business owner. Any pain that I worked through from the past is in the past." I hoped that would be enough for him to leave.

"I don't know if I've been able to leave that time behind me. I mean . . . I moved on, of course, and I have a happy life now. I just . . . I have a lot of guilt."

"Do you need me to say I forgive you, Brain? 'Cuz I did a long, long time ago," I said softly. "Maybe you need to forgive yourself."

"I think about what might have happened if I had gone back to Florida with you . . ."

"If you have regrets, let them go for your own sake." Somehow, it was easier to say the things that needed to be said while I was wearing a mask. "I don't have any animosity towards you, Brian. But I did. For a quite a while. You hurt me. You lied to me. You could have easily been honest, been a man and told me what you were going through or what held you back from coming home. You could have asked me to wait for you while you pursued your dream and worked things out. I would have waited. But after everything we had been through together, the plans we made for our future -- even considering all of that -- you decided to eject from my life with no explanation. It took a while to realize that you weren't coming back because I had so much faith in you. It took me a while to trust again. It took a while to stop loving you."

I looked Brian in the eyes and I could see he was really listening. "It's nice to hear you, finally, say that you're sorry. It really is. I appreciate that. But I think the thing that concerns me most is that you might not have learned anything. How long have you been with Sarah?"

Brian flinched a little hearing Sarah's name. "Um, seven years."

"You live together?"

"Yes."

"If she called you right now, would you tell her that you are standing outside my hotel room door?"

Brian blinked hard. "Uh . . ."

"See, Brian, you're letting it happen again. The vain imaginings you have of our past together, or the misguided belief that you have to have 'closure' on our relationship before you move on -- they're just excuses not to fully commit to Sarah in your heart. And if that's not the excuse, you'd find something else. In the meantime, you're missing out on the incredible perks of having one person in this world that belongs only to you in the deepest, fullest way. And when you give yourself, fully and freely back to them . . . Brian, stop waiting to see if something better is going to come along. You can have something better right now, today, with a woman who obviously loves you very much. She's been waiting seven years, for heaven's sake. All you have to do to have what everyone in this world wants more than anything else, is to make the decision that you are committing to Sarah and making her number one. Put her needs first, before yours. It's scary, but if you live like that, you both get more back. And, you won't be standing in a hotel corridor eighteen years from now talking to Sarah about your regrets."

"Hmmm." Brian nodded his head.

"Hmmm," I replied.

"I thought I was going to give the speech," Brain said half laughing.

"Yeah, well sometimes you get a lecture instead. I'm a mother. This is what I do." I laughed. "Brian, let's just play music and have a great time. 'Cuz lightening strikes quickly and then it's gone."

"Thank you," Brain said just as the room service cart came rolling around the corner. The young man pushing it didn't even flinch when he saw my face. *Increase the tip*, I noted mentally.

"I'll see you in the morning," I said to Brain as I signed my check.

Chapter Twenty-Seven

Sam Wintner, mayor of Commerce, Texas and Senate hopeful, couldn't believe that he was in a studio car headed towards a rehearsal in Hollywood, California. He was exhausted, a little hung over, and filled with remorse due to his snap decision to come out here and play with his old band for this talk show tour.

"Are we there yet?" Cassandra Wintner stirred a little, still half-asleep. Remarkably, even after waking up at three a.m. to drive to Dallas to catch the first flight to Los Angeles, she looked perfect. Her hair and make-up were flawless. She was beautiful when she slept. Then, inevitably, she woke up and started talking. The fact that she was here with Sam was almost more unbelievable to him than the absurdity him being here himself. Every band had a Yoko.

"No. Go back to sleep." Sam patted her leg. *Kind of like petting a sleeping grizzly.* Sam glanced at his watch; it was nine a.m. local time. Brian had told him rehearsal was at ten. Sam silently prayed there would be time to drop Cassandra off at the hotel and that she would agree to stay there. He was arriving two days later than everyone else had; he didn't want to make it worse by showing up with a wife in tow.

Brian's call yesterday had come right after he had a big blow-up with Cassandra. (Never, never Cassie or Sandra.) She'd wanted to attend a fund-raiser in Dallas that night. Alone. She argued that her attendance would be good for his political future. Sam had wanted to know why it was so important for her to go without him. He was free to go with her, which was rare. Her weak excuses made Sam suspicious, and it had all come down to the fact that her friends were more "sparkly" than Sam. And they were younger. It was out of consideration for Sam that she was willing to go by herself. So that Sam didn't have to endure their company, she'd take on the burden herself and promote his campaign. What a trooper.

Sam told Brian that he would come out to L.A. just to

shock the hell out of his wife. He hadn't taken the time to make many phone calls notifying -- or perhaps warning -- his colleagues of his intention to be away for two weeks. Even his assistant of twelve years, who knew more about his personal business than Cassandra, didn't know that he was off to perform with a band on a talk show tour with George Cooper. He wondered if any of Cassandra's high-flying friends could introduce her to George Cooper.

He would keep as low a profile as possible and hope to spin this experience into something positive with the voters during the campaign. He'd deal with the fallout from that later. For now, he was going to show his young wife that there was a side of him that she knew nothing about.

He was hoping to show her from their living room TV, though. When she insisted on traveling with him, he made excuse after excuse for why she shouldn't. The argument ended the same way as the hundreds before it had: Sam got tired and gave in to her. Now here they were, together, headed towards heaven knew what.

Sam lowered the partition between himself and the driver. "Do we have time to stop at the hotel to drop off my wife before rehearsal?" he asked.

Cassandra came to life instantly. "No, no, it's okay. I'm awake. I want to go with you."

"It's going to be a very long, boring day for you. Wouldn't you rather go shopping?" Sam cringed as the words slipped from his mouth. If Cassandra was loose on Rodeo Drive, there would be an audible sucking dry of all his bank accounts.

"No, baby. I wanna be with you," she said with her syrupy drawl.

Yeah, me and whoever might be around the movie studio, thought Sam.

"It's decided then, sir? On to the rehearsal? I'll drop your bags at the hotel after I drop you. It's out of the way and I don't want you to be late," the young driver said.

"That's fine." Sam longed for his position in city council

meetings where he was the authority.

They drove through the impressive studio gate and to the door of Studio 16. Just as Sam was getting out of the car, he heard Vi's familiar voice behind him. She was thanking the driver who was dropping her off in the spot next where Sam's driver had parked. She turned and spotted Sam, greeting him with a big smile. She looked beautiful and her warmth was already embracing Sam from several feet away. Sam relaxed at the thought of being affiliated with her band.

Cassandra peeked out the open car door into the bright California sun. "Let's go meet everybody!" As much as Sam resented her, he wanted her respect. Maybe this crazy stunt would make her look differently at her fuddy-duddy hubby. Sam, always a gentleman, helped her out of the car.

Chapter Twenty-Eight

I was just thanking Todd for dropping me at Studio 16 when I saw Sam Wintner for the first time in eighteen years. I was surprised that I hadn't remembered how tall he was. Wade was a big guy, but Sam was a few inches taller still. He wore a dark well-tailored suit that complemented his white, corporate, precisely-cut hair. He wore glasses and reminded me of a young Phil Donahue. I had always had a thing for Phil Donahue.

"Sam!" I walked over to give him a hug just as a young, beautiful blonde grabbed Sam's hand and got out of the car. She was much shorter than Sam, but her hair was teased up about three inches, lending her some height. She wore a full face of make-up, complete with begonia-pink lips. Aside from being slightly overdone for my taste, she was stunning and, apparently, Sam's significant other.

"Vi Francis, you're like a fresh drop of dew for tired eyes," said Sam. Texans had a metaphor for everything and I loved that about them.

"It's good to see you too, Sam. I'm so glad you decided to join us after all. It's great to have the authentic, original product together." I hugged my old friend. "And it's Francis-hyphen-Gates now; I'll bore you to death with pictures of my kids as soon as you sit down!" I laughed.

I felt Sam's counterpart bristle at the mention of kids, and I turned to greet her. Before I could introduce myself, Sam was *presenting his wife, Cassandra, to make my acquaintance.* Sam's fine manners were present in the everyday matters.

"Nice to meet you, Vi," Cassandra drawled and held out her hand.

"Ladies, shall we?" Sam was already holding the door open.

Jackson, Adam, and Brian were inside tuning up and tweaking the sound from yesterday.

"Sammy White! Good to see you, man." Jackson stood up to shake Sam's hand.

"Sammy White?" Cassandra repeated. Sam didn't respond.

"It's so good to see you, Jackson. How have you been?"

"Overworked and underlaid, my man. Oops, sorry, miss." If a black man could blush, Jackson was blushing.

Adam and Brian greeted Sam and met Cassandra. There were a few sideways glances among the guys as they wondered without words what she was doing there.

Once Sam had slammed back a cup of coffee, we were in place and ready to get started.

"I gotta know what you did in the bridge, Sam. It drove me crazy all night." Adam said.

Sam had taken off his jacket and rolled up his sleeves. He held up his hands and spread his fingers. "You couldn't have played what I played. I possess freakishly long tendons. I can reach one and a half octaves."

"I can't believe I didn't notice that before," Brain said. "I mean, I know you're tall, but . . . "

"So, is it true what they say about big hands?" I asked, laughing. Sam is so conservative he was the perfect target for embarrassment. "Sorry, Cassandra."

"Yes, Vi. It's true. Isn't it, Mrs. Wintner?" Sam put his hands back on the keys to demonstrate his reach.

"Mrs. Who?" asked Adam.

Sam said, "There are some things I kept to myself when I lived in The City. I had a stage name. Lots of people did." He started playing the keyboard that the studio had provided. "Nice action. . . . Mimics weighted keys. These keyboards have come a long way in eighteen years." The explanation was over. Sam was all business.

I watched Cassandra for her reaction. She was looking at Sam as if he was a stranger to her.

"Wanna take it from the top?" Brian asked him. "Are you ready for that or do you want to go over it?"

"I'm ready. I listened to the download I got last night from LimeWire. Can you believe we're on LimeWire?"

"I can't believe you stole us from LimeWire," I laughed.

"I'll buy you a coffee later," Sam promised.

I liked the atmosphere. It was good to have everyone together.

"Okay, band. Let's go . . . one, two, three, four . . . " Jackson smacked his sticks together. I sounded great, much to my own relief; but Jackson and Adam were having a tough time locking on the time signature changes so they decided to work together for a few minutes while the rest of us took a break.

"Vi, can I talk to you?" It was Brain. "Please. Just for a minute." He started walking out to the hallway and I followed. He closed the door behind us. "I thought a lot about what you said last night. You were right about . . . well, almost everything. Thanks for letting me off the hook, and thanks for the fresh perspective."

I smiled at him.

"I even wrote some things down when I got back to my room; it's in the form of a great song," He laughed.

"I can't wait to hear it," I told him.

"Fresh start?" Brian asked.

"Vi Francis-Gates," I said, "nice to meet you."

"Mrs. Gates." Brian shook my hand.

Two minutes later we were back in the studio. It was quiet when we walked in and I felt everyone trying not to look at us.

"I asked Vi to ditch Wade and run away with me, but she said no," Brain said sullenly. He couldn't pull it off and he started to laugh.

"You're an idiot, man," Adam said, throwing a balled-up napkin at him.

"No, Vi just gave me some great advice yesterday, I wanted to thank her, that's all. Nothin' to see here, go about your business," Brian said.

"He actually wanted a cover for calling the authorities in Texas and turning in Mayor Wintner for illegal downloads on LimeWire," I offered.

"Mayor?" Adam looked totally confused. I guessed that Brian had filled me in on Sam's new life, but maintained the veil of secrecy Sammy had always hidden behind with the rest of the band.

"The more we talk, the worse it gets, y'all. We might as well just play music. And Brian, you expose my computer activity and I'll release it to the media that you're in love with Jackson." Sam spoke softly.

Jackson broke up laughing. "We are a dysfunctional family, aren't we now?"

"Show me a band that isn't," said Adam. "Intensity is the greatest factor in making good music."

All at once, the band started playing "So Intense" By Lisa Fischer, a song I used to cover.

"See? You think I'm nuts, but we're still on the same page," Brain said.

"Let's go again, everybody," said Jackson, and we were back at work.

Chapter Twenty-Nine

The flashing light over the studio door indicated that someone was waiting outside. I looked at my watch and was surprised to see that it was already noon. The morning had flown by. The band sounded great now that all elements were represented and we were truly enjoying each others' company.

"I'll get it," I told the guys.

Jane, Brooke, and our catered lunch were in the hallway.

"Good Afternoon, Vi." Brooke greeted me with an air kiss. "How is it going this morning?"

"Really well. Want a preview?"

"Sure, why not? Make me a fan of The Francis Kelly Project." Brooke took a seat and Jane started uncovering our lunch.

"You're hurting my feelings, Brooke. I thought you were already our biggest fan," Brain told her, shaking his head. "By the way, this is our keyboard player, Sam Wintner."

"Very nice to make your acquaintance." Sam shook her hand.

"We need to get you to a stylist," Brooke stated.

"She's a bit of a viper," explained Brian, "but we think she might have a good heart. Still trying to figure it out."

"Please. I don't need a heart. I have all the other body parts that make 'heart,'" she made the quote marks with her perfectly manicured fingers, "an inferior desire."

"Why would a visit to a stylist be necessary, Brooke?" Sam asked naively.

"You need to modernize your look."

"Brooke? Is it?" Cassandra stood up. "I'm Sam's wife, Cassandra. My husband is an elected official with great political ambition and promise. Voters can base their opinions of a candidate on appearance alone, unfortunately, and my husband has to maintain his boring, ultra-conservative look so as not to offend his base." Cassandra continued to nod her head long after she stopped talking.

Brooke looked at Brain as if to ask what the hell Cassandra

was doing there.

"Know what? I don't care," she said finally. "Do what you want."

"Well, thank you very much, young lady. I'll be sure to present myself in a manner that neither shames you nor my constituents."

"Sam, you give us an air of elegance," I smiled.

Sam nodded to me.

"Okay, let's roll. One, two, three, four . . ." Jackson took us into the song. By the time we reached the first chorus, Brooke was smiling. Jane started bopping her head along to the beat and they were both on their feet by the end.

"That was great!" Brooke squealed. "Really!" She came running over to me and laid a hug/tackle on me, which reminded me of when Abrams was happy to see me. It was messy, it hurt, and it was pure emotion.

"Thanks Brooke. You seem surprised," I observed.

"Honest to God, I didn't think you guys would pull it together."

"Why, 'cuz we're old?" asked Adam. "See, that's what's wrong with the Hollywood attitude. Ex-per-i-ence." He pronounced each syllable. "That's what comes with time. Why would you want some green kids with no experience?"

"I don't make the rules, Adam, but you guys could break some. You sounded great. Better than on the record if that's possible."

Jackson was laughing, "You should hear the rest of the record. This is the biggest piece of crap on it."

By now, Jane had lunch set up. "Come 'n' get it."

"I have to go, but I'm going to call Mr. Cooper's people this afternoon to tell him that you sound awesome," Brooke told us as she headed toward the door.

"Mr. Cooper?" asked Cassandra.

"Yes, George. He stopped over to lunch with us yesterday," I said casually.

"I heard he's staying at the same hotel we're staying at,"

134

Sam had finally found a way to get Cassandra to agree to go to the hotel.

"He is? How do you know?" Cassandra took the bait.

"Isn't that true?" Sam asked Jane.

Jane searched his face for the right answer. "Yes, he is," she confirmed.

Perfectly on cue, Cassandra became very tired and didn't want to intrude on band practice any longer. Jane arranged for a car to take her to the hotel. Before she left we nailed down dinner plans as a group. I wanted to work out after rehearsal and Jackson wanted a nap so we decided to meet for dinner at seven o'clock in the lobby. Secure in knowing what time to be ready and, more importantly, what time Sam would be back at the hotel, Cassandra was on her way.

Yoko-less for the rest of the afternoon, we had a very productive rehearsal, musically and vocally. I felt ready to hit the road when we broke for the day at five o'clock. I had to laugh. Wasn't that exactly what my brilliant husband had predicted?

Compelled to tell him how right he was, I called to check in before I hit the gym.

"Hello, wife." Wade had checked the caller ID.

"Hi, honey, how are you?"

"Perfect. How was rehearsal today?" He was waiting to be told he was right. How arrogant!

"I'm ready for the tour, you were right, let's move on to something else." I laughed.

"Ah-ha!" Wade laughed too. "I'm very happy to hear that," he said. "I love being right."

"Yes, yes, yes . . . how are the offspring?" I asked.

"Just great. They are all home, so I can let them tell their own stories." He decided to tell on himself, "Megan is upset that we have had to go to Publix for groceries every day. Evidently you shop once a week, so I'm doing it wrong." He laughed.

"What about the meals in the freezer that I put together before I left?" I asked.

"I don't go for "food" I go for ice-cream. Dessert. I had to buy two varieties of cupcakes the other day because Megan and Henry couldn't agree."

I laughed, recalling my conversation with Henry. "The chocolate v. vanilla debate is always tough. The kicker is they both wind up eating both flavors." I found myself missing one of the very things about my goofy kids that typically drove me crazy.

"Hold on, Megan is standing right here." Wade told me.

"Hi, Mommy." She sounded so happy.

"How was your day?" I asked.

"Pretty good, but, Mom, Dad stops every day at the grocery store. Can you make him a list so we don't have to go every day?"

"I think he likes to get special treats for you guys. I don't think he knows today what treat he wants to get for you tomorrow. You like going grocery shopping anyway, right?" I tried to reason with her.

"Not every day of the world, Mom. Anyway, Henry is fine today, but he cried last night because he wanted Mommy." My heart caught in my throat. Then I heard Wade in the background, "Okay Meg, give someone else a chance."

"Love you Mommy, here's Henry."

"Love you from the top of the sky to the bottom of the ocean." I told her.

"MOMMY?" Henry talked so loudly into the phone.

"How's my little Mister?" I asked.

"I'm good Mom. Megan and I are playing Tinker Toys."

"I love Tinker Toys!"

"Yeah. Do you miss me Mommy?" Henry asked so sincerely that I thought my heart would explode.

"So very much, sir," I told him. "I am so glad we get to talk on the phone and take pictures for each other and that I won't be gone long at all."

"Well, it's a lot more days on my calculator," He told me.

"Oh honey. It's about a week now. That's how long Daddy's trips are and that goes pretty fast doesn't it? I bet Daddy has some fun things planned for the weekend."

"We're going camping!" Henry shouted. "Daddy says you

don't like it so it's good if we go without you." God bless Wade.

"That sound like so much fun! Are you going to sleep in tents?" I asked.

"Nope. Daddy rented a RB and we're going to Marathon, I think. I can fish there." He sounded very excited.

"That will be fantastic! Then, after those things happen, I'll be home."

"Don't come before camping though. Dad might not go if you're here." Henry wanted his camping trip.

"No worries, dude. I'll make sure I don't spoil it."

"Love you Mommy." I melted.

"Love you Schmenry."

"Hi, Mom." It was Lilly. "Can you believe we have to go camping?"

"What brought that on?" I hadn't heard Wade talk about camping for years.

"I dunno, but at least we don't have to sleep on the ground. I mean, it's Florida . . . snakes, gators, bugs. Settlers built houses for a reason." Lilly shared my opinion of camping.

"At least it should be cooler at night this time of year." I tried to sound encouraging.

"Dad rented a very cool RV. It has everything. We'll be comfortable and it's only a couple days. Abrams can even come." She answered my question before I asked.

"Sounds good, hon. Is everything else okay?" I asked.

"We're all doing fine Mom. I heard Megan tell you about Henry, but he was just overtired last night. Dad let them stay up for a movie on Disney Channel. You know how he gets." And God bless Lilly.

"Thanks for saying that, Lil. I swear I am never leaving home again until you are all married. It's killing me," I confessed.

"Is it fun though, Mom?"

"Yes. The band sounds great and it really is fun. The most fun I could have is being with you guys though."

"I love you so much Mom. I do miss you, but I'm excited for you."

"Thanks, baby. I love you."

I looked at my watch. "Put Daddy back on so I can say good-bye okay?"

"All right. Are you headed out?" asked Wade.

"I'm going to the gym and then out to dinner with the whole band and Sam Wintner's bitchy wife."

"So I could have come?" asked Wade laughing.

"You are not nearly as bitchy, not even close." I laughed. "Wade, do you think you could meet me in New York with the kids?"

"Do you think we're not already on the stand-by list?" Wade and I think exactly alike. "Don't let on that you know. It's a surprise."

I was elated. I would see them a few days sooner than expected. "Thank you," I said softly.

"I want to be there for you." Wade paused. "Are you okay?" he asked.

"Better now." I said.

"Get going then. I'll talk to you tomorrow." He blew me a kiss over the phone.

"Love you." I hung up and ran from my room to the gym. Everything was turning out better than I had hoped.

Chapter Thirty

I created my own circuit training program at the hotel gym and left there feeling exhilarated enough to run fourteen flights of stairs to my room. I had a shower and dressed in a pair of dark J Brand jeans, a funky Restricted high heeled sandal, and an asymmetrical plum colored top. One side had a long banded sleeve and the other side was off the shoulder. Wade teased me every time I wore it, saying that we could have afforded for me to buy the rest of the shirt.

I arrived in the lobby, stepped out of the elevator, and spotted Brain relaxing on a couch talking on his cell. When he caught sight of me he waved me over. I reached him just as he was wrapping up his conversation. "I love you too. Don't forget to set the security alarm, okay?" He paused for a moment. "I'll call you in the morning after my workout. Goodnight." He ended the call. "Sarah," He explained.

"I got to check in with my crew too," I told him.

"How are the kids?" He asked. "Are they doing okay without their Mom?"

"Yeah, they are. They have plans to go camping which would never have gotten off the ground if I was there, so they are making the best of me being away." I laughed.

"You like boating, but you won't camp?" Brain asked.

"I'll live aboard for months at a time but, no, I won't camp." As if trying to articulate a very deep thought I said, "Water is clean. The foundation of camping is dirt."

Brain laughed. "I never thought of it like that. I love camping in the mountains, the hiking, rock climbing, biking, and kayaking. I could disappear for years and be happy backpacking from one mountain to the next."

I smiled at him. "I'm a Floridian; I need water on three side of me at all times. But I love Colorado. It's so beautiful, it's almost spiritual."

"I went there on vacation to see Pikes Peak and I never left." Brain directed his attention to Adam who had joined us.

"Hey, man."

"You look great Adam." I said. He wore Seven For All Mankind jeans with a great belt. The buckle looked like a ship's brass porthole: chic with a sense of humor. His button down, probably Kenneth Cole, was half tucked in and strategically half untucked. His hair was a perfect mess and he wore sunglasses.

"You blend, dude," Said Brian who, himself casted a bit of a rock star shadow. He wore very nice dress slacks, I couldn't guess who made them, dress boots and a cashmere long sleeved shirt. His Maroon-Do was starting to look as if it belonged on him. These guys had adapted to Hollywood very quickly.

"Would you look at P. Diddy?" Adam nodded across the lobby where Jackson had just appeared.

Jackson was dressed in a black silk suit with a black shirt and a purple and black striped silk tie. He wore a black fedora style hat with sunglasses and the biggest, most ornate watch I had ever seen. "Good evening," We all heard his rich baritone voice greeting people in the lobby as he glided over to us.

"Hi, handsome," I said as he approached. I stood up to give him a hug. I wished that I could pack Jackson in my suitcase and take him back to Key Largo with me.

"You look lovely, Viola." Jackson used my full name. I had gone by "Vi" for so long that I almost looked over my shoulder to see whom he was talking to, but it sounded formal and sexy at the same time when he said it.
Made me think I should dust if off as I reached my middle years.

"You have half the people in here lookin' at you Jax. You're a star already, man," Brain told him.

Jackson laughed loudly, then said quietly, "They are trying to decide if I'm Forrest Whitaker or if Denzel has been eating too many spare ribs."

Sam slapped Jackson on the back. "Hope I can get seated, dressed as I am." He was wearing slacks and a light sweater vest over a polo shirt.

"You kidding? You give us credibility," said Adam. "You're the only one who looks like a big tipper. We're only getting seated because we're with you."

"Did Cassandra decide to stay behind this evening?" I asked Sam. She had seemed so excited to rub Hollywood elbows earlier; I was surprised not to see her.

"It seems that Cassandra has a little jet lag. She had dinner a few hours ago on Texas time and then decided to turn in early." Sam gave his wife's regrets, but I sensed that we were all relieved. I knew I had made a snap decision about Cassandra and after spending time with her I might have found her to be lovely, but I hadn't been ready to test that theory. I didn't have the mental energy.

"Does anyone know where we're going?" Brain asked. Jane had made the reservation and arranged for a driver.

"Francis Kelly Project?" A young bellhop approached us. "Your ride is here."

We followed him to the hotel entrance where a stretch Hummer was waiting. So much for my theory about everyone being "green" out here.

We piled in and were told by the driver that we were headed to Koi, a West Hollywood hotspot frequented by a lot of celebrities. I immediately thought about Cassandra. She would be sorry she missed this!

The ride was short and we were escorted by Koi security from our showy carriage past the paparazzi who were thick in front of the entrance. There were a few shots taken as we went inside and I thought I heard someone call my name. I probably misunderstood.

"Welcome to Koi," We were greeted by a beautiful Asian girl. "Do you have a reservation?"

"It was made for us by Jane . . .." Brain looked helplessly at me. What was her last name?

"Oh, yes, Mr. Cooper's guests. Welcome!" She upped her enthusiasm level. "You are in our private dining room. Please follow me."

"Private dining," Adam observed. "Last time I was here, I sat in the parking lot with a homemade sandwich waiting for the people I was driving, and today I'm in the private dining room."

I hadn't realized that Adam had been here before, but it shouldn't have surprised me. There were so many things that the band didn't know about each other.

"Will this be all right?" Our hostess showed us to a large U-shaped booth that would accommodate all of us easily.

"This will do nicely, thank you." I spoke for all of us and was the first to slide into place. Brain and Adam sat on either side of me and Jackson and Sam took the end spots.

"Could I place a cocktail order for you with the bar?"

We gave her our drink orders and settled into the atmosphere. The interior of Koi seemed to be lit only by candles, and there was a fireplace at one end of the room.
We had walked past beautiful bamboo plants; and warm, rich hues of red and burnt oranges combined with dark woods to give a very comfortable air to the place.

Our server appeared as if from a secret passage with our drink order and walked us through the menu. As soon as she finished, Jackson took her up on the Kobe beef filet mignon Toban-Yaki.

The rest of the band ordered the same.

"No sushi?" I asked, astonished. "This place is known for sushi!" I looked around the table, feeling like I was out to dinner with the kids. "Fine, I'll have the sashimi appetizer and the Miso bronzed black cod with seasoned veggies. You guys will have to ask me how incredible it is."

"A good Texan will always order beef, Vi. Not Kobe beef, but when in Rome. . . ." Sam laughed, raising his rocks glass. "Good whiskey, good friends, good memories yet to be made."

"Here, here." We all clinked glasses and sipped our drinks. Then Brian took a photo out of his wallet. It had obviously been there for a while; the edges were worn and it was somewhat faded. He set in the middle of the tabletop where we could all see it.

"Oh brother, why you got to bring my fade into this?" Jackson referred to his "Kid-N-Play" hair style. We looked at ourselves standing together on stage at The Bitter End. It was one of our last gigs together. I remembered the night. Brain had his arm around me and I was smiling and sweating. We had just finished our set and were standing in front of our gear.

Adam looked like a baby. We all did, I suppose. Sam's face seemed lit from within and his smile was as wide as mine was. Each face was that of a sincerely happy musician who had just had the opportunity to do what sustains life for every musician: perform. What a great moment.

"That's fantastic," I said to Brian. "Have you been carrying this all these years?"

"Yeah. I love that picture." Brain looked around the table. "I've had other bands, all of them better than this one, but there's something about that picture."

Jackson started laughing. "You son of a bitch."

Brain put the picture back in his wallet. "Speaking of other bands, I hear yours is pretty good, Jackson."

"Naw, man. We the shit!" he said. "Honestly, it's tight. The song list is stuff that works. We play a lot of bars, but we get some money gigs every now and then."

"I've heard good things about you, Jackson," Adam said. "I've played some of the same rooms as your group. The guy who owns Talliwags loves you. He says you're great every time you're there."

"That's nice to hear, man. You playin' around Jersey?" Jackson took another sip of his Hennessey.

"I'm living in Long Island right now with my sister and her family, but before this last rehab stint, I was in your neighborhood."

"You didn't call," Jackson said.

"I didn't want to be around me; you wouldn't have either. If I started drinking again, there wouldn't be enough liquor in this place."

I suddenly became aware that we were drinking in front of a man just released from rehab. "My God, Adam, I'm so sorry. We shouldn't even be here." I sat my wineglass down and looked at Brian.

"No, Vi." Adam grabbed my hand. "You don't have a problem with alcohol, I do. I knew we were going to be in this environment tonight. I can handle it. The smell is like the mother ship calling me home, but . . .." Adam laughed.

"I didn't know you had some trouble, Adam. I'm damn sorry to hear that," Sam said.

"I was stubborn . . . and really stupid. Took me three arrests for DUI, some jail time, and two rehabs, but I'm solid this time. Thank God for my sister, man. She saved my life. And thank God I didn't kill anyone." Adam smiled really big, as if posing for a toothpaste commercial. "So, what have all of you been doing?"

"Seriously, Adam, if you need a gig, I got you, okay? Call me when we get back. My bass player is a little flaky. We only stick with him because there's no other option knocking on our door. I would love to work with you," Jackson offered.

"Thanks Jackson. I don't know if I could be in bars every weekend. I'll think about it though. I'm gonna make it this time, so I gotta think through all my decisions."

"I understand, man. It's out there, all right?" Jackson put out his hand over the table and he and Adam bumped knuckles on it.

"So, you're the Mayor?" Adam asked Sam.

"Commerce, Texas. Just over an hour Northeast of Dallas. My Mamma would be proud," answered Sam.

"That's a jump from playing keys in the Village," Adam observed.

"Well, I was living a fantasy of sorts in New York. The guys back home wouldn't have understood me playing in a band. They probably still won't," said Sam. "Momma made me practice piano, but she wanted me to be a classical player. I wanted to be able to talk to nice young ladies who didn't give me the time of day until I sat in on keys one night at a party. After that, I was doin' it for the ladies and the beer." Sam summed it up pretty concisely.

"After I graduated from NYU, I went to law school and got serious. Got boring. Got old. Ask my wife." Sam knocked back the

144

rest of his first whiskey.

"Cassandra is a looker," Brain complimented Sam.

"Well, she is." Sam raised his glass to the server. "I did this to show her she doesn't know me very well. This might make her pay attention."

"She's young," I said. "She gets latitude for that. It takes a while to learn what life has to teach us. That's why I'm so freaking smart," I joked.

"You're the youngest one at this table, so you better stop right there, Franny." Brain winked at me and the server delivered my appetizer.

"Who wants to taste?" I offered.

"Raw fish," Sam shook his head. "Why would you eat that when there are perfectly good cows out there just waiting to be cooked?" The guys laughed.

"It's all you," Adam confirmed.

I felt like I had tasted heaven after my first bite. Wade would have loved this place. I hoped I'd have the chance to take him to the one in New York while we were there.

"So what about you, Brian?" Sam asked. "I don't know much about what you're doing now."

"I'm a high school music teacher, living outside of Denver in a beautiful community at the foot of the mountains. My girl's name is Sarah." Speaking under his breath to Sam, "who is younger than I am by the way." Brian shrugged his shoulders, "I don't think I've changed much, really. I still wanna play music more than anything."

"Sounds like you have all the ingredients to be happy," I said between bites.

"I don't sit around thinking about it much," Brian said. "Things feel okay."

I laughed, touching my napkin to my lips. I assured Brain, "If you weren't happy, you'd know it."

"I don't believe that," said Adam. "Life can get away from you. You have to constantly be taking inventory. Before you realize it, you could be someone you don't recognize and years could be lost." Adam sat forward a little. "You know the story about the frog and the boiling water, right?" All of us shook our heads. "Okay, if you boil water in a pot and try to put a live frog in it, he'll feel the heat and jump right out. But, if you put the frog in the pot when the water is room temperature, put heat to the pot and keep cranking it higher and higher 'til it boils, the frog will stay in the water and die."

"That's never going to happen to you, Adam. You're in charge of your life now. I can see that." I spoke softly as I continued to eat.

"I am taking responsibility for my life. And I've learned a lot." Adam smiled sheepishly. "Maybe someday I'll be married with children like you and Jackson are. I gotta make-good on the commitment I made to myself to stay sober so I can be worthy of that."

Our dinner arrived and we started talking about Hollywood and this unexpected lightening strike.

"I know that those kids in the picture believed it would happen sooner than this, but timing is everything and everything happens in its own time," Brain laughed. "This is an incredible experience we get to share. I'm honored to be here with you guys."

"I think the girl in that picture is very thankful that enough of her spirit is still alive inside of me to inspire me to finish what she started."

"What we started," Brian corrected me.

"Yes, what we started." I laughed.

"From my perspective, I want to finally introduce Sam Wintner to Sammy White." Sam dabbed at his mouth with his napkin.

I knew exactly what he meant. He had two very distinct people living inside of him. Until now, he didn't know if one's existence would endanger the other.

"Jackson, you've said the least tonight," Brain observed.

"Not much *to* say. It's all about work, baby. Life is work. Sometimes the work is more fun than other times. Sometimes George Cooper likes your work and things go Hollywood for a while. After this is over, it'll be work again." Jackson had finished his dinner and folded his napkin beside his plate. "I don't expect nuthin' more than that. Sharon and I are gonna work 'til we die, but that's okay. We're a solid team and we both know the score."

"This might change things for us long-term," Brain told Jackson.

"Naw, man. This is a great ride and I'm enjoyin' every minute. When it's over, it's over. I know how the world operates and so do you Brian."

"We'll see." Brain was finished with his dinner as well.

The fact that we all gelled so well together musically gave the impression that we were all similar, but we weren't. Brian was a dreamer, Adam a lost soul, Sam a pleaser, Jackson a realist and me . . . I tried to define myself in a tidy little package. I couldn't do it. Maybe that was part of what this journey was about. The part of myself that I had forgotten about, neglected, and silenced. Maybe I was a combination of all of the personalities at the table. Like Sam, I didn't want to risk giving the past a chance to adversely effect my present. Like Adam, I had to stick to my own rules. Like Jackson, I knew that hard work was the key to having the life you wanted. And a part of me was still like Brian; the part that wanted to believe that the wildest of dreams could come true.

"Vi?" Brain tapped my arm. "What about you; coffee?" Our waitress had returned and was inquiring about our plans for coffee and dessert.

"No thank you."

Brian addressed our server, "Just the bill, thank you."

"Your bill has been taken care of already and the gratuity was included. Thank you very much, please come back."

"Have you hugged George Cooper today?" I asked the guys.

We passed a lot of familiar faces on the way to the door. Jackson was right, this was fun for a moment, but it was going to end. I was very thankful for this experience, but glad that it was temporary. I'd happily go back to being "Mommy." The role that inspired me, motivated me, and brought me complete joy. As I suspected, my title was defined by all the characteristics I had considered earlier: protectiveness, dedication to providing strict guidance, working hard, and having faith enough to dream . . . I was Mommy. Being with the band again made me realize that I was always Mommy, even before I had children.

Chapter Thirty-One

Brian woke up at 7:00 a.m. and headed down to the gym. He grabbed an apple from the front desk of the fitness center and started running on the treadmill. He enjoyed his morning workout in Los Angeles more than his solitary routine at home. Lots of pretty young ladies also started their days working out, and some of them wore sheer little clothes that got clingy when sweaty.

As usual, he let his mind wander while he challenged his muscles.

He was thankful that Vi had seemingly let him off the hook after his shameful attempt to make his sins from the past go away. He was still very embarrassed by his visit to her room. What had he expected her response to be? He should have asked himself that question before he had found courage at the bottom of six beers and two shots.

Brian's cell started playing "If you want my body and you think I'm sexy . . . ," a ring tone Sarah chose for herself as a joke. She loved the idea of Brain being in public and having that song play from his pocket.

"Good morning, babe!" Brain was little perturbed at being interrupted.

"Hey! Are you alone?" Sarah sounded strange.

"I'm at the gym, but I can talk." Brain watched one of the thinly veiled young women perform a series of squats and lunges. Sure, he could take a break.

"I have some really big news."

"Okay, what's up?" Brian felt a tinge of panic.

"You're going to be a daddy."

Brian absorbed the words as he replayed them in his mind. "I'm . . . you're . . . ?"

Sarah started to laugh. "I hate telling you this over the phone. I should have sent balloons or something, but I just found out myself. The stick turned to a plus, and I couldn't wait to let you know!"

"Wow. Sarah. I am . . . how far along do you think you

are?" Brain couldn't think straight, but that seemed like an appropriate question.

"I must be only two weeks along which is really four weeks pregnant. It's weird how they count the weeks from the beginning of your cycle before you're even preggers. So, Daddy, what do you think?" Sarah was so excited she barely took a breath.

"I'm shocked. We weren't trying, were we?" Brain didn't know how to feel. What would this mean for his new music career? Was it over before it started because of a baby?

"No, but we were blessed anyway," Sarah said quietly. "Brian, you are happy about this aren't you?"

"Of course I'm happy. I'm just shocked, that's all."

"Well, you have about thirty-six weeks to get used to the idea," Sarah told him.

"Do you want me to come home?"

"What for?" Sarah laughed. "I'm pregnant, not disabled."

"If you need me . . ."

"I'm fine, honey. I'm so excited. I'll try not to have the nursery finished before you get home." Sarah was still giggling.

"Yeah, well, wait for that. Aren't you supposed to wait for three months to tell people anyway?" Brain asked.

"I'll wait till you get home so we can tell everyone together, but I won't be able to keep a secret this great for three months. Besides, that's in case something happens to the baby. Nothing is going to happen," she said firmly.

"No, of course not." Brain mentally kicked himself for saying something so stupid.

"I'll let this sink in with you a little and I'll call you later, okay?" she said.

"Good. Okay. Just be careful and stuff, okay?" Brain tried to say the right thing. "Take care of yourself."

Sarah laughed. "My dear, dear Brain, you need some time to absorb. I love you very much. I'll call you later."

"Love you too. Bye, babe." Brain closed his phone.

He felt as if a bus had hit him. *What does this mean? Marriage, for one thing.* Brain would propose as soon as he got home. They would have so much to prepare in the next few months. *Is it possible to have a new baby and a career in music at the same time?*

For the first time in his life Brian didn't finish his workout. He walked, without observing any scantily clad fitness felines, back to his room and took a long, hot shower.

Chapter Thirty-Two

Sam rolled over to find Cassandra sleeping soundly next to him. When he last checked the clock it had been 4:30 a.m. and she had still been out. Sam had attempted to call her several times between four-thirty and five when he gave up and went back to sleep. Her phone had gone directly to voice mail which meant that she had turned it off rather than just ignoring it, which, Sam thought was far more polite.

He eased out of bed to avoid waking her and made his way into the shower. He felt terrible. The long flight coupled with the late (for Sam) night out at Koi had left him feeling completely drained. Sam hadn't had much sleep in the last forty-eight hours, but he was adapting to sleepless nights. Cassandra had given him plenty of those lately. He wondered if his little stunt with the band was going to have the intended effect on her or if he was just kidding himself.

He felt trapped. A divorced political candidate had a disadvantage, even in this divorce-embracing culture. Leaders and politicians were held to idealistic standards, and their falls from grace were blown out of proportion when they displayed their humanness.

Sam turned off the shower and quietly got dressed, stopping to take a long look at his wife. Where had she been until the early morning hours? Did he really want to know? Why couldn't she just love him and honor him like she vowed to do? Hadn't he already given her everything he could possibly give? *So much for a new start out here,* Sam thought. *Same routine, different location.*

Sam shook his head and headed down to the lobby for breakfast and to read the newspaper.

He had regained a feeling of self-worth from being out here with the band. Playing music brought back of a piece of him that he really missed, although he hadn't seen that person looking back at him in the mirror for decades.

Sam decided to follow that glimmer of hope wherever it might lead. Screw the voters, his wife, his dead mother, and anyone else who wanted him to fit into their preconceived notions. Sam Wintner made a far-reaching and final decision. He was going to be happy. The rest of the world could fall into place or get left behind. Sam began to whistle as he waited for the elevator.

Chapter Thirty-Three

Alone in Studio 16, I began to wonder if I had missed a message. It was quarter past ten and rehearsal was supposed to have started fifteen minutes ago. Our sound man, Manny, had been late most days, but it hadn't hindered our practice. We were self-sufficient. Not having any other band members present would have made my rehearsal harder though.

The door swung open and Adam burst through as if being chased. "Vi, I'm so sorry I'm . . ." He took a minute to look around. "Where the hell is everyone?"

"Aren't they with you?" I asked. Then I noticed that Adam was wearing the same pants and shirt he had worn last night to Koi. I started to laugh. "You didn't stay at the hotel last night, did you?"

Adam had a sheepish grin on his face. "I should probably check out of my room. I haven't stayed there yet. I've kinda been hangin' with Tracey."

"From the salon?"

"Yeah. She's a really nice girl."

I laughed again. "You slick son of a bitch."

"I like her," Adam said. "It's too bad we leave for New York in few days."

The door burst open again and Brian and Jackson rushed in together. They too, looked flustered.

"Sorry," Brain started. As a band we used to fine each other for being late for practice and gigs. The money went to replace cords, light gels, and stuff like that. I guess the programming took. All three of the musicians were panicked; they all took out their wallets and gave me twenty bucks each.

"Brian and I were talking about heavy life stuff, and we just lost track of time," Jackson explained.

"Is everything okay?" I asked.

Jackson put his arm around Brain, "Tell 'em, baby."

"Sarah called this morning." Brain paused for second.

"Ready?"

"No," Adam said. "I can tell this is major. Wait for Sam. We'll do this as a band."

"Okay, yeah." Brain started for the coffee service.

I instinctively knew, as Adam must have, that Brian had just gotten the most life changing, miraculous, frightening news a person can get. I felt an overwhelming gush of happiness rise to the surface. I cleared my throat and wiped my eyes.

Brain looked up from stirring his coffee. "Oh God. What, you're psychic?"

"Adam knows too," I said quickly to deflect his attention.

"Congratulations, man." Adam shook Brian's hand.

I handed him the sixty dollars I still held. "Here, you have lots of fun things to buy."

Brian laughed. "I started thinking about how having a baby changes--everything-- and I freaked out, so I woke Jackson up after I got the news. I needed to talk to a father and mine isn't around, so . . ."

Jackson laughed his hearty laugh. "You're gonna be a great dad, man. Just the fact that you're worried about being a good dad means you're already half-way there." Jackson slapped Brian on the back just as he took a sip of coffee. Miraculously, it didn't spill all over him.

"I can't hold back any more!" I ran over to Brian and gave him a huge hug. "I am so happy for you both. You don't even know how great it is. Your life just gained color and purpose and . . . oh, you've never loved like you're going to . . ." I choked up all over again.

Brian started laughing. "Vi. You are the greatest." He hugged me again. "I wish Sarah had called you instead of me this morning. I wasn't quite so . . ."

"Emotional," I said flatly. "I know, I know. . . ." I blew my nose just as Sam walked in.

"I have no excuse whatsoever --" he began to search through his wallet, but stopped when he saw my face. "Vi, are you okay?"

"I'm just happy," I said, tearing up again.

"I just told her that I'm going to be a father and she's just happy," Brian explained, still laughing at me.

"Shut up!" I said at the same exact time that Sam said, "Congratulations!"

We laughed, Sam got some coffee, and someone suggested that we rehearse. We took our places and waited for Jackson to count us in, "One, two, three, four . . . "

Chapter Thirty-Four

Because of our late start, lunch came quickly. The light above the studio door let us know that catering was waiting for us outside. As had become routine over the last few days, I was the one who answered the beacon.

"Vi! You look great, as usual!" Brooke's greetings were becoming uncharacteristically warm and human. Still, the human element lacked authenticity. "It's so good to see you!" she gushed. Her enthusiasm seemed forced, premeditated, and a bit creepy.

"Brian, hi, how are you?" Brooke wheeled the cart into the room herself and began setting up our lunch. "I have missed seeing you guys these past few days. I've been so busy finalizing all the details of the promotional tour for you and making sure that you will have everything you need every step of the way." She spoke in her typical high-pitched, fast-paced manner.

"What's for lunch?" asked Jackson as he made his way to the folding table that we had come to think of as our dining room table.

"I brought three different soups." Brooke unveiled the selections with grand drama. "Lobster bisque, pasta fagioli, and chilled cucumber. There should be something for everyone's taste. And I brought three varieties of sandwiches. There are veggie wraps, I have grilled salmon with feta and tomatoes on faccocia, and then there's Italian meatball."

"To what do we owe the personal attention today, Brooke?" Brian asked. "Where's Jane?"

"Jane is tied up today, so I thought I would order for you and be your delivery girl. Nothing is more important to me than making sure The Francis Kelly Project has everything it needs!"

Silence exploded from each of us simultaneously. "What?" Brooke asked, evoking another round of speechlessness.

"It just seems like . . . well, you've gone from hating us to loving us in a very short time," Adam explained.

"Hating you? My God, Adam, where did you get that idea?

I was the one who made this all happen for you, really. I loved the song from the start and I . . ."

"Brooke, Brooke. It's okay. Don't worry about it. I think what Adam means," Brain looked at Adam to make sure it was okay to speak for him, "is that we're glad that we seem to have risen to the top of your list, so to speak."

"Lunch is great, baby. Thanks." Jackson had already begun to sample the goods.

"All right, fine. Can I be straight with you guys, no bullshit?" Brooke looked at each of us.

"I'm not a big fan of bullshit myself," I offered.

"Okay, here's the million-dollar question. What are you going to do after the country sees you with Mr. Cooper, and the radio play on this song increases when the soundtrack comes out?" Brooke's gaze settled on Brian, who remained silent.

"You know the studio gave you a shit deal, but a shit deal is better than no deal which is what you had before, so I'm not saying you're in a bad position here. But what you do next is very important. Can you use this as a springboard into the music world?

I think you can and I think you better start making a business plan rather than leaving your fate to chance." Brooke paused for effect. "What you need to do is form your own record company and sign a Pressing and Distribution deal which will allow you the most autonomy, the highest profit margin, and the most control. I think you might get offers from the major labels -- and that's an easier way to go, some might say -- but I think this is where the long-term money will come from. You can sign other acts and, hopefully, build yourself a nice little label."

I could see that Brooke's ideas were intriguing Brain. "What you're proposing assumes that The Francis Kelly Project would be on the label which presently only exists in the body of this conversation. We haven't discussed a commitment to each other, or to this project beyond this tour." I didn't want the cart to get too far in front of the horse.

"How much material do you have in the can as a group?" Brooke asked Brian.

"One CD with fourteen sides," Brian answered.

"There's your first release. Maybe next year you follow it up."

"That means being in the studio for the next year," I said. "Speaking for myself, I can't do that."

"It won't take you guys anywhere near that long. Brian has a lot of material. He gives you the music to learn, and you get together for a long weekend to bang it out. It can be done that way." Brooke had obviously been giving this more than casual consideration.

Sam spoke up. "Brooke, I think you have a great idea for Brian and for any of the other band members who may be interested in carrying this on. But I have to say, right here and now, that I can't continue with the band beyond this engagement."

"I can't either." I turned to Brian. "I think Brooke has a great idea and I think it's worth investigating, though."

Except for Jackson, no one had indulged in the lunch Brooke had brought with her and I was starving. "Let's sit down, have lunch and throw some ideas around," I said. "We might be able to 'think-tank' better if we eat."

Everyone agreed.

"How would I even get a record label started?" Brian asked Brooke. "How much up-front money would I need to get going?"

"I could help you find investors," she offered.

"Why would you do that?" Brian rolled his eyes after biting into the salmon. "This is incredible," he said almost involuntarily.

"Well, I have a motive," Brooke confessed. "I am about to get fired for fraternization. I was hoping to be valuable enough to you to be an employee if not a partner."

Adam laughed. "See, now I'm hurt. With whom were you fraternizing, and why not me?"

Brooke rolled her eyes and heaved a disgusted sigh. "That information is not germane to our conversation. Listen, I'm a trust-fund baby like everyone else out here. I have some money that I can bring to the table and I know people who could get involved. I know how this town works. I could be a huge asset to you."

"And you believe in this band enough to start the label with only one act?" Brian asked her.

"Honestly, what I heard last time I was here, coupled with the invaluable publicity you are about to receive, makes me believe that this could go all the way." Brooke nodded her head along with each of her last words.

"What if the band doesn't exist after next week?" Brian asked.

"I know a lot of unsigned talent as well. It would just be a lot easier to get off the ground by capitalizing on this head start Mr. Cooper has given to you."

"I think you should release the whole CD," Adam said through a mouthful of Italian meatball. "It's a good record. It holds up. My sister listens to it, and her kids love it too."

"If you think it would sell today, I already signed over my rights to everything we wrote together and I think you should go for it," I told Brian.

"I ripped that up." Brian was still enjoying his salmon.

"You what?"

"I couldn't take that, Vi. You wrote everything on that CD with me and we have about ten more songs that we never recorded. Good stuff, too." Brian winked at me. "We have kids to think about. Don't sign away what could mean the difference between state schools and Ivy League."

I laughed. "I never thought I'd be falling back on my music writing to make that happen."

"Okay, so you release the record in the can," Brooke said. "You can work out the details surrounding a follow-up if there is one. Brian, you have material, and a lot of talented bands don't write. We can sign the bands and they can record your stuff. That would make even more money for you."

"I'll have to talk to Sarah. It doesn't sound like this would work from Colorado. We'd have to leave a lot behind."

"You would have to be here," Brooke confirmed. "And we'd have to surround ourselves with some good people."

"If, ah, you need an A & R guy or anything . . . well, I'd be interested in making the move," Adam told Brian. "I could use a

162

fresh start."

"You could use it as an excuse to be closer to Tracey," I said.

"You hittin' that, man?" Jackson asked. "I told you you'd do well here." Jackson laughed as Adam turned red.

"That information isn't germane to the conversation," Adam grinned.

"You've given me a lot to think about," Brian told Brooke.

"Good. I figure if we are going to do this, we better sign the band before we go out."

Brian almost choked. "You're talking about setting this up overnight?"

"Damn close. I have a proposal for your perusal." Brooke handed a neatly bound presentation to Brian.

"You were pretty sure I'd be interested."

"It's the smart thing to do, Brian. And it's what you want to do," Brooke answered.

"Yeah, but I'd have to work with you. That's a huge drawback." Brian wasn't joking.

"You'll learn to love me, Brian. More and more with every dollar I make us."

"You do know more about this than I do, and you know the town . . . but I'm going to have to really trust you, and we barely know each other."

"Before you knew me, you weren't going to be on Leno day after tomorrow. Now you are. I rest my case." Brooke decided to leave it at that. "The video shoot is here on the Warner lot tomorrow in Studio 27A. The same transportation will pick you all up at nine a.m. for hair and make-up. Bring a few of the outfits you got from the stylists. Oh, and Mr. Cooper wants to be in the video as a gag. He'll fake playing guitar alongside you guys. This piece might never be used, but it might, so look rested." Brooke blew a kiss and left, sucking the air out of the room as she went.

"That's a lot of shit," Jackson observed.

"I'm having a baby, possibly starting a record label, maybe

moving to L.A., and shooting a video with George Cooper tomorrow. How was your morning?" Brian asked no one in particular.

Chapter Thirty-Five

Once lunch had been inhaled, we all seemed less than enthusiastic about running the song again. Personally, I felt that if I had to hear "So Beautiful" one more time, I might have a full-scale meltdown.

"Back to the grind?" asked Jackson.

"I guess so," Brian answered, but didn't move.

"Does anyone feel, as I do, that my corpse will probably be able to play this song for at least twenty-four hours after I die just from muscle memory?" Adam joked.

"Well, there is nothing new to cover. The vocals are perfect, the arrangement is flawless. I feel like we have nothing left to conquer unless we change songs on Mr. Cooper, and I don't think that would be wise." Sam folded his napkin neatly and placed it on the table.

"I'm good if you guys are. I could do Leno right now, man. In fact, I'm dyin' to get there," Jackson concurred.

"I think we're as prepared as we can possibly be. How about taking this afternoon off?" I suggested. "After tomorrow we're on a pretty tight schedule. This might be our last chance for some relaxation for a while. Besides, we want the performance to be fresh."

"Vi's right. Let's break for today." Brian grabbed the packet that Brooke had left for him. I could tell that he was eager to digest it.

"Brian, I think you should have a lawyer look that over. There is a lot at stake, and you don't know Brooke from Adam," I said.

"I hate that cliché." Adam shook his head.

"Sorry."

"I know you're right, I just don't know how to go about finding someone on such short notice." Brian would follow his heart and catapult right into this thing without taking the time to make an intelligent decision. I knew Brian, and the part of him that feared missing an opportunity was still in control.

"Let's call Jane. She'll be able to guide us, maybe even set an appointment. I'll go with you to meet with an attorney if you want me to," I offered. "Brian, you're talking about relocating your family and starting a business on the word of a girl you met for the first time a few days ago. I don't have partners for a reason. It was hard for Wade and me to come up with the capital when I opened my first boutique and it was tempting to take on a partner to ease that burden, but partners generally mean trouble." I hoped I hadn't overstepped my boundaries.

"When I present this to Sarah I had better have a good understanding of the details or she's going to ask something I can't answer, and then she won't entertain the idea ever again." Brian began to look over the proposal. "I just don't know enough about this to know what the industry standards and practices are." He tossed the packet back onto the table. "Would you really go with me? Two sets of ears are better than one."

Sam cleared his throat. "If I wanted to be ignored I could have stayed at home where my wife perfects the practice more impressively with each passing day."

"Oh, shit, Sam!" Brian snapped to the realization that he was sitting at the same table as a lawyer.

I laughed out loud. "Well, I think I've been replaced by a person far more capable than myself." I stood up and grabbed my purse. "If you need me to do any legwork or anything, call my cell. I'm going to pick up a few touristy things for the kids."

"Thanks, Vi." Brian waved me off and moved over to where Sam was sitting. Sam had taken out his cell and was already speaking to a colleague in Dallas to ask for a referral while preparing questions based on the proposal for an entertainment attorney.

As I waited for the van, I thought of how naturally it had come for me to step in to take care of Brian. Oddly enough, it didn't make me feel uncomfortable. It was just habit.

I climbed into the van and asked to be dropped off along Rodeo Drive. I checked my watch; it was just after two o'clock;

166

just after five p.m. back home. Wade and the kids should be at their campsite by now. I dialed Wade's cell. His voicemail came on immediately.

"You have reached Captain Wade Gates, please leave a message. If you are my incredibly hot wife, please make it dirty. BEEP."

I laughed for the first few seconds of my message. "You guys must be busy doing what campers do. I love you and miss you beyond words. I'm on my own for the rest of the day, so call when you get this. Oh, and when I get home I want to do that naked floating edible flower thing . . . is that dirty enough, Captain Gates?" I laughed again and closed the phone. Unfortunately, the driver had heard every word and was smirking to himself. I couldn't wait to drive myself around again.

Chapter Thirty-Six

Sam and Brian had made their way through Brooke's proposal, made several notes and crossed out a few paragraphs. Sam's colleague in Dallas had been able to call in a favor from a friend and they had a four o'clock meeting with one of the biggest music attorneys in Los Angeles. With Sam at his side, Brian felt very confident and damn lucky.

The two men went to their rooms to shower and change for their meeting. Sam was surprised to find Cassandra in his room.

"Well, hello," Sam said coolly.

"Sam, I have something to tell you," Cassandra began.

"Be quick about it because I have a meeting," Sam told her very matter-of-factly.

"I want a divorce," she announced.

Sam noticed that her bags were packed. The realization left him surprisingly unaffected. "What time is your flight to Dallas?"

"Did you hear what I just said, Sam? I want a divorce." Cassandra stood indignantly dressed in her favorite Dolce and Gabbanna suit. Sam remembered what that suit had cost and knew he didn't own such an extravagant outfit in spite of the fact that his money clothed them both.

"Haven't I always given you everything you want, dear?" Sam met her gaze.

"I'm going home." Cassandra shifted her weight from one hip to the other.

"I'm still not sure why you came in the first place." Sam calmly undressed and headed for the shower.

"Don't you even want to know why?" Cassandra followed him.

"Specifically or generally, Cassandra?" Sam turned on the shower and stepped inside.

"What do you mean by that?"

"Specifically, that you have found a young man, perhaps even had him tag along to L.A. with us, and you can't stand the duplicity of your life any longer. Or generally, that you never loved me, but were lured by my money and the lifestyle I have been able to provide, but you just can't bring yourself to love me in the way a wife should love her husband. Both scenarios are paramount to living a lie, so does it really matter?"

Sam turned off the water and toweled off. He wrapped a towel around his waist and headed to the armoire where he had hung his clothes.

"I gave you a lot, Sam," Cassandra spat.

Sam took his pants from the hanger and put them on. "Thank you."

"Don't you want to hear it from me? The reason?"

Cassandra was dying to tell him something, but Sam truly didn't care. And it felt great. Not to care about her and what she thought, where she was, what she was doing, or with whom she was doing it. Sam laughed out loud. "No, darlin'. I don't care." He finished dressing and retrieved his watch from the bureau. "I hope you'll be well and safe. Good luck to you." He kissed his wife on the cheek and left the room for his meeting with Brian.

In the elevator, Sam dialed his assistant. "Mayor Wintner's office," answered the assistant who had been with Sam for most of his professional life.

"Hi, Martha, it's me. How's the office?"

"Everything is under control, Mr. Wintner. You told me you wouldn't be checking in unless something went wrong, so what can I do for you?"

"This is of a personal nature and certainly not in your job description."

"You know you can ask me anything. Out with it."

"I need you to remove some things from the house. Cassandra may be returning back there tonight and I don't want my mother's jewelry and my valuables to come up missing. Also, I need her name taken off all of my bank accounts and her credit cards cancelled."

"Mayor? Does this mean . . . ?"

"Yes, Martha. Cassandra has asked me for a divorce and I am going to give her one."

"Yeeeeeeeeeeeee-haaaaaaaaaa!" The sixty-two-year-old, perfectly proper assistant couldn't contain her excitement. "Ding-dong the witch is gone!"

"Yes. Well, I guess I don't need to ask you how you feel about that."

"Can I change the locks on the house?"

"Not yet. Just please remove the following items. . . ." Sam listed the valuables that were irreplaceable family heirlooms and a few other big-ticket items.

"I'll have May gather those things up and I'll run right over to get them." Martha referred to Sam's housekeeper.

"Thank you. I'll be home in another week. If you need anything, please call without hesitation." Sam hung up.

He was shocked by the sense of calm he felt. He guessed he had already worked through the sadness each time the evidence had presented itself, when the realization of her lack of commitment to their marriage was new. It wasn't new anymore; in fact it was very, very old. Sam started to feel more and more confident with every step. Coming out here was the catalyst for a miraculous event. Now he had to help Brian structure a deal that would give him the best chance at succeeding at his dream. Sam felt needed, valued, and productive. Funny, given his profession and the role he played in his community, this was the first time in a long time he had felt these things.

Sam imagined Cassandra's face when she saw the empty jewelry box or the first time she tried to use her credit cards. He laughed out loud. He hoped her new man had a lot of disposable income because Cassandra could dispose of a man's income faster than Sam had imagined was possible. She was young. The lessons would come hard to her, but she had time to get her life together if she chose to do so. Sam knew she wouldn't though, she'd just find the next gullible man willing to donate to the Keep Cassandra Beautiful Foundation.

Maybe the divorce would play badly with the voters, but he had to live his life for himself. Let the chips fall.

He saw Brian in the lobby. He was dressed in one of the

suits he got from the stylist and looked very much like the president of his own record label.

"Thanks again for coming, Sam, I appreciate this so much."

Sam slapped Brian on the back, "Don't mention it, friend. You've done more for me than I can possibly repay."

Chapter Thirty-Seven

Brian pressed his cell phone more tightly to his ear, sure that he must not have heard what Sarah said correctly. He had mentally prepared a list of facts and figures to support his cause and developed counter-arguments for every line of reasoning she might present. Brain had barely gotten through his opening statement when Sarah interrupted him, stopping him in his tracks with a single word.

"Okay."

Brian paused. "So you mean *okay, we'll talk about it when I get home okay?*, or *okay, Brian this is just crazy and I'm hoping you'll forget about it okay*, or *okay,* as in *okay?*"

Sarah giggled softly. "Okay, Brian. If this is what you've dreamed of and there is a chance that your dream can come true, we'll never forgive ourselves for not giving it a shot. Let's go for it. That kind of *okay.*"

Brian paced in the hallway outside the offices of Wesley Taggat, Esq., one of the most powerful men in Los Angeles. Taggat was a major contributor to the campaign of the current governor of California and supported The Republican National Committee. He had known of Sam's political ambitions and was friendly with the people Sam was affiliated with. Moments earlier, the entertainment attorney had been very helpful in structuring a California corporation for Brian which had been dubbed "Advanced Band, Inc.," named after his sixth period band class. Taggat also reworked the proposal Brooke had presented to Brian. One or two keystrokes from now, Brian would be in business. Before giving the go-ahead, Brian had excused himself from Taggat's office, coming out in the hall to call Sarah to get her consent.

"You just had to top my big news, didn't you?" Sarah teased.

"Sweetheart, there's no topping the news that I am going to be a daddy. That's a huge part of the reason I really want to do this. The television exposure we're going to get on these talk shows with Cooper is invaluable. It's not like we're starting out on a wish and a prayer. It would be irresponsible not to capitalize at this point. "

Brian felt more certain every minute. "Brooke says she can get us some investors and Mr. Taggat offered to introduce me to some very influential people after this tour. I really do feel that we have a great chance for success out here, Sarah."

"I'm with you. *We* are with you." Brain knew he had never loved her more than he did at that moment. "I guess it's a good thing I didn't start decorating the nursery," Sarah laughed.

"Sarah, I want you to know that you aren't moving and having this baby without a commitment from me. When I get home . . ."

Sarah squealed, "No, no, no, stop right there! I've waited for this for so long. You are not going to do it over a phone. You're going to do it right."

"I just wanted you to know . . ."

"Shut up, Brian Kelly." Sarah sounded as if she had taken the receiver away from her ear a bit. "I mean it, shut it." She was laughing again.

"All right. All right. I love you and mini-you. And I'm going to do my best to give you ladies the best of everything."

"Ladies? It could be a boy, you know."

"Not if God loves me." Brain was picturing a mini version of himself, complete with all his flaws.

"Go back in there and get your record label off the ground. Congratulations."

"I'll call you later. Thank you, Sarah."

"Don't you mean the future Mrs. Kelly?" Sarah laughed.

"Can I be this lucky? I'll call you later."

"Bye, babe."

Brian stepped back into the office. "We're set to go." He announced feeling an energy surge through him that he thought had been long lost.

Brian was on cloud nine, but already thinking about his

next step. He'd call Brooke tonight and ask her to meet him at the hotel bar. He needed her to be a principal of this corporation, but he wasn't offering her any shares in the company. He was prepared to offer a generous, tiered salary based on the investment dollars Brooke was able to attract. Taggat had assured Brian that she would take the deal and that it was more than fair. Brian felt a little guilty that he had acted on what was essentially Brooke's idea without offering her shares of the company. Like all good lawyers, Taggat had protected Brian's best interests and advised him to retain all the shares for now. Brooke's bonus structure was very generous and would motivate her to find new talent and investors. Brain knew that if he set Adam loose in Los Angeles for a week, he would find authentic talent. Adam would be a terrific A & R guy. Hoo-ray for Hollywood.

Chapter Thirty-Eight

After a long afternoon of shopping, I headed back to the hotel and began to run a hot bath. I ordered my dinner from room service and decided to try Wade's cell phone again. He answered on the first ring.

"Hi, honey."

I loved the sound of his voice. "Hey, I called earlier, did you get my message?" I asked.

"I did, Vi, but we're pulling out tonight and I promised the kids a laundry list of things we could do before we go."

"Weren't you going to stay another day?" I wondered if I was losing track of time out here.

"We were, but *your* children are more like you than I suspected." Wade pulled the phone from his ear for a minute to yell at Abrams. "Lilly tried to put on a brave face, but this RV isn't the cleanest. In spite of our best efforts, it stinks. The fact that Abrams has been doing a lot of swimming and then sleeping on the carpet hasn't helped." He pulled the phone away again, "*Abrams. NO! Come, boy!* You know, this dog doesn't listen to anyone but you. He just started to dry off, I don't want him to jump in and get soaked again."

"Put me on speaker," I joked, "I'll get him in line."

"Henry is having fun, but his schedule is all messed up. He missed his nap yesterday and today so he's crabby. Megan doesn't like the water on the gulf side because the bay is a little brown, so we have to go to the ocean side to swim and the beach is really narrow there. It drops off pretty quickly so Lilly and I are constantly on lifeguard duty. And the damn bugs . . . we're getting are carried away."

I could hear the frustration in Wade's voice. I know what it feels like to plan something special and not have it play out the way you imagined it would.

"I'm sure when they tell me about this camping adventure they will only remember the great parts of it and they will tell me I missed a really good time." I wanted to hug Wade. He tries so hard and hits the mark ninety percent of the time.

"I hope so. I can't wait to see you, Vi. You're the glue that holds this circus together."

"Three days until New York. You're coming the first day I get there, right?

"Yeah, we're on the stand-by list and it looks good. We'll make the morning direct to JFK unless one hundred people book the flight between now and then. In fact, we'll get there before you do."

"You're the greatest husband of all time. I miss you too and I can't wait to see you. Are the kids close by?" I asked.

"Lilly took them up to the campground shower. *Abrams, NO!* Vi, I'm sorry but he's got that look. He's inching down the dock, I had better put the phone down to go get him or I'll be pulling a hundred and sixty pound dog out of the drink for the third time today."

"Go ahead, Wade. I love you."

"Love ya."

My dinner arrived and I decided to eat in the tub. Unorthodox, yes, but delightful.

I said Grace and thanked God for the abundance of gifts he had given me before I ate. Once I started counting my blessings I felt like it was almost too much. Other people were struggling with serious issues and I was living a dream. Then it hit me, like a message from Above. Maybe this wasn't a blessing just for the sake of blessing members of The Francis Kelly Project. It was given to us to pass through us for a greater blessing. The right thing to do was to magnify the blessing, make it reach farther.

One of my favorite authors was Marianne Williamson and one of my favorite quotes from her popped into my mind. In *Return To Love*, which I had read at least ten times, she wrote: "As we let our light shine, we unconsciously give other people permission to do the same."

My mind started concocting possible ways to keep the gift going. Philanthropic Foundations, children's charities, and causes close to my heart rushed into my thoughts, all vying for my attention and begging to be considered. All of a sudden I became comfortable with this opportunity in a way I hadn't been before. I was going to turn it into something that blessed others.

I laughed and said out loud, "Sorry, God, that I didn't see it sooner." I knew he understood. He had known me for a long time. I didn't have to explain. He knew I'd catch on eventually. Some people felt comfortable talking to God in church, I, on the other hand, was most productive at deciphering messages while dining in the tub.

Chapter Thirty-Nine

Brian waited for Brooke in the hotel bar. He had chosen to sit outside because the deck was empty except for one couple who didn't seem to notice, or care, that there were other people on the planet. He wanted to be as isolated as possible because he anticipated that Brooke might not take this offer well and might get all high-pitched and crazed.

As if drawn to him by his thoughts, Brooke appeared in the doorway. "I'm glad you're out here," she said as she sat down across from Brian. "I don't really want to run into anyone. I got fired today. I knew it was inevitable, but it still stung."

"I have a sneaking suspicion that you are going to find a new position very quickly," Brian said.

"I certainly hope so. I have some pretty expensive beauty habits." Brooke ordered a Sex on The Beach cocktail from the waitress.

"Sam and I spent the afternoon at Wesley Taggat's office."

Brooke's eyes widened. "You are *kidding* me," she said. "How did you get past the front desk?"

"Sam is an attorney and the mayor of Commerce, Texas. He's part of a network of very powerful people. And Taggat is aware of who you are, Brooke. We discussed you and took action on what you suggested to me earlier today."

"No shit, Brian? I am impressed with your initiative." The waitress brought Brooke's drink over and she took a sip. "What advice did Mr. Taggat give you?"

"He set up a corporation, Advanced Band, Inc., and filed the necessary documents with the state. The record label is called Advanced Band Records.

"I get it, Teach -- first-class name." Brooke raised her glass to both Brian's achievement and her clever pun. "You called me here to tell me that I'm involved in some way, I hope?"

"Well, Taggat advised against taking on partners at this point, but he felt you would be invaluable as a principal. He drew up an employment agreement that outlines the position I'm offering you. The tiered salary is commensurate with your productivity and there is a generous bonus structure. The company currently has no bank account and nothing to deposit into it, but you were confident that you could help us raise some capital. . . ."

Brooke was taking it all in and she showed no expression. Brian wasn't sure how she was taking this.

"Do you have a copy of the Employment Engagement?" she took another sip of her drink.

"I do." Brian slid a manila envelope across the table.

"Give me a second to look at this?" Brooke raised her eyebrows.

"If you want to take it to a lawyer . . ."

"My dad is a lawyer; he can look it over, but I'll understand what I'm reading." She took another drink. After a few minutes, Brooke slid the document back into the envelope and set it on the table.

"I can earn my way to a pretty nice position." Brooke tapped her fingernails on the tabletop.

Brian nodded.

"Eventually." Brooke ticked things off on her fingers as she spoke. "But, you need capital and you need talent and you need connections within the industry to get this off the ground. I can provide those things for you. Without what I bring to the table, you're dead in the water. The resources I bring are worth fifty percent of the shares of the corporation."

"I am not going to do that, Brooke. This is the only offer I am prepared to make."

"This was my idea," Brooke said evenly.

"And it was a great idea."

"I'll do it." Brooke said. "My dad will probably be very disappointed in my willingness to sell myself short."

"Taggat told me what you currently make -- or made -- with the studio." Brian tipped his hand.

"Oh. Well, I was almost due for a big increase." Brooke took another sip of her cocktail.

"Welcome aboard, Ms. Vice President." Brian held out his

hand.

"Thank you." she shook his hand. "You leave in two days for New York and you'll be very busy between now and then. I'll get started doing whatever you'd like me to start doing."

"Taggat's office is sending over investment agreements. Get 'em signed and get us some money. Find us respectable office space that we can afford on a shoestring budget."

"Okay. I won't make any commitments without your approval. Are you coming straight back here after New York?"

"I'm going to Colorado first. Sarah is putting the house on the market tomorrow. We have to quit our jobs and tie up some loose ends. I hope this thing takes off quickly because we don't have a ton of savings. We need to find someplace to live out here . . ." Brian tried to run his hands through his hair, forgetting that he didn't have much anymore.

"It's a lot, I know."

"You know about half of it, but I have two very capable women helping me out and I think it'll be okay." Brian let out a long sigh.

"What about the band? Do you think they'll make more records for the label?" Brooke asked.

"I just don't know. Vi, Sam, and Jackson are pretty entrenched in their own lives. I guess we'll have to play that one by ear."

"We'll take one step at a time. We can release the CD though, right?"

"Yes. We have one." Brian tried to sound enthusiastic.

"Get some sleep, Brian. You've had a long day." Brooke downed the rest of her drink. "I'll stop by tomorrow in an unofficial capacity. I guess you'll meet your new studio contact tomorrow."

"I heard that the studio isn't going to replace you right away. Sort of implies that your position wasn't as--"

Brooke interrupted before Brian could finish the friendly jab, "I got your whole world in my hands, Brian. Be nice." Brooke pointed her finger at Brian's nose, displayed a rare genuine smile

and made her exit. Brain ordered another drink. After today he felt
he deserved it.

Chapter Forty

When Hollywood wanted to protect one if it's most valuable assets, the Secret Service could take notes on procedural security. Brooke had told us yesterday that the location of the video shoot was on the Warner lot, but that had been a cover. The actual location of the shoot was known only by a select few people and was disclosed to our driver while in route.

Jane and Todd, our driver, had met us in the lobby of our hotel and escorted us to a rented van. We drove around a while to ditch some paparazzi, then pulled into a parking garage where we left the van and piled into an SUV with heavily tinted windows. We drove around a little longer until Todd got the call on his cell, directing him to our final destination. The paparazzi had found our hotel earlier in the week and Warner was worried that they would follow us, hoping we would eventually lead them to Mr. Cooper.

We reached our destination, which appeared to be an abandoned warehouse in an industrial section of L.A., but turned out to be filled with a surprising cache of high tech audio/video equipment, complete with a crew. We met the director of our video, someone famous enough to be recognized by Brian, Jackson, and Adam. He was introduced to me as "Mick Gee." The band gear was hooked up for the sake of authenticity, but the audio track for the video wouldn't be recorded today. The track would come from the CD and sync with the video. A green screen surrounded our staging area, where the equipment was set up. The director could use whatever computer graphics he chose to make us appear to be performing in whatever location or under whatever circumstances struck him as "awesome."

We were told to proceed to hair and make-up and that Mr. Cooper was scheduled to be on set in an hour.

"We were never really told how the video would be used," Brian told Mc G. "Do you know anything more about that than I do?"

"I can tell you that if they're paying me, there's a plan. I was just told to keep in simple, but put my signature on it. If the song climbs the charts, the video will get spins on MTV 2, VH1, like that. It might be tacked onto the end of the film depending on editing. The film is finished, so I'm not sure." Mc G shrugged his shoulders. "I like B-I-G productions, man. I like to blow things up. This is kind of low-key for me, but Cooper asked, and I think I can get some dynamic stuff going on behind you and make something revolutionary from a very analogue concept. It's a challenge. And I love that guy, Cooper. I haven't worked with him before."

"It's easy to have a man-crush on him," Brian joked. "He's the coolest guy I have ever met."

"I know, dude. Go let the girls make you look alive and I'll see you in a few. I have some computer shit to do." Mc G tinkered with his Mac and nodded as if the song was going through his head.

"C'mon, Mr. Kelly, let's go *make you look alive*," I laughed.

Sam, Jackson, and Adam were already chatting up the stylists, and I discovered why the boys had been distracted since our arrival. The young stylists were so gorgeous it was hard to believe they were here to be behind the camera.

Sam was in a chair with a mud mask on his face, Jackson was making the girls giggle, and Adam was having his hair done while talking on the phone.

"Jane." Adam called her over. "Do we get tickets to invite guests to The Tonight Show tomorrow?"

"How many do you need?" Jane asked, already whipping out her phone.

"Just one. For a friend," Adam answered, still on his phone. He laughed a little in response to the person on the other end and replied into the phone, "It hasn't even been a week. I'm not asking for a title yet. 'Friend' is good."

"What name do I leave at Will Call?" Jane asked, talking with someone at NBC.

"Tracey Napoli."

"Done," said Jane, snapping her phone closed. I had to admit I missed the snapping closed of a flip phone. That's one

186

thing Blackberry's just couldn't do. It was like the satisfaction you used to be able to get by slamming the phone receiver down into the cradle. You just couldn't get that satisfaction by pressing the "talk" button on the cordless phones of today.

"Okay, Trace. You're on the list. I'll call you later to see if we can meet for a late dinner. Bye." Adam hung up.

"I'm glad things are going so well with Tracey," I told him, giving his arm a squeeze as I passed by to sit at my station. We were lined up next to each other at stations covered with make-up, hair products, and lit by bulbs a few candlesticks brighter than the sun.

"She's a nice girl." Adam wasn't ready to say any more than that. After all he had been through he deserved to be guarded, so I changed the subject.

"So, Brian, we never heard how it went yesterday." I had to raise my voice to address Brian, who was three stations down.

"Thanks to Sam, I'm on my way. I have a lot to talk to you guys about, actually," Brian semi-yelled back.

"I didn't do anything but make an introduction, my friend. But Brian is on his way," Sam confirmed.

"Adam, I need a senior A & R guy. I can't think of anyone better for the gig than you man. But you'd have to move out here."

"You're moving, right? " Adam asked.

"I talked to Sarah yesterday. She was very enthusiastic. She's putting the house on the market today."

"If you're going all in, I know you're going to make happen." Adam was sitting in the chair next to Brian so their conversation was less boisterous than Brian's and mine.

"I don't have a house to sell, dude. But I'm coming out here with almost nothing and I know better than to expect much in the way of salary at the beginning. Maybe I can do some session work. I did a lot of that the first time I was out here," Adam thought out loud.

"Hopefully, we'll have capital to start. Brooke is finding investors. We want to get The Francis Kelly Project CD out as soon as we can to take advantage of all this media attention. We should have respectable record sales without having to spend too much on marketing," Brian explained. "The band search practically made us a household name. This talk show tour with Mr. Cooper surely can't hurt. If we have to get side jobs to get started, it shouldn't be for too long, but I want to think that we're going to be able to focus on the label from the beginning."

"Wouldn't the band get more money signing with a major label than with you?" Jackson asked from the end of the line next to me. He could hardly contain his laughter as Brian struggled to sit forward in his seat and look down the line to see if he was serious.

"I mean, that's major label distribution, man." Jackson was bursting at the seams.

"We'll have distribution--" Brain started. Jackson couldn't let the joke breathe any longer. His laughter shook the room.

"You son of a bitch." Brian threw a brush in our direction, which narrowly missed the head of the girl doing my hair.

"This is your shit, dude. I told you from the beginning that you paid me fair and square as work for hire." Jackson was laughing pretty hard by then. "You shoulda seen your face dude. You were purple."

"Is that what color your face turns when you shit yourself?" Brian asked. "'Cuz that's what I almost did. I thought one of Sam's lawyer friends had gotten a hold of you."

"From hero to scum sucker in less than five minutes," Sam observed.

"What do you call ten lawyers at the bottom of the ocean?" Jackson asked.

"Keep going, I've never heard that one before. Then someone sues you or you get divorced and you come running to a lawyer, don't you?" Sam joked. "By the way, Cassandra left yesterday, we're getting a divorce."

"Sam, I am so sorry." I turned my head to look at him and my stylist grabbed my chin to keep me straight.

"Don't be darlin'. I feel better already," Sam replied.

"So, you're a lawyer and a musician?" Sam's pretty, young

stylist asked for clarification.

"It's true, I am cursed with talent and brains," Sam boasted.

"And you're damn good-looking," I added. "I'm not too worried about you Sam."

"Thank you, Vi. I do think I will be no less than a hell of a lot better off than I was before."

"There's room for everyone at the label if any of you want to take the chance," Brian offered.

"My wife has four sisters in New Jersey. There's nothin' that could make her leave," Jackson said. "Brooke was talking yesterday about us recording a new record to follow this one next year. I don't even know about that man, but I'm not ruling anything out."

"Thank you, Brian," Sam told him. "I'll be available for free legal advice and possibly keys on a new project. It will depend on the timing. I have a lot of people depending on me and I have to take care of those obligations first."

"I understand," Brian told both men.

I was silent for a minute and Brian answered for me.

"Vi, I know you have your family and your boutiques. If you ever want to put your music industry hat on, the door is always open and I will probably never stop asking."

"Thanks Brian."

My face was taking shape and my hair looked great. The guys had been finished for some time, but we were enjoying the conversation.

"We look good," Jackson observed.

"We're plugged in to those stacks, so we might as well actually run the song a few times while we're here," Brian suggested.

"Good idea, man," Adam said. "Let's get back to the main studio and see if we can get a few turns in before we start filming."

"I'll sing, but I'm not dancing yet," I announced. "My hair looks too good." I told my stylist as she put the finishing touches on me. I stood up and assessed myself in the mirror.I wore Jennifer-Aniston-on-a- wavy-day hair, glowing make-up, a short flowy white dress, and the Monolos. I was happy with the finished product.

Jane commented on how great we all looked and then asked if anyone else needed tickets for any of the upcoming performances.

"As many as I can get for anything in New York," Jackson told her.

"Four for my sister's family for anything in New York if I could get them," Adam echoed.

"Four tickets for my family for anything in New York as well." I added to the total as Jane scribbled. "My family will be there the whole time, so it doesn't matter which show."

"That's great, Vi. You'll get to see your family in a few days." Sam was genuinely happy for me.

I suddenly felt very sorry for him. He didn't have anyone to share this with, other than us.

"I can't wait for them to meet you," I told him.

A voice came over a loud speaker: "Francis Kelly on the set, please."

"Let's go," said Brian.

Mc G was talking to some staffers when we came into the sound stage, and he introduced us to his team individually.

"Okay, so here's the plan," Mc G said. "There will be several backgrounds going and the shoot will seem three-dimensional because we have you surrounded on five sides. The different camera angles will help us to achieve what we're going for. It's going to look like nothing at all to you at this point. Don't react to anything; just play the song along with the audio track. We'll do some takes acknowledging the camera and some where you don't look at the camera at all. Your work is simple. I've got the hard stuff to do in post."

"Good," said Adam. "I'm not an actor, so I'm glad there's not a storyline."

"I'm not an actor either, but I keep getting jobs," said a voice from behind Mc G. Mr. Cooper always seemed to appear from thin air and never with an entourage. He wore black pants and a black dress shirt open at the neck. He had a hat and a five-o'clock shadow. His attempt to blend in was admirable, but impossible. It was almost as if he shone from within.

"Mr. Cooper, I am excited to work with you." Mc G shook his hand.

"This is going to be fun," he responded. "Thanks for letting me sit in, guys. I want to be in the background, kind of as 'Pop Up Video' trivia ten years from now, if anyone remembers me in ten years."

We all laughed at the thought of an anonymous George Cooper.

George picked up his guitar and took direction, as we all did, to act natural and play along with the song. I was amazed by how normal it seemed to have him there after a while.

It took just over an hour for Mc G to get enough material that he could create his "awesome" video from.

"Thanks again, guys. That was fun." Mr. Cooper shook each of our hands.

"Mr. Cooper, could I bother you for a picture? My daughter Lilly is thirteen and I would be the coolest mom in the world if I could give her a picture of us together."

"Of course, Vi." While Jane took some shots with my camera Mr. Cooper asked if any of our families would be able to come to any of the shows.

"Jane just took our wish lists for tickets, but we understand if it doesn't pan out," said Adam.

"I was actually wondering if you'd like to invite some people to the premiere party. If I had a table for, say twenty? Would that work?" Mr. Cooper asked us.

"That's very generous, Mr. Cooper. Thank you very much." Brian shook his hand. "Thanks for everything. I can't tell you what all of this has meant to us. It completely changed my life."

"You did it. Don't give me more credit than I deserve." Cooper slapped him on the back.

"Now, getting back to the party. The movie is rated R, Vi,

not appropriate for the kids, and the party might get a little crazy as it gets going."

"The kids wouldn't expect to see the movie or to stay at the party past the band's performance, which Jane already told us kicks off the night. Believe me, they will be thrilled to be there for any amount of time. They will talk about this for years!" I smiled at him.

"That's great. Okay, well, I'll see you guys tomorrow for Jay. The next day is Ellen, Oprah, and Luke, right, Jane?"

"Yes, sir."

"Good thing I have highly organized people telling me where to go and what to do all day." Mr. Cooper winked at Jane who immediately turned crimson.

"I didn't know you were married, man." Jackson laughed and held out his hand.

George shook it. "Not falling into that trap."

"Good man. Give the rest of us something to dream of." Jackson laughed again as Mr. Cooper shook hands with Adam and Sam.

"Thank you all for coming once again," said Mr. Cooper. "See you tomorrow."

It was only noon, and we had the rest of the day to ourselves. Brian wanted to open some bank accounts for Brooke to fill, among other things. Adam decided to tour around and map out the local music scene. Sam had some divorce-related calls to make, and I was headed back to the hotel to soak up some sun by the pool.

We said our good-byes and headed in our own directions. The promotional tour was finally starting tomorrow and the day after that, I'd be with my family again. My smile was so big; there was a chance that my face might split in half. Five days from today, I'd be at home again with my beautiful family. I had some singing to do first, though, and I planned to enjoy every second of it.

Chapter Forty-One

"Dear Lord." I squinted to make certain that I was seeing clearly. "That woman is wearing a T-shirt with my face on it." I couldn't believe my eyes. As we got closer I could see that *Soccer Moms Rock!* was written beneath my picture.

The band, Brooke, and Jane all looked out the window of the studio van to see what I was freaking out about. We were pulling into the NBC Studios in Burbank and there was a line of people waiting to be seated for this afternoon's taping of "The Tonight Show." Many of the potential audience members seemed to know that we were expected there today.

"I made a few calls this morning," Brooke told Brian. "We need to maintain the buzz heard 'round the country when people were looking for you. Things have died down these past few weeks and we need to fuel the fire again and let Mr. Cooper help us fan the flames."

"Check out the Francis Kelly Project T-shirts and, oh hell, what's that one?" Adam squinted his forty-three-year-old eyes to make it out. "I Lick Brian Kelly?"

"Bullshit," said Brian.

"No, man. That's what it says."

Brooke asked the driver to drop us off where the ticket holders and audience hopefuls waited in line, rather than taking us to the private rear entrance. She had tipped off some members of the media and she wanted us to take advantage of the photo op. It was important that we be seen greeting "fans" and signing some autographs.

"It looks like your demographic is more in the habit of buying Reunion Tour tickets than downloading the latest titles from iTunes," Brooke observed.

"People our age have money," Brian reasoned. "We're not worried about filling stadiums with screaming kids; we just want to sell some records."

"Well, get out there and let some of those old women lick you then," Brooke ordered.

"We better not have fans in New York because my wife will kick the ass of any woman who looks directly at me, even if it's by accident," Jackson said as he climbed out of the van, garment bag in hand.

"I hope these people have Republican family members in Texas," Sam mused as he climbed out behind Jackson.

When Brian opened his door and stepped out a few people yelled, "Brian! Hey, Brian Kelly! Good to see you!" Brian waved and smiled, walked over to the line behind the barricade, and started signing autographs.

Adam waited for me and held out his hand. "Ready?" he asked, laughing.

"No. This is weird. Are we really a big deal? I clean my own toilets, you know? How big of a deal can I really be?"

"Vi! There she is! Vi!" A few people began calling my name and I wondered how many of these "fans" were planted. It didn't seem possible that someone would spend good money on a shirt with *my* picture on it.

I followed the rest of the band with Brooke and Jane in tow.

"Vi, hi, could you sign this, please?" It was a soccer ball.

I had to laugh. "You know I don't play, right?" I asked lightheartedly.

"I'm at the field every Saturday. It's so great to see a soccer mom get plucked from the sidelines."

Perfectly on cue, Brooke slipped a Sharpie into my right hand.

"Thank you. That's very nice," I said, giving back the freshly autographed ball.

"Vi, I think you're fantastic." Another ball was presented to me. Each of the band members chatted, signed, and schmoozed. I wished Wade could see this, he wouldn't believe it!

"Thank you so much for listening to the band," I said to someone else; a younger girl this time who came with her family.

Jackson was posing for a group picture with some women who were giggling at his self-deprecating one-liners. Sam and

Adam were shaking hands, but steadily continuing toward the studio door.

"I've got to run." I told the group as I handed back yet another soccer ball.

Just as we were about to cross the threshold of the studio doorway, I saw a young man with a T-shirt bearing my face and the letters MILF. "What does . . . ?"

"Don't ask, Franny, don't ask." Brian steered me inside.

"That was crazy!" Jackson said as we traveled through security towards our dressing room.

"That was only about a hundred people," Brooke told us. "Wait until I really get the PR machine rolling. But you'll have to enjoy it now because media outlets have very short memories and great big appetites. You have to feed them constantly to keep them around. In a few days they'll move on to the next story and you'll turn back to pumpkins."

The guys had one large dressing room and I was given a separate one across the hall. I hung my clothes on a hook and joined the boys in their dressing room. Just like old times. When the time came to actually get dressed, I'd spend a few minutes on my side of the hall, but we stuck together until then.

We arrived two hours before the taping of the show to run sound check and rehearsal. I was happy for the chance to go onto the stage and see the studio before the audience was seated. I always felt better playing a room that was familiar to me and even a half-hour on a stage before the audience came in made it "mine." I had seen the stage on television many times and I didn't want a million witnesses to the shock I'd feel when I stood on the iconic platform for the first time.

We walked onto the set together and stood quietly for a moment, letting it sink in.

"Woah," said Jackson.

I nodded my head in agreement.

There were sound guys running in every direction and the gear we had been practicing with had been set up.

I walked to my mic stand and looked out over the seats that

would soon be occupied. "I am so glad I came," I told the band.

"Hey, guys, I'm Rick. I'm running your monitors. Wanna get some levels?"

We keyed in each piece and then it was time to do the mix.

Jackson counted us in and we were playing "So Beautiful" on "The Tonight Show" stage. I was so glad that we had the chance to do this privately because before it was over I had tears rolling down my face. We never sounded so good. *I* never sounded so good.

As the last chord rang, I turned around and saw both Brian and Adam wiping their eyes. I started to laugh. "You're worse than women!" I pointed at them as my cheeks got wetter.

"Aw, now. No, no no, none of that," teased Jackson. "You white boys cryin' over nothin'. I'll show you something to cry about."

"Please, Jackson." Sam held his hand up to his eyes. "Never again. I still have nightmares."

Brian and Adam started laughing so hard they had to sit down.

"What did I miss?" I asked.

"Just thank God, right now, that you're a woman and that Jackson respects you," Brian told me through his laughter.

"Damn pussy white boys," Jackson muttered.

"Are you guys comfortable with that?" Rick was asking about the sound, but his question started the guys laughing all over again.

We headed back to the dressing room to give the stylists plenty of time to get us ready.

All I could think about was the reaction Wade and the kids would have while watching us on TV later that night. I planned to call them and watch it with them over the phone. I tried to anticipate each response. Wade and Megan would love my dress. Lilly would sing along and dance, never taking her eyes of the screen, and Henry would probably jump up and down the whole time yelling, "Mommy, Mommy, Mommy!" while everyone else tried to shush him so they could hear. Abrams would pace around barking just to be involved. As if by telepathy, "Home" appeared on my phone.

"Hi there!" I answered.

"Hi, Mommy!" The chorus came via speakerphone on their end.

"We just wanted to wish you luck, honey. I didn't want to call too close to the taping because I figured you'd be busy." Wade sounded so excited.

"Thank you so much, guys. Mommy just did sound check and it was fantastic, so I am really looking forward to getting out there." I lowered my voice as if divulging a secret. "I'll be singing just to you guys, okay? Don't tell anyone."

"I KNEW IT!" yelled Henry. "I told Megan Mommy would be singing for us, but she said lots of other people would be watching you on their TVs too."

"What color dress are you wearing, Mom?" Megan asked.

"Black, Meggy, what do you think?"

"Only if you have a tan," Megan advised.

"I got some sun yesterday by the hotel pool."

Lilly leaned in to the phone. "Knock 'em dead, Mom."

"Thanks, babe. I will."

"Are you in good voice, even after all the rehearsing?" Wade asked.

"You know me, I'm a workhorse. The more I sing, the stronger I get. I'll call you guys tonight at 11:30 your time when it airs, okay? We can watch it together."

"Great, Vi. We'll be here. I invited a few people over. Mary, Bill, and Anna are coming, and Isabelle and Doreen are bringing their husbands."

"Of course!" I said, not having thought about it before. "You'll use any excuse to have a party. A fish just jumped in the bay, let's have a party!" I laughed.

"I think this is a little bigger than a jumping fish," he chuckled.

"All right. I'll call you guys after we tape to let you know how it went."

We said our "I love yous" and I hung up.

A stylist for the show introduced herself to me and asked how I wanted to be done up. I showed her the picture I still had on my phone from the first day in L.A., and she got to work.

Chapter Forty-Two

We were all perfectly silent throughout the make-up process. There was little chit-chat as we got dressed and picked at the food provided by the show. I drank three cups of ginger tea, just to be sure I ingested enough of the voice-soothing properties. Then I worried that I'd get on stage and have to go to the bathroom. Just when the waiting seemed to become torture, the monitor clicked on in the room and Jay Leno was doing his monologue.

"We have a great lineup tonight --Cameron Diaz is here." The audience cheered with excitement. "Mr. George Cooper is here!" The audience went wild. "He has a new film coming out and he brought us a band -- The Francis Kelly Project is here!" The audience went wild again.

"That applause sign must have an electric charge attached to each seat. Clap or get zapped," I muttered. I was still skeptical about the whole "people actually know us" concept, but it was nice to hear applause rather than crickets.

Cameron Diaz was the first guest.

"Now, why didn't Girlfriend come back and say hi?" asked Jackson.

"Guess we're not big-time after all," Adam said as we watched her.

"I've always liked her," I said. "She seems very down to earth."

"Yeah, well the earth I live on doesn't have many girls who look like that down on it," Adam said.

"Is she an actress?" asked Sam.

"Dude, you've got some catchin' up to do," Brian laughed.

"... I do like The Francis Kelly Project. I was following the whole search for them. It was really cool." Cameron was talking about us! "No one knew anything about them other than the fact that they had recorded this completely awesome song. It was intriguing, you know? And what happens after you find them? It was a cool reality-slash-news show." Cameron laughed her signature, hearty laugh.

"Did you meet them backstage?" Jay asked.

"No. I got here really late -- I pretty much just got here." She laughed again. "I want to meet them if I get the chance."

"That's right, baby!" Jackson clapped his hands together.

". . . I think it's kind of cool how they quit music, but the music came back to get them, right? It shows you can do it all, but you can't ever forget who you are."

"And who are you, Cameron? We'll find out and talk more with Cameron Diaz when we get back."

"Freakin' cool as hell," Adam said almost to himself.

"I can't believe anyone knows us, let alone celebrities." I shook my head.

"Hey, did you guys hear that?" George Cooper stuck his head in the room.

"Crazy, right?" Brian asked him.

George laughed. "Have a great time out there. I can't wait to hear you."

"Thanks!" we all yelled.

"So, have you ever met George Cooper before?" Jay asked Cameron. "You're old friends, right?"

"We're married and have six kids, Jay. We're just quiet about it." Cameron laughed.

"Then let's bring out your husband. He has a new movie opening this weekend -- Mr. George Diaz, ladies and gentlemen!"

George shook Jay's hand, slapped him on the back, and kissed Cameron.

"Who's babysitting the kids?" he asked her. "You didn't even tell me you were going to be here." Then to Jay, "After years of marriage, you just don't talk anymore."

The audience laughed, completely taken with George Cooper.

"Tell me about this movie and this band."

"This is the best movie I have ever made, Jay," George started. "It's very close to my heart and I let it sit for a while because I didn't have all the elements perfectly placed, the title track being one of those elements. So one day, I'm having Stromboli at Joey's here in L.A. . . ." He turned to the camera. "Joey you owe me big, man -- and I hear this song. I immediately fell in love with it. It was perfect for the movie. Better suited to the film than songs I had songwriters write specifically for the film. I had to have it, but it took some doing to find out where it came from. And you know the rest."

"But the funny part is," Jay said, "this isn't a band of starving artists looking of their big break; this is a recording of a band from eighteen years ago whose members are now parents, business owners . . . the keyboard player is a lawyer and the Mayor of a small town in Texas."

"Yeah. That's the great thing about this. They came back together to help me promote the film because the song is actually a lead character in the movie, and when you see it, you'll know what I mean. You don't wanna interview me you need to hear the song. You listen to it while I catch up with my wife, okay?" He leaned toward Cameron.

"When we get back, The Francis Kelly Project."

Just then the door opened and the stage manager peeked in. "Places on set."

We filed out the door to the stage where the curtain had been drawn back to reveal our section of the stage.

I glanced over at Mr. Cooper who winked and nodded at me. Cameron mouthed, "Awesome dress," and gave me a thumbs-up. I loved her before, and I loved her more than ever at that moment.

Within moments, the lights came back on. After hours of waiting, things seemed to be happening so fast. Jay gave us our cue: "The Francis Kelly Project!"

Jackson counted us in with the loud smack of his sticks. "One, two, three, four . . ."

The band played in perfect sync and I started to move as if the music didn't give me a choice. I could feel my smile growing. My mic felt like an extension of my arm the way it did so many years ago. For Wade and the kids, for the younger Vi who had such big dreams, and for everyone who would never get the chance to stand where I was, I sung my heart out. The band achieved perfect synergy and the audience was pulled along with our energy. It was a perfect moment.

I looked over at Brian who was grinning widely and then, in the other direction, at Sam who had taken on the air of a true rock star. Adam's playing was locked with Jackson who never generated a heavier, funkier groove.

I found the camera that was on me and sang right to my family. I'd had those moments on stage before, but not in a long time. I felt euphoric. Then, before I knew it, the song was over. The last chord rang and there was silence for half a second.
Then the audience exploded. Brooke and Jane were backstage, out of sight, but I could hear them screaming above the din.

George, Jay, and Cameron were on their feet. I got tackled from behind and Jackson whipped me over his shoulder as I laughed hysterically. "Gotta get some face time somehow!" he yelled. I laughed even harder.

Chapter Forty-Three

The musical guest always performed at the end of the show, so Jay came over to shake our hands and wrap up the broadcast. Cameron and George joined us on stage and I embraced George like he was an old friend.

"You sounded incredible, Vi," He told me with a big George-Cooper smile.

"Thank you so much. It felt great." I knew I was beaming.

"Awesome!" said Cameron as we hugged. "You sound better live than you do on the CD!"

"That's so nice of you to say." I told her. "I love you by the way. I've seen every movie you've made just because you're in it."

"Oh, thank you. You and my Mom," she said laughing.

At that moment Brian grabbed me and lifted me off the ground from behind. "Franny, you were great!" he shouted while he spun me around.

"Okay, okay, don't make me puke in the middle of my moment!" I laughed.

He set me down and I turned around to face him. "We did it," he said.

"We did it." I took both of his hands into my own. For just a moment I saw Brian exactly as I had seen him eighteen years ago on the sidewalk on Fifty-Fourth Street when he was trying to keep me from leaving New York and trying to keep my dreams alive.

Jackson was chatting up Cameron Diaz and Sam and Adam were head to head with Mr. Cooper. Jay came over to offer his congratulations to Brian and me.

"It's obvious that you all have a lot of live performance experience," He told us. "A lot of 'studio creations' fall apart under the pressure of a live audience. There's only so much the sound crew can do in those situations, but you guys were great."

"Thanks for noticing, we are the real deal," Brian assured him.

"I wish you lots of luck," Jay said. "Take your time out

here if you want to, I've gotta get home for dinner." He shook our hands again and headed home from another day at the office.

We were off-air so Brooke, Jane, and Tracey came out on stage. Tracey ran to Adam who lifted her into a big bear hug. Watching them really made me miss Wade. In another 48 hours or so my family would be back together.

Brooke punched Brian in the arm, "What a great performance." she told him. "I am so glad that I've attached myself to your rocket." she said with a big smile.

Mr. Cooper overheard her comment and leaned into their conversation, "Me too." He said, winking. "Advanced Band had better be the next Arista, huh?"

"How do you know about Advanced Band Records?" Brian asked him.

"Meet your first investor," Brooke announced.

"All right!" Brian reached for Mr. Cooper's hand. "Thank you for your confidence, sir. We're going to work our asses off."

"I know you will Brian. It's a sound investment." George nodded. "I'm funny today." He observed. "Extremely witty."

"We have a lot to celebrate," I said, putting my arm around Sam's waist. "I don't think I can go back my hotel room and sit there by myself. I think I have to go somewhere. Any takers?"

Jane looked at her watch. "It's a few minutes after five o'clock now. I made reservations for six at Mr. Chow. It'll be a little early for the Hollywood crowd, but I figured you'd need to blow off some steam and get something to eat."

We took one last look into the theater from the stage and headed back to our dressing rooms to wash our faces and get dressed in street clothes again.

Cameron and George had exited down another corridor.

I dialed 'Home' and waited for only a half ring before Wade picked up.

"How did it go?" He answered anxiously.

"Phenomenal," I answered. "Absolutely awesome. Thank you so much for encouraging me to come out here. It was so much fun, I can't believe I get to do this again seven more times!"

204

"You sound very happy."

"I am. There is a big void, but it will be filled when you guys are with me in New York."

"Honey, we can't wait. I'm going to tell the kids that it went perfectly and that they can talk to you tonight while the show airs, unless you want to talk to them right now."

"We're going to grab some dinner, so I don't want to keep everyone waiting. I'll call back later."

"Love you Vi."

"I love you too." I hung up feeling like the luckiest person who had ever lived.

Chapter Forty-Four

Mr. Chow in is Beverly Hills just off of Wilshire Blvd. it's a celebrity hang out, making it a reliable showcase for the paparazzi, but at six o'clock in the evening, it's pretty quiet.

The band, Tracy, Jane, and Brooke (we've worked our way up to a respectable entourage of three) were seated right away in the very elegant black and white dining room. Our fantastic performance, and the relief we felt to have it behind us, induced an incredible high and none of us had floated down. There were toasts and accolades amid an atmosphere of celebration.

Brooke gave Brian the good news that Mr. Cooper's investment in Advanced Band Records was more than just a token gesture of support; he contributed one hundred and fifty thousand dollars. And she had firm "maybes" from three other backers who had very deep pockets. She was confident that once "The Tonight Show" performance aired, many interested parties would inquire about the hottest start-up in town. Brooke was sure that the subsequent TV appearances would help create a frenzied atmosphere that would put her in the position to receive offers rather than having to solicit them.

As we savored Mr. Chow's fine offerings we got to know Tracey better and we counted the days until our families became part of our entourage. We compared the ages of my kids to Adam's nieces and Jackson's daughters and decided that they were going to be inseparable once they got acquainted, based on their shared love of High School Musical, 1,2, and 3, Wii games, and tiaras. Henry, being the only boy in the group, would certainly be made to feel like a little prince, considering all the attention he was likely to get from the girls.

After a while, the pace of the conversation slowed down. I decided the time was right to share my idea.

"I have been thinking about all this good fortune that landed at our feet and I've been trying to come up with a way to pass it along." I took a deep breath, hoping my idea wouldn't be met with choruses of *No way, crazy lady.*

"A few years ago, Wade and I bought a parcel of property in Key Largo that had a large warehouse on it. We intended to hold inventory there for the boutiques and store some personal items. It's air conditioned and fairly new." Everyone's eyes were on me. "We haven't made use of it and it's just sitting there."

"My vision is that it could be a music camp for underprivileged kids who might not otherwise have the chance to learn to play instruments or explore their musical interest. We could work with the public school systems and host camps there throughout the summer." I had used the word *we* and no one had stopped me. "I know there are school districts around the country that don't offer music anymore. A program like this one might be the only chance some of these kids have for a well-rounded education."

"Wade and I could convert half the warehouse to living quarters, cut the rest into rehearsal and recording studios, and we could have a small auditorium for live performance. The Francis Kelly Project could come for a week to do private instruction and perform. I haven't researched grants or endowments or anything and the plan is young, but maybe Wade could solicit the airline to get involved as a national outreach program to help provide transportation.

There are a lot of details that I need to work out, but I think the concept has a lot of potential. And I was hoping that you would all be as excited about it as I am."

"I love it," said Brian. "Teaching music is important to me and the down side of having a label is that I have to quit doing that. I'm in, Vi. Work it out and I'm in. Maybe Advanced Band can sponsor a few kids."

"Okay, Spendy Spenderson, before you give away the money I've attracted, we should get rolling a little," Brooke cut into the conversation.

"I want to call it the Francis Kelly Gates Foundation," I continued. "To tie all of us in together."

"I'll do whatever you need me to do. I'd love to teach

music to kids and get a Florida vacation out of it. I've never been to the keys," Adam volunteered.

"I know I'll need a full-time staff, but you guys could be the big finale. Guests rock star instructors. And it gives us an excuse to stay in touch," I added.

"Oh, oh, oh, you said there will be a recording studio there? That's where you guys could record a new release!" Brooke found her carrot.

"I guess that would work." I remembered my speech to Brain about relationships requiring give and take. I hadn't planned to record at the new facility myself, but, if that's what it took to make the foundation work for everyone, I could give a little.

"I think Sharon and the kids could stand a week in Florida, but in the summer, Vi? Are you sure about that? Isn't it a hundred and twenty degrees every day down there in the summertime? I'm sweatin' just thinkin' about it." Jackson was worried.

"That's when the kids are off school Jax," I reasoned.

"Personally, I would relish the opportunity, Vi. It wouldn't make me look too bad as a politician either; donating my time to a foundation to teach music to kids. It kind of makes what I'm doing right now perfectly acceptable." Sam's logic made us all laugh because, as cynical as it seemed, it was true.

"Okay, I'll start researching this once I get home and that will be our plan." I was thrilled.

We had finished our meals and were enjoying coffee.

"A lot of important people will be coming in here in a little while. It might be good to stick around," Brooke suggested to Brian.

"Okay, I'm not ready to go back to the hotel anyway," Brain said.

"I'll keep you company, if you don't mind," Sam offered.

"Us too." Adam spoke for himself and Tracey.

"If you guys have everything you need for today, I'm going to make sure everything is set to go smoothly tomorrow." Jane had finished settling the tab and was ready to leave. She reviewed the schedule one more time. "You'll need to report to the hotel lobby at nine a.m., we go from Ellen to The Really Late Show, and then to Oprah in L.A. After that we're off to the airport, so make sure you call for bellhop service to bring your luggage down in the morning. Brooke and I will take care of it and make sure it gets on the plane with you tomorrow."

"Long damn day," Jackson observed.

"You'll get some sleep in New York before we tape Letterman if you aren't good at sleeping on the plane." Jane offered some hope for a nap.

"Well, I had better get back to the hotel to pack and to call Sharon," Jackson said.

"She and the kids are gonna be all excited about tonight, so I wanna to be on the phone to watch along with them."

"That's exactly what I'm doing," I told him.

"We'll grab a ride together then."

As we walked toward the door, Jackson eyed a few girls arriving for a fun night at Mr. Chow. "I am happy to be going home tomorrow, but I will miss the sights in Los Angeles," He laughed.

"Men." I laughed along and shook my head.

"Don't you tell my wife I said that," Jackson warned. "Sharon is cool. She knows I love to play music but she thinks no one notices me and I don't notice anyone else. She thinks I am so focused on my playing that I don't have time for anything else."

"Because that's what you told her." I filled in the blanks.

"Well, sure. She's cool that I'm there for the music, it's my love for watching women dance to my music she wouldn't approve of so much." We both laughed.

"Aw, Jackson. You're harmless." I told him. "If a woman propositioned you right now, you'd run screaming from the room."

"Sharon's cool with my love for music, but she would kill me if I looked at another woman. I have a very healthy fear of that woman," Jackson said seriously. "A very healthy fear."

Chapter Forty-Five

I watched the opening of the Tonight Show with greater attentiveness than I ever had before. I was more nervous as a spectator than I had been before the actual performance. I sat on the edge of my hotel room bed and leaned forward so that I was within a foot of the television screen.

I picked up my cell and dialed home.

"They just said the name of the band on TV!" Lilly screamed into the phone. I could hear the television surround sound blaring in the background.

"It's going to be such a long hour!" I told her.

"Dad invited everyone over here. Each of us kids got to invite some friends from school, so there are eight kids sleeping over tonight. We're all so excited, Mom. It's like New Years' Eve!" Lilly took the phone away from her ear to yell over the noise, "Hey, everyone, Mom's on the phone!"

I could hear cheering and hellos coming from my living room.

"I have a stupid question, Lilly. Are you TiVo-ing this?" I asked.

"TiVo is set, then I'll burn some DVDs," she answered.

"I should have known."

"Hey, I'm *your* daughter. Of course, I'm organized."

"Thanks, honey. I'll call you back when the band is on. Keep the line clear if you can, otherwise I'll call your cell."

"Okay, Mom. I'll put my phone in my pocket just in case. Good contingency plan."   "Talk to you in a little while Lil. I love you!"

"Love you too, Mom."

I hung up and watched Cameron's full interview and chuckled all over again when George started cracking jokes. Even though I knew what he was going to say, I still found him funny.

After the longest fifty minutes of my life, the commercial break before our performance finally arrived. I called our home phone and Wade answered.

"I've been hanging up on the calls that weren't you," Wade told me.

"I'm so nervous," I whispered into the phone.

"Here it is, Vi, here it is!" The show was back on and I saw myself on the screen.

I could hear the roar of our friends and family in the background. "You look beautiful, babe," Wade yelled above them.

It got very quiet on his end as the band started playing. I heard Henry yell, "Mommy, Mommy, Mommy!"

I laughed to myself. Just as I predicted, I mused.

I held my breath as the TV Vi started to sing. Perfect phrasing, perfect pitch; nice, even transitions between full and head voice. I was glad I was alone, because I started to cry big, happy tears.

"Hey, hey, hey, none of that," Wade said on his end, hearing my deep breaths.

"I can't help it," I choked out. "It's so good . . . "

"It's great. You're great, Vi. I'm so happy for you and so proud."

We listened together until the last note. I got chills all over again and the partygoers at my house raised their voices in a deafening cheer.

"Mom, that was incredible!" Lilly grabbed the phone away from Wade.

"Thanks, babe." I told her.

Lilly had passed the phone to Megan. "Mommy, your dress was fabulous. You sang really great, too."

"Thanks Meggy."

"Henry wants to say something," she handed the phone off.

"Mommy, can you believe how late I'm awake?" Henry sounded very proud.

"I can*not* believe it," I told him. "Did you have a nap today?"

"Yup. Spencer did too, at his own house. He's sleeping over tonight and we're both up this late." He had the world by the toe.

"You and Spencer are cool, big kids to stay up this late."

"Yeah, I know. I better go brush my teeth, Mommy because I ate a lot of chips." Henry tattled on himself.

"Take Spencer with you and make sure he brushes as well, okay?"

"You got it Mom. Oh, and Mom, I saw you on TV."

"Was that cool?" I asked.

"Very."

"I can't wait to give you all the kisses I've been collecting for you." I told him.

"Don't give 'em away, Mommy."

"I won't."

Henry gave the phone back to Wade. "You killed Vi. You were fantastic." Even if I had bombed, he would have said that, but I knew he meant it.

"I'm really happy with the performance," I admitted. "I hope I can do it just like that three more times tomorrow."

"This one was a big one. Daytime TV is what it is, but this was huge and you nailed it." Another signature Wade pep talk.

Wade and I said our good-byes and I was asleep before my head hit the pillow.

Chapter Forty-Six

On Manhattan's Upper East Side, Benny Bernstein laid in bed with his wife Angela. They watched "The Tonight Show" every night before going to sleep. Benny was polishing off the last bite of his liverwurst sandwich, lettuce hanging out of the corner of his mouth. He wiped away a dollop of mayo that had set up camp on his upper lip.

"See, Ange? All I need is a band like this to shop around for a deal. A sure thing. If a band like this came into my office, I'd have 'em signed to a major inside of an hour and we'd all be depositing big, fat checks."

Angela rolled her eyes and tried to breathe through her mouth to avoid the odor of Benny's sandwich. "Bands like the Francis Kelly Project don't just walk into your office, Benny. You have to go out there and find 'em."

"Rhythm Syndicate walked in, Angela," Benny reminded her in a condescending voice.

"How long ago was that, Benny? Eighteen years? Twenty? Good Lord." Angela put down her nail file and turned off the lamp on her side of the bed.

Angela's words triggered the realization and Benny flashed back eighteen years. He choked on his liverwurst as it hit him. He leaped out of bed to put his nose right on the TV screen. Benny Bernstein watched Vi and Brian celebrate a terrific performance with their band as the credits rolled. On The Tonight Show. National television. Promoting an international film for which their song was the title track. "Son of a bitch!" he yelled to no one in particular.

Chapter Forty-Seven

"This is the life". Jackson reclined his seat to the prone position. "I'd better not tell Sharon about this or she might start thinking I've gotten soft."

"*You* can't tell *your* spouse?" I was experiencing a guilty pleasure, but trying to remain firmly focused on the pleasure aspect. We were aboard a private Bombardier Challenger 605, courtesy of Brian's new attorney. "Wade flies for American, and I loved flying with the company until today. Now I know that commercial aviation ranks right down there with bus travel."

Adam finished his tenderloin and roasted vegetables and poured himself more Perrier. "So, does Mr. Taggat own this jet?" He asked Brian.

"He's a fractional owner with Flex Jet so he uses a plane from their fleet whenever he needs a ride." Brian finished his mahi mahi and folded his linen napkin.

Sam had just returned from the restroom and was wearing a matching pajama top and pants with slippers.

"Make yourself at home." Brian's words dripped with good-natured sarcasm.

"On the red-eye, I bring lounge clothes to be more comfortable." Sam didn't seem the least bit self-conscious. "I heard you talking about fractional ownership airlines from the head. It's the only way to go." Sam enlightened us to the obvious as he settled in his seat and reclined. "You set up your ownership plan and call for service whenever you need to travel. The crew only needs two hours to meets you at the private FBO airport you request for departure. They load your luggage, provide you with high end catering, and set up your transportation on the other end. Cassandra had contacted a sales person from Flex Jet hoping to avoid TSA, waiting at the gate, delays, flight cancellations, and flying with 'common people' as she put it."

"Sounds like a good idea to me," I admitted.

"I suppose it is well worth the investment for frequent fliers, but I like Texas and am very rarely tempted to leave it." Sam explained.

I looked around to take it all in again. There was a small galley area and eight seats that fully reclined, plus the couch I occupied. Rich cherry wood accented the leather seats and the LCD screen that received Direct TV. Each seat also had a personal DVD player with a small DVD library and a snack drawer containing things you could only find in specialty markets. The cabin was twenty-eight and a half feet long, eight feet wide and six feet high. I asked the first officer for as much information as I could when we boarded. I wanted to be able to give Wade all the details about my flight. I realized that I was gathering information on the luxurious interior and creature comforts and that Wade would be more interested in the performance and limitations of the jet, but, I thought, the other details would be noteworthy to anyone in any walk of life.

As we were leaving Oprah from L.A. earlier today, Mr. Taggat called Brian on his cell inquiring about our travel arrangements. When Taggat found out that we were flying commercial, he offered us the use of his hours with Flex Jet. Oprah's personal assistant was nearby and overheard Brian's half of the conversation. She encouraged him to take Taggat up on his offer, having flown on Ms. Winfrey's G5. "It's the only way to fly; private jet." She was adamant.

"Which show do you think was best today?" Brian asked.

"Oprah felt the best," I told him.

"The sound was perfect; I could hear you guys really well. They have a hell of a crew. I was nervous when I found out the show was outdoors, but it was great," Adam agreed.

"Ellen went well." Sam chimed in. "It seems like forever ago, but that was good, too. I'm looking forward to seeing the tapes."

"Me too." I thought back to Ellen. It was the first show we had taped that day. I probably looked the best on that one, being that I was still freshly made-up. "I think the Oprah performance was explosive. Being outside gave us a different energy."

"Yeah, the Ellen thing was clean, but there was something

about being outside that made it more alive, I think." Adam sounded tired.

"Can you friggin' believe we met Oprah?" Jackson had his arms crossed and his eyes closed.

"She is powerful," I said.

"I was a little bit afraid of her," Brian joked. "Like if I said the wrong thing she would have me ejected from her planet."

"I know what you mean, dude," Jackson replied.

"So are we not talking about The Really Late Show or what?" I acknowledged the elephant in the cabin.

"I don't think it was our fault," Adam's voice was getting softer and softer.

"Luke Walker was pissed off that Cooper never accepted an invitation to come on his show before today. I think the whole thing was set up portray George as if he's too good to be there and it backfired." Brian was thinking out loud.

"Maybe that's it all it was," I replied. "But, he really went out of his way to insult the movie. He didn't have anything nice to say about us either. Do you think it will hurt us?"

"When the CD comes out, critics are going to review it, it'll be public domain. So are we. Not everyone is going to love us." Brain tried to blow it off.

"I know this for damn sure, more people watch Oprah than The Really Late Show and she pretty much made it law for each citizen of these United States to buy our CD when it comes out, so I'm not gonna let Mr. What's-His-Name bother me none." Jackson's eyes were still closed.

"You're right." I turned out the light above my seat. I was too tired to read.

"I bet Luke Walker flies commercial," Brian continued the conversation.

"Like Brooke and Jane." I pulled a thick wool blanket over me. "I feel terrible that they stayed on the commercial flight."

"It's their own fault for taking control of our luggage first thing this morning. They should have waited to see if a private jet ride popped up. Anyway, someone has to watch over my Armani suits," Brian reasoned.

"You're really a terrible person," I joked, throwing my Jila gum box at him. Then I realized what I had done. "Please give that back to me," I begged. "That gum is really hard to find and it's really good for my voice. Really strong peppermint."

"Then you shouldn't throw it at people," Brian chided.

"Okay kids, Daddy is going to sleep. Shut it up," Jackson commanded.

"G'night," Adam whispered.

Sam was already out.

New York City, The Francis Kelly Project is coming back. And this time we won't be invisible. This time, we are pampered guests.

Chapter Forty-Eight

Our Flex Jet Challenger touched down at Teterboro at 6 am. Ground transportation was waiting planeside to drop me off at JFK to meet my family and then continue on into the city to take the rest of the band to the hotel. We had collectively chosen the Marriott Marquis because it was close to The Late Show.

Inside the American Airlines Terminal I found my family's flight on the monitor and confirmed that it was on time. I was nervous about showing up to meet them because Wade had told me that kids had planned to surprise me when I arrived at JFK. I didn't want to ruin their plan, but I didn't want Wade to worry when I wasn't on the flight he expected me to be aboard. I hadn't gotten the chance to call him and tell him about my change in travel plans. I was turning the tables on them due to my earlier than expected arrival and I hoped they wouldn't be disappointed.

I set out to find the inevitable Starbucks. If I was going to stay awake until their arrival, I needed a boost.

Once I had my cup of caffeinated goodness in hand, I tried to pass through security to await my family's arrival at the gate, but was stopped because I didn't have a boarding pass.

I apologized profusely; explaining that I should have known better considering that my husband was a Captain for American.

The young TSA worker looked so closely at me that I was sure I had aroused his suspicion. I was waiting for bells, alarms, and a strip search. Instead, he became apologetic and accommodating. He called on the radio for a celebrity escort and a few seconds ticked past before I realized that the celebrity he was referring to was me. A heavyset woman in a motorized cart had accelerated to a slow speed crawl in response to the radio call and was heading in our general direction. The TSA worker nodded towards the cart and told me *"Here's your ride, Ms. Francis."*

I wished Wade was around to witness this. Flight crews were given priority when going through security checkpoints and they didn't have to wait in line. Evidently flash-in-the-pan celebrities were given privileges as well. In my case, I doubted that I'd still qualify for special courtesy in a couple of days when we flew back home. My "fifteen minutes" would be over by then. Wade would have to walk us through showing his crew ID and I would be just another face in the crowd like Cinderella after midnight. Which was fine, I hadn't been a 'celebrity" long enough to get used to it anyway.

I settled into a chair in the waiting area, took my book from my purse, and got lost in a Jeffrey Archer masterpiece. I was shocked when I looked at my watch and found that forty-five minutes had evaporated. I went to the Ladies' Room and tried to spiff up a little, filled with excitement that I would be seeing my family in just a few short minutes.

I washed my face using the harsh hand soap from the bathroom. Thank goodness I had my jar of Borghese Cura di Notte in my purse to reconstitute my taught skin. Upon application, I began to look dewy and fresh. I pulled my hair back into a ponytail and brushed my teeth. I was still wearing the clothes I had on twelve hours ago, but, under the circumstances, I had done the best I could do with my overall appearance.

I began to pace back and forth along the windows beside the gate, waiting for the plane to arrive. Finally, finally, it came. It took far too long to attach the jet way.

I was so excited I thought I might have to visit the Ladies' again.

The first two passengers entered the terminal through Gate 19 and I refrained from tackling them. They didn't know how close they had come to an overly exuberant greeting from perfect stranger.

I heard my family before I saw them. Megan and Henry were singing "New York, New York." I laughed out loud and started to cry all at once. I stood outside the door and locked eyes with Wade, who was carrying Henry's blanket, three carry-ons, and pushing the stroller. My knight in shining armors! His eyes showed surprise to see me, then delight, then relief that he had his "right hand" again and was no longer a single parent. I knew he

222

had already forgiven me for trumping their surprise.

"Mom!" Lilly saw me next and the little ones started running and screaming, "Mommy!" I was the one on the receiving end of an NFL-worthy tackle. I had my babies in my arms. My oldest baby was trying to help me counter balance so that I didn't wind up on my tail.

It was a happy, sloppy airport scene for the ages. Wade and I didn't say a word to each other, we just held on tight. The kids were so happy to see me that they never questioned how I knew they were coming, what I was doing at their gate, or if I was surprised to see them.

"Mom, we had snacks on the plane and the lady let us it in the big chairs in the front. The comfy ones!" Henry reported.

"It's called first class Schmenry," Megan said. "He kept calling it first grade," she told me.

Their words were a blur. I felt like I was having an out-of-body experience and was watching the happiest woman in the world greet her family.

"Okay, guys. We have Mommy with us from this moment on, so let's get down to Baggage Claim and get to the hotel," Wade said.

I sprang Henry's stroller, picked him up, kissed him again, and put him in it. There was a stand for Megan so that she could ride rather than walk, and she jumped into position after another kiss and hug from me.

When the little ones were situated, I hugged Lilly again. "Thank you so much for helping take care of them while I was gone, Lil."

She shrugged. "Just remember all this when I turn sixteen, okay? A little BMW convertible is a nice way to say I love you." She put her arm around me as I started to push the stroller.

Coming down from the anticipation of seeing my family hit me like a ton of bricks and I fell asleep in the cab before we exited the airport. I was in Wade's arms, beside my children, just as it should be.

Chapter Forty-Nine

"One, two . . . " Sam counted down and looked at the LCD screen on the back of my camera as the Gates family posed on the stage of the Ed Sullivan Theater. "Three." Click. The remarkable moment was frozen for all time.

Thanks to Jane, all of our ticket requests had been fulfilled and our families were going to be able to see us perform on The Late Show. Jane arranged for them to watch our sound check and rehearsal as well. After wardrobe, hair, and make-up we rejoined our guests to document the extraordinary circumstance of having the Ed Sullivan Theater stage to ourselves. In a few minutes, the doors would open and the audience would take their seats.

"This is incredible." Wade told me. He was grinning from ear to ear. "How amazing is it for you to be performing on the same stage where so many entertainment icons have performed?" he asked.

"It's surreal," I told him. "Thank you so much for bringing the whole circus up here." I tried to kiss him.

"Nope. I'm not smudging that beautiful face." He laughed. "Not until later anyway."

"Five minutes . . . doors open," A voice announced over the theater P.A.

"I love you." I pecked Wade on the cheek anyway. The kids and I got in our last hugs and kisses before my performance.

"Mommy won't be on until the end, okay. So you have to be quiet and sit in your seats like ladies and gentlemen. Does anyone have to go potty?" I didn't want Wade to have to leave the show twice to take each of the little ones to the restroom.

"I'll take you, if you have to go," Lilly told Megan. Both kids decided they wanted to see what the bathrooms looked like.

"Guess that puts you on potty duty too, Daddy." I gave Wade one more peck before he picked up Henry and asked to be directed to the facilities.

Jane appeared on the stage with a staffer from The Late Show. "I'll show you guys to the green room, if you're ready," the young girl offered.

Jackson was recreating the picture we just took with his own family. "I'm coming," he said over his shoulder.

Adam waved to his sister and her family and we all headed backstage.

I expected to love Jackson and Adam's families, but I thought that we might require some "getting to know you" time before that happened. I was wrong. It was instantaneous. I realized that we were all experiencing this dream-come-true together and it bonded us quickly. After all, who else could really identify?

"Wade is a great guy," Brain said as we walked through the backstage area to the green room.

"Thank you," I answered. "I got lucky."

"Your kids are cool little people too. Lilly is so mature, I can't believe she is the same age as some of my students."

"She's a very enlightened person." I told him. "Megan is too intelligent for her own good and Henry is going to be the sweetest strong safety in the NFL. He'll pick 'em up and dust 'em off after he throws 'em down."

Brian laughed, "Man. I'm going to be having this conversation. The 'Let Me Tell You About My Kids' conversation."

"You're going to be a great father." I squeezed his arm.

The monitor was on in the green room, which was empty except for some delicious looking snacks. I helped myself to cup of ginger tea, now a superstitious ritual, and sat in a very comfy chair to watch Mr. Letterman warm up the audience.

I loved David Letterman and had been watching him since he had a morning show. I had heard gossip and ascertained that he wasn't particularly social, so I hadn't expected to meet him before the show. I understood his desire for privacy. He was so good at what he did and we were lucky to share that with him in the appropriate venue. I felt he had the right to live privately off-camera because he gave us so much of himself on-camera. He always congratulated the band after their performance on stage, so I'd be happy to get a handshake at that time.

"Who are the guests tonight?" asked Jackson, no doubt hoping for a Jessica -- Biel, Simpson, or Alba, it probably didn't matter which. Just a sexy Jessie.

"Tonight we have Stupid Human Tricks; those people are in another waiting room," the show staffer told us. "And there's a kid who knows the presidents in order and their legacies -- he's six years old -- and Mr. Cooper, I hope. He has yet to arrive."

"He'll be here," Jackson told her.

"Do you know where he is?" The girl asked, somewhat desperately.

"Naw, he's just the greatest, so he'll be here," Jackson reasoned.

"Okay. Enjoy the show," The girl told us. "Break a leg."

Paul Shaffer's band started playing and we watched Letterman's monologue. We all laughed out loud several times.

". . . And Cooper travels with his own band now. Maybe you've heard about this, the whole country was looking for them, they were even featured on 'America's Most Wanted,' I think. The Francis Kelly Project is here."

The audience applauded loudly.

Mr. Cooper leaned against the doorframe. "Flex Jet, huh? Man, you guys are catching on to the rock star lifestyle pretty quickly."

Brian got up to shake his hand. "Mr. Taggat insisted. I'm actually kind of nervous about what he's going to ask of me now that I owe him one," Brian confided.

Mr. Cooper laughed. "I think he just likes you. And I think he's going to like telling everyone within earshot today that he flew The Francis Kelly Project from L.A. to New York in his jet. He loves to talk about himself and how great he is."

Brian looked relieved. "We felt like he was pretty great as we flew cross country on a private jet last night."

Mr. Cooper laughed. "Vi, did your family make it in okay?"

"Yes, thank you, they did. They're in the audience." I gestured toward the monitor.

"Great!" He looked genuinely happy for me. "What's your oldest daughter's name again?"

"Lilly."

"Do you have a pen?"

"Right here, sir." Sam had a pen in his wallet. It was the coolest little compact thing I had ever seen.

"Thanks, Sam." Mr. Cooper turned the pen over in his hand. "I have got to get one of these," he said almost to himself before he wrote "Lilly" on the palm of his hand.

"You're not . . . ?" I asked, hoping he was.

"I think I can come up with a way to work Miss Lilly into my conversation with Dave." He winked.

"Do they have EMTs in the building? We better have one standing by, because my daughter is going to have a heart attack."

Mr. Cooper shook hands with Sam, Adam, and Jackson, gave me a kiss on the cheek and saluted Brian. "Knock 'em dead, guys," he said, leaving the room.

"I love that man," I blurted.

Dave introduced George Cooper and the crowd showed their overwhelming appreciation for the actor through their enthusiastic applause. The host and guests acted like they were old friends, effortlessly setting up jokes for one other.

"So, this band you travel with in your carry-on, what are they called again?" Dave asked.

"I think you're referring to The Francis Kelly Project, Dave."

"Yeah, that's it. So you're so big now, I mean, I know you're big, but you're so big now that you have a band march in front of you and play for you wherever you go," Dave stated.

"Yes." George Cooper dead panned.

"Good for you." Dave slapped his desk and the audience laughed.

"This band is more well-known than I am these days, actually. They are great musicians, they have a great style, and they wrote a song, eighteen years ago, that has essentially become the lead character in my new film. I couldn't imagine the film without the song."

"Okay, so we'll hear them later, but tell me, how much do they charge to march in front of you and play for you wherever you go?"

"You feel like you need a little pomp and circumstance, Dave?" George asked.

"I've got all the pomp I can handle; I just need a new circumstance." Dave laughed. "Know what I mean?'

"No," said Mr. Cooper, as Dave laughed. "Hey, can I do something?"

"You're the man with the marching band, you can do anything."

"I want to say hi to a friend who is here in the audience tonight."

"Oh, my . . . she's gonna die!" I said with my hands pressed together in front of my lips.

"Where is Lilly Gates?" George asked. The camera panned and found Lilly because Wade, Megan, and Henry were waving their hands and pointing.

"Lilly, thank you for coming. I'll see you after the show." George spoke directly to Lilly and her smile lit her entire face. She nodded to him. She looked so beautiful.

Backstage we all laughed out loud.

"What was that about?" Dave asked.

"None of your business," George answered quietly.

"Okay. The Francis Kelly Project when we get back."

We got up and headed for the stage door. "Here we go," Brian said.

The lights were low, but I could see my family from the stage. I waved and they waved back. The stage manager counted us back in for the next segment. David Letterman introduced us and we started playing the song that changed our lives. Flawlessly, perfectly, and with great style and energy.

Once again, before I was ready for it to be over, it was. Dave shook hands with the band members and Henry yelled over everyone, "Mommy! Mommy!" I could see Megan standing on her seat as Wade tried to coax her down, and Lilly was crying. I wished I could run into the audience to hug them all.

We had three live shows to do the next day and the premiere party the following night. It had seemed like the time was dragging while we were in Los Angeles, now it seemed to be moving at light speed. I guess this was what it felt like to experience a miracle.

Chapter Fifty

Our entourage, now a very healthy size, gathered backstage. Mr. Cooper generously took the time to introduce himself to each member of our families and posed for pictures. Lilly was especially delighted.

After milking every ounce of euphoria from the after-performance high, we dressed in our street clothes and rinsed off our stage make-up.

Jane briefed us on our schedule for the next day. Every show would be a live broadcast and we would be darting from one performance to the next. We would be finished for the day by noon and on our own until the premiere party the following night.

Once Jane was satisfied that we were up-to-date regarding our itinerary, she asked to be excused. She was eager to get back to the hotel and get some sleep. "Flying the red-eye in coach just doesn't make for a restful night of sleep," she joked.

"Where is Brooke?" Brian asked.

"Brooke asked me to tell you, after the show, that she stayed in L.A. to meet with some money people. She didn't want you thinking about business while you were on stage, but she did have a few calls after the Tonight Show aired from parties she had pitched the day before. It sounded so promising that she wanted to jump right on it." Jane told Brian.

"Isn't that, like, exactly what got her fired from her last job?" Adam raised his eyebrows.

"I don't care what she does to get the money." Brian tried to cover his eyes, mouth and plug his ear, "As long as she gets the money." We all laughed.

I told Jane to get some rest and told her not to worry about us. We'd be ready in the morning. Live shows didn't allow for rehearsal or a sound check, which increased the pressure, but I wanted to spend more time celebrating today's great show before I started worrying about that.

"I have a suggestion for dinner," I told the group. "I explored the hotel after I worked out today and I saw The View

Restaurant. It revolves, has a huge dinner buffet and great views of the City. We're all dressed for it and I think the kids would love it."

"Sounds great, Vi," said Sharon. "I've always wanted to go there. Now we have an excuse."

"I'm so sorry to be a party pooper, but we have to drive back to Long Island and we don't want to get buried in traffic." Adam's brother-in-law made his apologies. "It was so great to meet you all and you sound . . . " He shook his head. "Incredible. I can't believe I know you!" He shook the hand of each band member and gave Adam a huge bear hug. "I'm proud of you."

Adam had tears in his eyes. He hugged his sister. "This would never have happened if you hadn't been there for me," he told her.

"Never mind." She didn't want to cry, I could tell.

Adam's nieces gave him big hugs. The girls were seven and ten, old enough to understand the enormity of all this. "Pretty cool band, Uncle Adam."

"Thanks guys." He let go of them so they could get underway. "We can't wait to meet Tracey," the youngest called out.

"Who's Tracey?" Adam's sister asked.

"No one, just someone I told the girls about who they promised to keep secret." Adam looked deflated. "Nice job on that Jenna," he gave her thumbs up.

"Sorry Uncle Adam. I won't tell Mom," she yelled back as the family walked away together.

"Okay. Good," Adam replied, then turned to us. "My sister is fantastic. I owe her my life, sincerely. But she is someone I want as far away as possible when I'm dating someone. She gets overly excited, you know?"

"Did you tell them about L.A.?" Brian asked.

"No. Today was too good. I know they'll be happy for me, but it's bittersweet. I doubt we'll see much of each other anymore." Adam choked up a little.

"Well Wade," Sam sensed that Adam didn't want to be the

center of attention. "Let's go talk about airplanes. I'm getting instrument rated and I love hearing aviation stories from someone who has good ones."

"I have a few that'll scare the hell out of you," Wade laughed.

* * * *

"Dinner was fantastic and it was fun to hear about all your early New York memories," Wade said as he tossed his room key on the large credenza in our King size room.

"Nice people, huh?" I smiled to myself as I began to peel off clothes.

"Nice people," Wade confirmed. He always repeated what I said. It was an occupational hazard. The Captain and First Officer routinely confirmed that they heard the call-out by repeating it out loud while in the cockpit.

We dropped off the kids in their room next door where they were going to take baths and put on their jammies. Wade and I had told them that we would do the same and would be right over to hang out in their room to wait for The Late Show to air. Wade and I had the same idea, of course, but we needed to be fast.

"How many trysts like this have you had in this City?" Wade asked as he grabbed me and threw me on the bed.

"Counting my days on 42nd Street hooking or just recreational romps?" I asked.

He gave me a dirty look and attacked.

Twenty minutes later we were next door having a pajama party with the kids.

"So, Mom what is it like? Waiting to see yourself on TV?" Lilly asked.

"You should know. The camera was on you while Mr. Cooper was talking to you." I sat beside her on the bed and helped myself to one of the quesadillas Wade had ordered from room service.

Lilly displayed a typical teen-age reaction. Here eyes grew

wide and her mouth gaped, "Are you kidding me?" she asked. "How do you know that?"

"We were watching backstage. We had the TV feed back there. I can't imagine they would cut that out; it was cute." I cupped the side of her face and she laughed.

"That's what I'm going for 'cute'," she imitated my inflection.

"You looked beautiful. And they showed all of you guys. We're all on TV tonight."

"Can I call Spencer and tell him to watch?" Henry asked.

It was only nine o'clock and Spencer was the youngest child, so I thought it would be all right.

"I'll dial for you," I said grabbing my cell.

Lilly was already typing on her phone. "Do you want me to send to Anna's house, Megan?" she asked as she composed her email.

"Yes, please." Megan said politely. " I wish you could email my whole class at school, but I don't know all of the addresses."

"Honey, I bet every household in Key Largo will be watching because the local paper listed the show times of Mom's performances," Wade told her.

"They did?" I asked.

"Oh yeah. I was brilliant in my interview. I made sure they got Francis and Company in there too." Wade flopped down on the bed and started pushing kids off the edge to make room. Happy, screaming protests filled the air.

Megan rallied against the injustice. "I bet Amnesty International would like to know about how we kids have to sit on the floor while the grown-ups are on the soft bed."

Wade looked at me, "What kind of reading material are you buying her?" Then to Megan, "And how old are you?"

Megan put one hand on her hip and pointed at him with the other. "You know how old I am, so hushy hush hush."

"That's it." Wade launched himself off the bed and wrestled Megan to the ground in a heap of giggles.

Henry laughed out loud and I wiped some cheese from his adorable little chin. I forced him to finish chewing and swallow before he threw himself into the writhing pile of people on the floor.

"Sent," Lilly announced. "I asked fifteen people to watch."

Wade sat upright, still being climbed on from both sides. "Guys, tomorrow we're going to stay here and watch Mom's live performances on TV and then we'll all go out and see the City. Do some shopping, things like that, okay?"

"I thought we were going to go along," said Megan.

"I have to leave at six in the morning," I told her.

"No way. I'm not doing that. Not after yesterday, or today, getting up before the sun. No way." Megan put her foot down, although the decision had already been made for her. The schedule was too tight tomorrow to ask them to keep up.

"I have to sing at the movie premiere party day after tomorrow and Mr. Cooper said it would be okay for you to come watch me." I didn't get the reaction I had hoped for. "Movie stars will be there," I added.

"Yeah!" Megan and Lilly jumped up and down. That was more like what I had been expecting.

"Will Zac Efron be there?" Megan wanted to know.

"I don't know Megs . . ."

"He's a huge star," She told me.

"He is, but he might not be in town. We'll have to see."

"Mommy, will Buzz Lightyear be there?" Henry asked. "He's a huge star."

"I guess it just depends, dude. He might not even be on earth right now."

"You're right, Mom. He's pretty busy d'fending the Galaxy."

We played charades, name that tune, make-shift basketball with the waste basket and the pages of the USA Today, and had talent show. I was almost out of time-killing ideas by the time The Late Show started.

We gathered on the bed and watched stupid humans and

one very smart, young human. Then Mr. Cooper came out. The shot of the Gates family was terrific. You could see each of them clearly and the camera stayed on them for about ten seconds. That was a long time on TV. Lilly blushed all over again watching Mr. Cooper single her out in the audience and Megan and Henry were thrilled to see their faces on the screen. Wade looked incredibly handsome and, mocking conceit, he said he felt the need to apologize to George for stealing his limelight.

We held onto each other as we watched the band's performance. It was very good. I spent more time watching everyone else this time, rather than critiquing myself. Sam had great stage presence. Brain was very camera friendly. Adam looked very relaxed and Jackson was the biggest ham. He stood out, even sitting down behind a drum kit. We looked like a band. Each of us had an individual style, but we looked like we belonged together. I was really proud to be a part of the product. The background vocals were a perfectly blended shadow around my lead vocal. I needed to give the guys more props for that. They sounded great.

Wade laughed. "Jackson is smooth. His smile is neon."

"He is the personification of cool."

"I'm a cool person too, amen't I Mommy?" Henry asked.

"The coolest," I replied without hesitation.

Dave was shaking our hands on television. I had to do that again in a few hours. The realization gave me anxiety.

"Let's say prayers and get to bed." I rallied the kids. They had a King room like Wade and I did and all three of them planned to sleep in the same bed. Our rooms adjoined, so we would be within earshot. Now that Wade and I had taken care of each other, the dividing door would stay open. The kids were exhausted and didn't protest. Once again, I was so tired I could feel every muscle in my body.

One more day of television appearances and the whole experience would be behind me. Tomorrow night at this time, there would be no show to watch; it would be over. I was a little sad. Funny, at first I didn't want to be here, now I didn't want it to end.

I decided to fully enjoy every remaining second. I was sure that when it was time to go home, I'd be more than ready. I missed my house and Abrams. I hoped he was behaving at Mary's. I missed Francis and Company and the girls. I had to get to work on developing my new venture as well. That would be fun. I wondered when I should tell Wade that I'm converting our warehouse into a music camp.

Chapter Fifty-One

Sam watched the credits of "The Late Show" from the comfort of his hotel bed. He aimed the remote toward the screen and hit the off button. He was pleased with the performance of The Francis Kelly Project -- relieved, actually. The band came across as a group with abundant talent, style, and class.

As he reflected on the path each of the band members lives had taken since their first time in New York, his cell phone rang. The display revealed a phone number he didn't recognize from the Dallas area.

"Sam Wintner," he answered.

"Sam, it's me, don't hang up," Cassandra said in a single breath. "Sam?"

"Yes, Cassandra, I'm here." Sam wasn't completely surprised to hear from her.

"I've been watching you on TV the past couple days. I haven't missed a one," Cassandra drawled.

"Haven't you better things to do? Finding yourself a place to live, for example." Sam turned the television on once again and began to flip through the channels.

"I was hoping we could talk about that, Sam. I think once you get home, maybe we could go back to the way things used to be --"

"Cassandra, please spare yourself the humiliation. The decision has been made. You asked me for a divorce and, honestly honey, this is the first thing we have agreed on in a long time."

"But, Sam, I still love you."

"I have to wonder if watching me on television the last few days has had anything at all to do with that development." Sam started laughing.

"Sam, it's not that. I made some mistakes, I know. You're a good man; I know you can find it in your heart to forgive me. Please give us a second chance. I love you, Sam. I need you. I don't know who I am if I'm no longer Mrs. Sam Wintner."

Sam mulled it over for a moment before deciding on the

perfectly satisfying, trite retort from cinematic history. "Frankly, my dear, I don't give a damn." Sam hung up. He laughed out loud picturing the temper tantrum Cassandra was sure to be having somewhere in Dallas. Sam felt lighter, younger, and hopeful. He turned off the TV once again and, this time, turned off his cell phone as well. Sam relaxed and quickly fell asleep.

Chapter Fifty-Two

"Wow." It was all I could say.

Jackson laughed his deep, hearty laugh. "Well, all of a sudden I don't feel so pissed off about having to get up this early."

"The Today Show" was somewhat of a spectator sport in New York City, but I never imagined this many people would get up this early to come to see us. We were greeted by signs, T-shirts, and wide-ranging Francis Kelly Project mania as we got out of the van and headed into the studio at Rockefeller Center.

As we walked between the barricades, Today Show cameras followed us while we signed autographs and greeted the people who had gathered to see us.

"Thank you for coming out so early," I told one woman as I signed a well-used soccer ball.

"I told my husband he was on kid duty. I wanted to see you and tell you that you inspired me to go back to school."

"Really? That's fantastic. Congratulations!" I gave her a hug.

"I thought I was too old to go mix with those kids, but if you can shake your booty and sing your heart out better than the twenty-somethings, well, I can sure sit next to them in a lecture hall."

Jackson was doing his thing, chatting with the women and taking pictures with people. Sam posed for a few shots, and Adam was signing the backs of T-Shirts. I caught up with Brian who had gotten farther ahead of me, closer to the door.

"Brian, Vi. Could we get a picture?"

We paused to smile for a moment and went back to signing.

"Mr. Kelly, could all five of you sign this for me?" A young man handed Brian a cracked CD case. "The Francis Kelly Project" and Brian's old New York telephone number were written on it.

"Where did you get this?" Brian asked him.

"I've had that for as long as I can remember, sir. My mom brought the CD home from work when my brother and I were little. She used to play it for us all the time."

Brian signed the CD cover and passed it along to each band member.

"Where did your mother work?" Brian asked the young man. He was wearing a ball cap that said "Joey's Diner, L.A."

"She cleaned office buildings here in the city. There was one guy, I think he was an entertainment lawyer, you know?" Brian nodded. "He threw a lot of CDs away. My Mom brought home what he threw out and we rated it. Some stuff sucked, man, but some of the music was really good. We loved this CD. It became our official family soundtrack. I took it with me when I moved out to L.A. so I would have a piece of home out there, but, like an idiot, I lost it. At least now I know who recorded it so I can get a replacement."

"Do you still live in L.A. or are you back here now?"

"I'm here again. I was on the Left Coast to try to get a deal for my own band. I worked as a cook to pay the rent, but it's too expensive out there. We tried really hard, but we weren't getting anywhere so, one by one, the band members came back home to New York. We all have family here so it's easier."

"What's your name?" Brian asked.

"Kenny Kramer, sir." The young man held out his hand. "It's Kenneth Sharkey, really, but I record as Kenny Kramer. Sounds cooler, I think." He seemed incredibly sincere.

"Kenny, do you have a demo on you?" Brian asked.

"Mr. Kelly, I have a demo in every pocket of my cargo pants. You never know who you're going to see walkin' down the street. Or who will come into the diner where I work at for lunch, you know? I mean, it's random how these things happen. Dumb luck. That's all it comes down to sometimes."

Kenny handed his CD demo to Brian who opened the gel and looked inside. Brain handed him the Sharpie he had been using to sign autographs. "Write your name and number on the CD in case it gets separated from the case. Put your email address on there as well."

"Good idea, sir. Thanks."

"I'm starting my own label in L.A., called Advanced Band Records." Brian told him. "If I like what I hear, I'll give you a call."

"Thanks, Mr. Kelly. That's all I could ask."

Each band member had signed the cracked CD cover and Brian gave it back to Kenny. "Thanks, Mr. Kelly."

"I feel like I should be thanking you, Kenny." I overheard the end of Brian's conversation with the young man who had asked that we all sign his CD case.

"What was that about?" I asked Brian.

"I can't explain it, but I feel like I just met the missing link."

Before Brain could explain any further, Jane asked us to keep moving and hurried us into the building.

Once inside, the pace was much faster than it had been on the taped shows. People were moving at lightning speed to change sets, set graphics, and move segments along to allow for commercial breaks. The band had gotten ready at the hotel and arrived camera-ready. After quick touch-ups The Francis Kelly Project was in place, waiting for Meredith Viera to interview George Cooper.

We stood quietly off-camera, but on a stage very close to where the interview was taking place. I wondered how Mr. Cooper said the same thing over and over with the same enthusiasm on every show. We were paying close attention to the exchange, waiting for our cue, when Meredith directed a question to us.

"We've all been following The Francis Kelly Project from the band search to the television appearances. How does it feel to be thrust into the national spotlight?" She was looking in our direction and the camera was on us.

"Meredith, it feels like the fastest, most unpredictable roller coaster you have ever been on. You think you're going to throw up one minute and find yourself laughing your head off the next." Jackson got his 'face time' and Meredith and George both laughed.

"How about you, Vi? You've become an icon for women in their forties almost overnight. What's it like to know that you are inspiring women all over the country?"

"It's humbling," I said. "So much good fortune has that effect."

Back in the hotel, Wade and the Gates children jumped up and down on the bed screaming for Mommy. "She talked on TV!" Megan squealed.

"And Brian, I hear you have two babies on the way; one with your long-time girlfriend and a new record label."

"I'm very excited," Brian replied. "I think when success comes later in life and you work for it as hard as we have, you have a respect for it . . . almost a reverence. We're not going to take this for granted," Brian said. "Becoming a dad on top of it is incredible. I'm surrounded by great parents, so I can ask for advice from experts." He gestured towards Jackson and me.

"And, Sam, you're the mayor of Commerce, Texas. There are whispers that you may be considering a run at the Senate."

"I have been approached to consider such an endeavor. I have dedicated my professional life to public service and I will continue to do so whenever I am called to action," Sam answered politely.

"And, Adam, George tells me you're the most talented musician he's ever encountered. You're from this area, correct?"

"New York is my home. And I'm an adequate musician, but thank you for the compliment," Adam laughed.

"I like you guys. What a lovely group of people. Why don't you do your thing for us?"

Jackson counted us in and we were playing "So Beautiful" once again. Before we knew it, the stage crew and Today Show team were clapping for us as we went to commercial.

George joined us and we were all escorted off-set.

"You handled yourselves very well. Sorry you got thrown under the bus," he apologized. "That's live TV . . . gonna happen all day. You never know what to expect." He flashed his trademark grin and took off for the next event.

Jane appeared and directed us to follow a long hallway that lead to an exit. Outside on the street, our van and driver were waiting.

"Great job, guys. That was fabulous." Jane gave us the thumbs up from the front seat next to the driver. "Next stop is Regis and Kelly."

I pulled out my make-up bag and mirror, retouched my lips and brushed on some translucent powder. There wasn't much time to enjoy the 'high' from the Today show performance. I felt like I had to refocus for the next one.

"How are we doing on time?" Sam asked Jane.

"We'll have about twenty minutes once we get there if we get there now."

"Jane, I'm doin' my best here." The driver took her comment personally.

"The good news is that we have plenty of time between Regis and Kelly and The View." Jane reminded us. "The two shows are shot in the same building so the commute between those performances will be delightfully simple compared to sprinting with our hair on fire like we're doing now."

I was glad that Wade and the kids were back at the room watching from a comfortable, non-stressful location. Trying to keep up with us this morning would have been impossible.

"Okay, pull around to the 67th Street entrance," Jane told the driver as we got close to Columbus Circle. "Across from that Starbucks, please."

We had made the trip from midtown in ten minutes, which was great considering that it was not yet nine am. We were scheduled to be on-air at nine-thirty.

We piled put of the van and were met by another mass of well wishers.

Jane handled them for us by explaining that we were on a tight schedule. I was afraid of getting pelted with a soccer ball, but it didn't happen.

We met Mr. Cooper who was having a coffee in the green room, sitting contentedly in an oversized leather chair and wearing a different gorgeous suit than the gorgeous suit he had been wearing a few minutes ago on Today.

"Did you 'beam' over here?" Brian asked him.

"I might be slightly more pampered than you guys. I didn't take a van," he joked. We all laughed. Compared to a few weeks ago we were major celebrities, but compared to Mr. Cooper we could hardly be classified as anything more than 'popular'.

We changed our clothes and waited for our segment. Live on the air, Regis and Kelly played off of one another as effortlessly as ever. They were a wonderful team and their timing was perfect.

"I want to meet Vi." Kelly told Regis when they were telling the audience who their guests were going to be.

"So. Do. I." Regis spoke in a sexy voice.

"Vi, there you go, baby," Jackson teased me backstage as we watched on the monitor.

"I think she's incredible," Kelly told him.

"So. Do. I." Regis hit the same joke twice for an even bigger laugh the second time around.

Blocks away at the Marriott Marquis, Henry pointed a French toast stick, dripping with syrup, at the TV. "They're talking about MOMMY!" Henry screamed.

"Isn't that cool?" Wade marveled with him. Allowing the three year-old to have French toast and syrup in bed was something that only happened in a hotel room. He would never have allowed it at home.

"Is he hitting on Mom, Dad?" Lilly asked. "That's gross. He's old."

Wade laughed. "I think Mom would be flattered by the compliment. Hey, I don't mind a television legend noticing that my wife is hot."

"Ewwww, Dad. It's Mom. I don't wanna hear that." Lilly was finished with the conversation. She wanted to watch the rest of the show in silence and without any references to her mother's looks.

Mr. Cooper did it again. He was witty, charming, and sold the movie in such a way that left you feeling that your best friend had just recommended it for your weekend viewing. Then we were called to take our place on stage and we waited to be introduced.

Kelly waved "hello" and we all waved back. George and Reg had their heads together discussing whatever legends discuss when they are together. The stage manager indicated that we were about to go live again and Regis introduced us to the viewing audience.

"Here's the band that caused a nationwide stir performing their song from George Cooper's newest film. He produced it, directed it, stars in it, and picked the music for it. Are you gonna play in the band, too?" Reeg asked George.

"I already taught them everything I know," George said.

"Here they are. The Francis Kelly Project." The lights went down as Jackson counted us in and I was glad for the atmosphere. The studio had remained bright this morning on 'Today' and I liked this better.

Following Mr. Cooper's example, we played as if this was the songs debut performance. It was the first time many of these people had heard it and we wanted them to love it. We had more fun this time, sensing the imminent end of our television performance career. We interacted with each other more. I used the wireless mic to roam around the stage and sing to each band member, lending the mic for shared background parts and resting back-to-back with Brian as he played his guitar solo. The audience ate it up. We got a standing ovation and we actually took a bow when it was over. It was a spur-of-the-moment thing that we hadn't done after any of the former performances.

Backstage we were laughing and talking over each other.

"That was great. That was the best so far," I said.

"No, Oprah was still the cleanest," Adam said.

"Don't forget the first one. What's Leno's show called?" Sam asked.

"You're so unaffected," Brian teased him.

"Know what? This is a nice problem to have. Not being able to agree on which performance was the best," Jackson laughed.

Mr. Cooper came into the green room. "You're starting to look comfortable," he told us. "You just get better and better. See you next door."

"Let's go rock those mouthy broads at 'The View,'" Jackson joked.

Chapter Fifty-Three

The ladies at "The View" couldn't get themselves close enough to George Cooper and I didn't blame them a bit. Once again, he told the story about producing and directing the movie and his quest to select the perfect soundtrack. Once again, our story was marveled at on nation television. Once again, we were brought on as the world's luckiest show and tell. And again, we made ourselves, our families, and George Cooper proud. Then suddenly, the television appearance portion of our contract had been fulfilled.

The following night, after the movie had made it's premiere to a privileged audience, we played the last engagement of our media tour. Our middle-aged band of regular folk captivated stars of the silver screen, world class musicians, and people we recognized from the society pages. Their genuine admiration barely registered with us because our table, right up front, was the focus of our attention and energy as we performed. Our families sat together applauding and cheering for us. Brian had called Sarah so that she could hear us over the phone and Sam was content and happy in the moment. It was an incredible night.

Our good-byes were quick in an effort to make them painless. We were all headed in separate directions first thing in the morning. There were hugs, a few tears -- all shed by me -- and promises to be in touch. We were looking forward to the release of the CD and the trip down memory lane we'd happily take as we shared the rest of our old tracks with new groupies excited to hear them. We all hoped, especially for Brian and Adam's sake that it did well. We took lots of pictures and then, as quickly as we were transformed into rock stars, the clock struck twelve and we returned to our normal lives.

* * * *

Adam relocated to L.A. and moved in with Tracey. During his first week as the Senior Vice President of Artists and

Repertoire at Advanced Band Records, he signed three bands, each having unlimited potential.

Jackson went back to New Jersey and started a corporate function band, capitalizing on the recent publicity. He formed a five-piece product and played events everywhere from Manhattan to Barcelona. His "at-home" price was fifteen thousand per night and he paid his side members two thousand each. They commanded a higher price for fly-away gigs, and Jackson quit selling Buicks. Sharon quit her job, got her agent's license, and became the band's exclusive booking agent and manager.

Sam flew back to Dallas and picked up his Ford Expedition from the parking garage where he had left it at DFW. It reeked of Cassandra's perfume, so he drove it directly to the Audi dealership and traded it in for an Audi R8 Spyder -- which, Sam knew, would look completely out of place in Commerce. It might send the wrong message to voters as well; but, Sam believed, playing in a band on national TV had already given him a certain distinction. Maybe he'd garage the R8 if he decided to run for Senate, but he had promised himself he was going to be happy and it was easy to fulfill that promise from behind the wheel of a technological dream like the Audi. He laughed the whole way from Dallas to Commerce, traversing the distance in half the usual time.

Brian proposed to Sarah as soon as he returned home. They got married in Vegas on their way to California. Unlike the stereotypical Vegas bride and groom, they were sober and serious about the life commitment, but they were drunk on Vegas. Brian wore a powder blue tuxedo and the bride wore sequins. "Elvis" was the officiate and the newlyweds "honeymooned" at the Paradise Garden Buffet at the Flamingo Hotel--the pregnant bride was hungry--before getting back on the road. Sarah's mother moved to L.A. with them to help them set up the new household and get ready for the baby. Sarah worked with Brian, Adam, and Brooke at the label managing the office. The first phone call Brian made on his first day of work as President of the label was to sign a band of young, talented musicians with a unique sound. The bandleader, Kenneth Sharkey, a.k.a Kenny Kramer, was pretty happy to get the call and tell his Mom that his band had finally gotten the big break he was looking for in the music industry. Brian had high hopes and great fondness for Kenny's band. He devoted much of his time and energy to developing and marketing the act.

I went home to Key Largo and was overjoyed to see Abrams and my beautiful house. My first day home, it was as if I had never been away. I was surrounded by familiar comforts: the smell of the bay, the sound of my children laughing and screaming, Abrams barking . . . I fell back into it immediately. It felt perfectly natural.

I was bombarded with questions at the grocery store, and the boutique became a tourist attraction. Wade loved the idea of turning our unused warehouse into a music camp for kids, and the band remained on standby to be involved once we got it off the ground.

Wade requested some personal time from the airline and we decided to take the kids and Abrams and head to the Bahamas on the boat for three weeks, just to be together.

As I sat in the fly bridge, taking my turn at the helm, I heard the kids cheering and Abrams barking below as Wade presented the dinner that he prepared for us in the galley. Looking toward the horizon I saw turquoise blue water meet an indescribable sky. The salt air soothed my senses, the wind blew through my hair and the setting sun warmed my face. I was, literally, sailing off into the sunset.

Chapter Fifty-Four

SIX MONTHS LATER

Wade grabbed the phone before I was conscious enough to realize that the ringing is what had interrupted my sleep. I didn't know what time it was, but my tired eyes let me know I was opening them sooner than they wanted to be disturbed.

"Captain Gates," he said, convinced that only crew scheduling could be calling the house so early.

"Sure, Brian. She's right here, hold on." Wade handed me the phone and sat up in bed. He looked concerned.

"Brain, are you okay? What's wrong?" I sat upright like Wade, all my faculties sharp in an instant as I prepared to hear the bad news that typically accompanies early morning phone calls.

"Vi, did you hear?" Brian was completely out of breath.

"Did I hear . . . what?"

"'So Beautiful' has been nominated for an Academy Award!" Brian was laughing. "Best Original Song!"

My mouth fell open. Wade motioned for me to tell him what Brian was saying and I simply gave him the thumbs-up sign.

"Vi, are you there?" Brian asked.

"Yes, I'm . . . wow." I started to laugh. "Wow"!

"I know! Congratulations!" Brian laughed along. "And, Vi, you know they have each nominee perform the song live during the Academy Awards."

I fell back onto my pillow, laughing harder at the impossibility of it all.

"That's great, isn't it, Vi? That's an audience of about eighty million in the U.S. and one thousand million worldwide."

"It's great, Brian. Better than great. Congratulations."

"I'll let you go back to sleep. I'll call you later," Brian said before hanging up.

Who says lightening never strikes the same place twice? If you carry that lightening rod around long enough, you might be lucky enough to get hit three or four times.

Author's Note

February 12, 2010

If you have muscled this far into my first literary effort, I feel compelled to say, "Thanks, Mom and Dad. You have always been my biggest fans." In the unlikely event that you, dear reader, are *not* one of my parents, I admire your intestinal fortitude and thank you for your patience.

The Francis Kelly Project was a pleasurable escape for me and I hope that it provided the same light-hearted journey for you as the reader. I intended this book to be a literary bubble bath. On this day, there is enough tension, strife, and uncertainty in the world. As you may have noticed, I allowed my characters to avoid those pitfalls, for the most part, while safely residing in a world where dreams do not have a shelf life. I may be naive, but I don't think dreams have an expiration date in the real world either. I will hold tight to my faith in all that is good and beautiful and teach my darling children to do the same. Because, when it's all said and done, God is in control, and life can't possibly be *too* rosy in His view. Whatever your dreams may be, cherish them. Believe in them. Expect them to come true. And even if it gets heavy, seems impractical, or doesn't match your outfit, never set down your lightening rod.

Sweet Dreams,

Marci Giebels

Marci@MarcisVoice.com

www.MarcisVoice.com

Please read further for a sneak peek at my next novel, *Twenty Weeks*.

TWENTY WEEKS

Chapter One

Paul Mason parked his Smart Car in the corner of the garage. Before getting out of it he paused for a moment, closed his eyes, and tried to recapture how he used to feel when he sat in the Jeep Sahara that he had traded for the beefed up golf cart. He missed the Jeep from time to time. It was big and burly, confident on the road. It could pull a trailer, power through stormy weather, and allow him to get a suntan while calling on his accounts. Paul and his wife, Ann, had traded the fun yet impractical vehicle when the cost of gas began to creep higher and higher. Making sensible choices hadn't been one of their wedding vows, but they had made a practice of it since becoming man and wife. The Jeep had been a remnant of Paul's days as a bachelor. It felt good to be responsible though; better than the instant gratification of driving a car you chose for emotional reasons. The couple agreed that, in the long-term, practical choices would lead them to a comfortable retirement.

Paul stepped out of the car and started to unload the six small bags of groceries that he had purchased at the market. There wasn't enough space for both Ann and the groceries, so she had stayed home. On the plus side, having a tiny car made Paul's six-foot frame looked much taller when he stood next to it and the single stall garage looked quite roomy when the Smart Car was parked there.

The garage, and the house attached to it, had been another responsible purchase. Rather than throwing rent money out the window every month, Paul and Ann bought the house so that they would be building equity in an investment. It wasn't a big, flashy house like the ones some of their friends owned. It was an older home in a well-established neighborhood. The trees in the yard were mature, as were the elderly neighbors. There weren't any young families on the street. Most people in their late twenties, as Paul and Ann were, got sucked into the new developments that had amenities like tennis courts, fitness centers, and amusement style playground equipment. The homes in those communities were significantly more money per square foot than what Paul and Ann's house had cost. They were too wise to be lured by such extravagances.

Paul went into the house and found Ann sitting at the kitchen table, which was covered with piles of bills.

"Hey, I got the football food," He announced.

"Okay, good. Did you get the Digiorno pizza because it's -"

"BOGO, I know." Paul referred to the buy one get one free offer from the supermarket that the couple had seen in that morning's newspaper ad circular. "Since we saved some money on the pizza I spent a couple extra bucks on the beer to get the stuff we like so we can have our choice brew while we watch our boys deliver the smack down."

"Give me one." Ann looked stressed.

"It's eleven-thirty on Sunday morning. Isn't it a sin to drink before noon?" he teased.

"Give me one," Ann barked.

"Okay, okay." Paul opened the beer and set it down on the table in front of her. "What's wrong?"

"I'm so, so sick of this. We can't keep up, let alone, God forbid, get ahead."

Paul opened his own bottle and sat down in the chair next to Ann. "Let's have a look." He sifted through the pile closest to him and lifted the envelope from the top. "This one was due last week, so it has to get paid this week, right?"

Ann pointed her beer bottle at the pile to Paul's right. "Those were due two weeks ago."

"How is this happening? Where is our money going?"

"Basics, student loans, mortgage, utilities, insurance . . ."

"We factored all of that into our budget and we always had room before."

"Yeah, *before* they demoted me from management to sales. *Before* your boss started asking you to wait a few weeks for the commission checks he owes you." Ann closed her eyes and sat back in her chair.

Paul could see the stress was affecting her. Ann's skin had lost the glow she used to have. She looked tired and drawn. The once shiny, lustrous, brunette hair that she had considered her crowning glory was pulled back into a neglectful ponytail that resembled a bale of tied hay. Her eyes, formerly as vibrant and clear as the aqua blue water surrounding their Bahamian honeymoon resort, appeared clouded. Paul put his arms around his beautiful, but battle-scarred wife. When he married her five years ago, he had promised her the life of luxury that he felt she deserved. And he had tried hard to provide it, but his bachelors degree in communications hadn't delivered and his job selling radio advertising wasn't covering their expenses.

"Maybe we should sell the house. We could pad our savings account and rent for a year or so. It would make us feel better to have a cushion," he suggested.

"You don't have any idea what you're saying, Paul. We would wind up selling the house at a loss. The market value is almost fifty thousand below what we owe on our mortgage."

Pauls' mouth fell open. "Dollars?"

"The assessments came out this week. The astounding news is that our taxes increased sharply due to the number of foreclosures in the county."

"The value went?" Paul asked.

"Down."

"And our taxes went?"

"Up. Yeah, you heard correctly."

"I wasn't aware . . ."

Paul and Ann's terrier-mix noticed that Paul was home. Most dogs ran to the door to greet their owners, their tails wagging and tongues kissing. Not Dog. Dog acted more like a cat, which was why they had named him Dog; to remind him of his species every time his name was called.

"Hi, Dog." Paul waved. Dog promptly ran into the living room adjoining the kitchen and tore at the upholstery of the couch. He had been systematically shredding it since Paul and Ann brought him home from the pound six months earlier.

"Did he wait for me to get home to do that?" Paul asked.

"Yeah, he hid under the bed while you were gone."

"The asshole wants an audience while he rips up our stuff." Paul went into the living room and gently lifted Dog off of the couch. "I got a dog so that I would have a furry companion to love, not because I wanted my house destroyed."

He held Dog's nose to his own while he lectured him. Dog wiggled frantically to get loose, then bit Paul on the hand to guarantee his escape.

"That's the perfect metaphor for our lives," Ann laughed. "We try to do the right thing and we get bitten for our trouble. That never happens to anyone but us. I mean, look at my sister. She makes decisions by the seat of her pants, or while not wearing pants at all, and she falls into a bed of flower petals every time. I cut ties with her because she was destructive and draining, always asking me to catch her fall, and then stupid choice number 1,008 gets her the pot of gold at the end of the freakin' rainbow."

"Just because the bartender she married hit the lotto for sixty million dollars two days after the wedding doesn't mean she and Dolph will ever have the true wealth we have . . . Our true love for each other . . ." Paul picked up the TV remote and turned the set on. "And our mutual love of football."

"Ann, the pregame show is starting in a few minutes. I *know* the bills are important and I *know* you're trying to get them out and I *promise* to help you with them later. But, for now, let's watch the game and forget this for a few hours, okay? It's Opening Day. It's a new season for the Galveston Gladiators." Paul puffed out his chest to fill up the Gladiators jersey he was wearing. "C'mon. Our thing is back; every Sunday for the next sixteen weeks, well, seventeen if you count the bye, but longer than that if they suck less than they did last year and make it to the post-season."

"They always suck though. It's even more depressing to put my hope in them than trying to figure out who to pay this week and who could be held off longer."

Paul went back into the kitchen, grabbed Ann's hand, and led her to the couch. "Please? Watch with me. You know there were trades during the off-season; there are new faces. I mean, it's the NFL. Free agents drift from team to team, every year is different. We traded Dip-Shit; we have a new quarterback this year and he's a cinch for the Hall of Fame."

"Make it interesting," Ann challenged him.

Paul considered his wager as Dog resumed tearing the stuffing out of the couch.

"If the Gladiators win we take Dog back to the pound."

Ann laughed. "You're not serious."

"The hell I'm not. If our team wins, we let another family try to tame that little demon."

Ann felt that not wanting Dog made her a heartless person. But the reality of Dog versus her imaginings of cuddling with a canine companion was a sharp contrast. She resented the mongrel ruining what little they had while he flipped them off with his attitude. If he had fingers, Dog would be giving them the bird all day long, Ann suspected.

"It *is* a no-kill animal shelter," she reasoned. "You're on."

She held out her hand to confirm the bet.

"You're future is on the line, Dog." Paul shook Ann's hand while he informed Dog who seemed to understand. His reaction was to accelerate his destruction of the couch so he could finish what he started before his chance was lost.

* * * *

"I feel so good. So unburdened and relieved!" Ann sat in the passenger seat of the Smart Car. She was winded from the pleasure she felt. Like the fabulous moment just after orgasm, but better.

"That little son-of-a-bitch is back where he belongs." Paul clapped his hands together in celebration.

Ann noticed that two families outside the shelter were scrutinizing their celebration and she was fairly certain she and Paul could be easily heard through their thinly constructed transportation. She cleared her throat and motioned for Paul to start the car.

"Don't take the terrier!" Paul shouted as he reversed the car and drove away from the animal shelter.

Anna laughed hysterically. "I feel like we're making a get-away like we just robbed a bank!"

"I would never have guessed that abandoning something could feel so good," Paul agreed. "Thank God they're open on Sundays."

"You know what's funny? We would never have made that decision on our own. And it was obviously the right thing to do; we haven't been this happy in months."

"Thank you Gladiators!" Paul shouted.

"Let's do it again."

Paul eased the car into traffic and patiently coaxed it up to speed. "What do you mean?"

"Let's bet on the Gladiators again next Sunday."

"What do you mean? You want to put money on the game?" Paul focused on keeping the Smart Car from drifting into the other lanes of traffic as the sheer from passing SUVs blew them this way and that.

"No. I mean letting the Gladiators make some life decisions for us."

Paul took his eyes off the road for a minute to try to read the expression on Ann's face. "You're serious."

"Yeah, I am. We analyzed every major life decision we have made together from every angle and it's buried us so far. The 'good' decisions haven't turned out so good, so let's leave some things to fate."

"Okay, let's imagine for one insane second that I agree to this. What do you propose for next Sunday's game? I made the first wager, so it's only fair that you should make the next one."

Ann scrunched up her face the way she did when she was thinking. "I think it should be about this car. It made sense to buy a cheap, fuel-efficient car, but I hate it. People look at us like we should be wearing bulbous red noses and fake hair and I'm scared to death that we're going to get smushed to the grill of a Hummer."

Paul laughed. "It's a safe car, in spite of its size. You know that. The crash test rating was very good."

"Do you like this car? Driving it every day. Having it as our only car?"

"I . . .hate this car. I hate the practicality of this car. I hate feeling like I *have* to drive this car. I hate that every time I hit a gum-wrapper in the road, I feel it."

"Okay, so let's trade it in."

"That's not a responsible decision. We weighed our options when we bought the Smart Car and we made a good choice."

"We made a choice we hate, but we feel bound by a sense of responsibility to be loyal to it. That's crazy."

"What's crazy is letting the outcome of a football game direct your life."

"Okay, so let's turn back around and get Dog." Anna crossed her arms and smirked playfully at Paul.

"Hell no."

"So the process worked in our favor. Why not try it again?"

"Almost anything we buy will cost more than this car, so where are we getting the money for that?" Paul asked.

"We'll figure it out."

"We're not the type of people who take action first and 'figure it out' later, Ann."

"We are now, damnit. Yes we are."

"You've lost it, entirely," Paul told her.

"And don't it feel good?" she teased.

"I do feel pretty good."

Ann reached the short distance to Paul's seat and loosened his belt. "And it's exciting."

Paul squirmed in anticipation. "It is exciting."

Ann tried to lean over her husband's lap, but her head hit the steering wheel. "Ow . . .it's too close." She sat up and rubbed her head.

"That settles it," Paul announced. "This car is on the line next Sunday."

"So we trade it if the Gladiators win?" Ann asked.

"Man, I don't even know if we're home or away next week, I'll have to look at the injuries -"

"Absolutely not." Ann pointed her finger at Paul. "This is random. It's not fantasy football. Don't weigh and measure the facts surrounding the game. Neither of us can look at the line or listen to the analysts' picks. We know the opposing team but we both know that the "Any Given Sunday" factor gives every team in the NFL an equal chance to win any match-up. This has to be as random as possible. That's the whole point."

"This from the woman who struggled for three days last week over whether or not we could afford to go out for pizza Friday night. Really? You know it's a big jump from wagering Dog to taking on a new car payment. I feel a little bit like my brother from the Garden of Eden. His wife wanted to live on the wild side too."

"Well then, since you already think I'm crazy. What if we expanded the wagers to follow the whole season?"

Paul turned into the driveway and pressed the button on the garage door opener. As he drove in to the garage, Ann focused her attention on freeing him from his jeans once again.

"C'mon Mr. Mason, wanna live dangerously for a change?"

"I do, but the shock of witnessing what I hope you're about to do might kill off any one of our nearly-dead neighbors, so I think we should close the garage door first."

"Say you're in this with me for sixteen weeks. We'll take turns making up the wagers. We'll let the Gladiators take the place of our well-thought-out approach to life and see what their record is in sixteen weeks. I mean, it's only sixteen weeks . . . what could happen?"

Ann batted her eyelashes at Paul, smiled a sexy smile, slipped herself into an impossibly small space and began to persuade him in a manner no man could resist.

Paul let out a deep moan and hit the button for the garage door to lower itself into place. "Whatever you want, Ann," he breathed as he lightly placed his hand on the back of her head.

www.ingramcontent.com/pod-product-compliance
Lightning Source LLC
Chambersburg PA
CBHW050923120626
46552CB00001B/15